the best of Friends

OTHER BOOKS AND AUDIOBOOKS BY SARAH M. EDEN

THE LANCASTER FAMILY

Seeking Persephone

Courting Miss Lancaster

Romancing Daphne

Loving Lieutenant Lancaster

*Christmas at Falstone Castle**

also in *All Hearts Come Home for Christmas* anthology

Charming Artemis

THE GENTS

Forget Me Not

*The Holly and the Ivy**

in The Holly and the Ivy anthology

Lily of the Valley

Fleur-de-Lis

THE HUNTRESSES

*The Best-Laid Plans**

The Best Intentions

The Best of Friends

THE JONQUIL BROTHERS

The Kiss of a Stranger

Friends and Foes

Drops of Gold

As You Are

A Fine Gentleman

For Love or Honor

The Heart of a Vicar

Charming Artemis

STAND-ALONES

Glimmer of Hope

An Unlikely Match

For Elise

The Fiction Kitchen

Trio Cookbook

*Novella

CHRONOLOGICAL ORDER OF ALL RELATED SARAH M. EDEN GEORGIAN- & REGENCY-ERA BOOKS

Forget Me Not
*The Holly and the Ivy**
Lily of the Valley
Fleur-de-Lis
Seeking Persephone
Courting Miss Lancaster
Glimmer of Hope
Romancing Daphne
The Kiss of a Stranger
Friends and Foes
Drops of Gold
For Elise
As You Are
A Fine Gentleman
For Love or Honor
Loving Lieutenant Lancaster
Christmas at Falstone Castle
The Heart of a Vicar
The Best-Laid Plans
Charming Artemis
The Best Intentions
The Best of Friends

SARAH M. EDEN

the best of Friends

A HUNTRESSES REGENCY ROMANCE

Covenant Communications, Inc.

Cover image © Shelley Richmond / Trevillion Images

Cover design by Michelle Fryer

Published by Covenant Communications, Inc.
American Fork, Utah

Library of Congress Cataloging-in-Publication Data

Name: Sarah M. Eden
Title: The Best of Friends / Sarah M. Eden
Description: American Fork, UT : Covenant Communications, Inc. [2024]
Identifiers: Library of Congress Control Number 2023936695 | 9781524424510
LC record available at https://lccn.loc.gov/2023936695

Printed in the United States of America
First Printing: April 2024

31 30 29 28 27 26 25 24 10 9 8 7 6 5 4 3 2 1

Praise for The Best of Friends

"Sarah M. Eden's characters are so real and so charming that they linger in your heart long after her books end."

—Sian Ann Bessey, award-winning author of the Georgian Gentlemen series

"A masterfully woven tale of an impossible love match historical fans will eagerly devour!"

—*InD'tale* Magazine

"There is a classical feel to this story that called to me, and I was helplessly drawn in by the amazing, distinctive characters, the smooth plot, and the beautifully described setting."

—*Readers' Favorite* five-star review

"Eden is a talented writer who makes historical, Regencies, Westerns, or whatever genre she tackles exciting and informative."

—*Meridian Magazine*

"What a treat! Old friends and new ones abound in this delightful new series."

—Esther Hatch, author of the Proper Scandals series

"Sarah Eden hit a home run with this engaging historical fiction."

—NetGalley five-star review

"This is such a tender story with raw emotions."

—NetGalley five-star review

dedicated to that one time in eighth grade when my best friend and I created a stick-figure comic strip in which we were Olympic gymnasts cursed with poorly constructed equipment, leading to inevitable hijinks and hilarity

ACKNOWLEDGMENTS

Many thanks to

- Traci Abramson, Sian Bessey, and Jolene Perry, for support, encouragement, and celebrations, for being there through all the ups and downs
- Annette Lyon and Sammie Trinidad, for writing sprints and get-togethers that kept me going through countless deadlines
- Dr. Shane Frazier, for saving my wrist from the consequences of my own poor decisions
- Jesse Perry, Ginny Miller, Liz Swick, and Jonathan Eden, for invaluable assistance in keeping things running
- Pam Pho at Stevens Literary Agency, for tirelessly advocating for me
- Everyone at Covenant Communications, for making each book we create together something truly lovely
- Paul, for everything

CHAPTER ONE

Yorkshire, spring 1819

Daria Mullins had always known she was unremarkable, but she felt certain even extremely ordinary people were entitled to dream of extraordinary things. However, her dreams had changed over the years, growing more reasonable. And of late, even the most ordinary dreams felt out of reach.

"Three Seasons without a match. Don't you think that is enough embarrassment?" Mother had made that argument more than once already during the family's discussion of their plans for the Season. "It is important to know when to set new goals. You can decide on a few while your father, brother, and I are in London."

To which Daria had responded, "I do have goals, and all of them are based in London."

But no matter how ardently she had insisted that she ought to make the journey to Town and that she wouldn't be an embarrassment, her parents had yet to be swayed. Mother and Father had spoken more of Great-Aunt Theodosia's loneliness in Anglesey than they had about Daria's anticipated isolation at the family home in Yorkshire.

This was, unfortunately, not unfamiliar footing for Daria. Her parents were often dismissive of her. At times, they were unkind. She didn't enjoy it, but she was too accustomed to it to be surprised any longer. And arguing with them had never helped in the past.

Daria was making a third circuit of the knot garden with her brother, Tobias, walking beside her, recounting her frustrations with the situation. The sky was particularly gloomy, which she thought terribly fitting.

"We could tell them that going to London would be good for your health," he suggested.

"Going to London is not good for anyone's *health*," she countered with a smile.

"Remind me again why we're working so hard to convince our parents to let you go to this place of illness and misery." Tobias liked to tease her, but he never did so unkindly. He was a prince among brothers. He deserved a sister who didn't cause him as much trouble as she did.

"Regardless of the lack of health benefits, London is where I see my friends. It is where I get to see and do so many lovely things. The theater and soirees and musical evenings." She swallowed the all-too-familiar lump of anticipated sorrow that rose in her throat. "If I can't ever return to London, when will I do any of those things again? Or see my friends?"

"I do think they would make certain you weren't entirely abandoned." He picked a poppy and set it in her hand. He'd done that since they were children, ever since she'd told him she thought poppies were pretty.

"But you have said you won't go to London if Father and Mother don't allow *me* to." She brushed the poppy petals against her cheek, another holdover from childhood. "In London, you can spend time with the gentlemen you knew in school. You see no one when you're here."

"I see *you*." He bumped her with his shoulder.

"I don't count, you absurd man," she said with a laugh.

"*I'm* absurd? You're the one who cannot count."

"I *don't* count. Not *cannot* count."

"Ah." The laugh he didn't quite keep out of his eyes undermined his attempt at a very serious demeanor. How he lightened her heart. She couldn't bear to be the reason he didn't go to London.

"We could tell Father and Mother that a wealthy, well-connected young gentleman has developed an interest in me and nothing will come of it if I do not journey to London. It is my matrimonial failures that sit at the heart of their objections, after all."

But Tobias looked as unconvinced as ever. "They would insist on knowing who this gentleman is, and we'd not have an answer."

"I hadn't thought of that." Heat stole over her face. She knew she was not the cleverest person, but heavens, it was embarrassing how often that was obvious.

He put an arm around her and gave her a brotherly squeeze. "That you are not a dab hand at deception is a testament to your good character, Daria. No need to be embarrassed about that."

"Only a truly wonderful brother would find a means of explaining his sister's lack of intelligence as a mark of her good character."

"There are many ways of being intelligent," Tobias said. "No matter that our father does not acknowledge as much, it is, nonetheless, true."

"When you stumble upon the type of cleverness I can lay claim to, do let me know." She spoke with both dryness and a bit of a laugh. She'd always been one for keeping her chin up and finding means of being happy even in great difficulty, though that had grown more difficult of late.

"You rescued Mother's soiree last Season when her plans proved insufficient," Tobias said.

She shook her head. "Planning gatherings does not require intelligence."

"It does though. If *anyone* could do it, then *everyone* would."

Daria linked her arm through his as they continued walking. "You are kind to be impressed by that. Heaven knows our parents aren't."

"Mother and Father *were* impressed that I spent a bit of time with Charlie Jonquil in Bath," Tobias said, his eyes narrowing in thought. "I think they were hoping I might become one of his particular friends, he being the son and brother of an earl."

"And I am closely connected to him now that he is married to Artemis," Daria said.

Artemis Jonquil was the creator of Daria's group of friends known to all of Society as the Huntresses. Artemis was quite well connected in her own right, being sister-in-law to an earl as well as to the most powerful and influential man in the kingdom: the infamous Duke of Kielder.

Daria's connection to Artemis had not been beneficial enough to outweigh the burden, social and financial, of a daughter with no prospects undertaking a fourth Season.

"What if," Tobias said in conspiratorial tones, "we convince our parents that I could not hope to build a connection with the husband of your dear friend and his group of close-knit gentlemen without you to facilitate the connection?"

An interesting thought. "They would be more likely to allow me to make the journey to London if they thought *you* stood to benefit."

Tobias stopped their forward movement along the garden path and turned to face her. "We tell our parents that you will be able to facilitate my entry into the social circle of Charlie and Artemis Jonquil if they permit you to take part in the Season."

"That could be accomplished in a fortnight." Daria shook her head. "They'd likely send me home after that."

"Arranging a journey back to Yorkshire for only you would likely seem an unwarranted inconvenience in their minds." His lips pressed together, and his eyes narrowed. "They go to great lengths to avoid inconvenience. I am convinced that if we can only get you to London, you will be permitted to remain as long as they do."

"And as long as *you* do," she pressed. "I could not imagine London without you."

His smile had been such a balm to her over the years. It was again now. "I think this plan will work. Your presence will allow me to interact with those in the Huntresses' sphere, and it will be the easiest thing to convince our parents of how beneficial that would be for my future, which they repeatedly tell me is important to them."

His future was important to her as well. She wanted him to be happy, to build a wonderful life. He deserved that more than almost anyone she knew.

"Will you make me a promise, Tobias?"

He nodded.

"If our parents still don't permit me to go to London despite our efforts, you have to promise you will go for the Season without me."

"Daria—"

"One of us has to have a chance at happiness," she continued before he could protest further. "You missing out on that opportunity because I didn't make a match in the three Seasons I was given to attempt it would not improve anything. It certainly wouldn't make me feel any better should I be left behind."

"You ought to be permitted a fourth Season. Our parents are being unfair." He spoke with firmness, defending her as he always had.

"You have to promise," she insisted again. "I cannot move forward with any of this if you don't solemnly swear to me that you will go to London regardless of their decision."

"I promise, Daria," he said. "But I also do not think it will come to that. We will convince them, and you will have your Season."

"What forfeit are you willing to place on that declaration?"

Tobias laughed. "We are to undertake another wager, are we?"

"We've done so all our lives. There seems little point changing that now." They'd indulged in some rather ridiculous bets over the years. It had helped them weather difficult storms. Perhaps it would help them endure this one.

"If our parents agree to allow you to journey to London, you will have to let me buy you a ribbon for your hair in whatever color I choose, and you will have to wear it at a gathering also of my choosing."

She tightened her arm more snugly around his. "Agreed."

"And what is your required forfeit if I am proven wrong?"

"I have already told you. If I am left behind, you will have to go without me."

Their steps took them back to the house. Tobias eyed the structure with a hint of uncertainty that must have been in her expression as well.

"Shall we toss ourselves into the fray once more?" Tobias asked.

"The fray will find us either way, I suspect."

The usual nervousness tugged at her as they walked inside to speak to their parents. Facing them *with Tobias* had seen Daria through a lifetime of being unimportant and insignificant. Her brother loved her and liked her and cared about her happiness. She tried very hard not to think about what life would be like once he was married and gone.

Mother and Father were in the small sitting room, where they passed most every day, Mother with her needlepoint and Father with a newspaper.

"Do you suspect the Duke of Kielder will be in Town for the Season?" Tobias didn't bother to *slowly* introduce the topic. Daria hoped that wasn't a misstep.

"He doesn't neglect his duties in Parliament," Father said, looking up at his son. "And the duchess and her sisters and sister-in-law are sought-after guests and hostesses in Society. I suspect the entire family will be in London for at least part of the social whirl."

Tobias and Daria sat in adjacent chairs, facing their parents. To her, Tobias said, "I'm certain the youngest of the duchess's sisters will be in Town."

"Artemis never misses the Season," Daria confirmed.

"And her husband's family will, no doubt, be in London as well." Tobias did a fine job of making his conjecture sound like a randomly seized thought.

Daria nodded. "And many of her husband's close friends."

"Do you think—" Tobias stopped himself short. "I would consider it an honor to meet both of their families and Mr. Jonquil's friends. They are all such significant members of the *ton.* Meeting them would . . ." He shook his head as if unable to finish the thought.

While she hadn't her brother's ability to enact complicated plans or navigate tricky waters, she had gained some confidence through her association with Artemis. She at least didn't fall to pieces any longer. "I cannot extend any invitations on their behalf, but I could introduce you to those I know because of Artemis and Charlie."

"Tobias already knows them both from our sojourn in Bath." Father employed his usual tone of strained patience. "He has no need of your introductions."

They'd not thought of that. The all-important first introductions had been undertaken in Bath. What were they to do now to convince her parents?

Tobias was quick to adjust the approach. "Bowing acquaintances are seldom invited to more exclusive gatherings nor eagerly introduced to others in the acquaintance's sphere. I had hoped to make greater inroads this Season." He allowed a small sigh tinged with disappointment.

Mother watched him with concern. "For my part, I cannot understand why the important gentlemen of your age have not eagerly pulled you into their friendships. How could they not wish for you to be part of their circle?"

Three years earlier, her parents had expressed shock when Artemis Lancaster—as she'd been then—had befriended Daria. Father and Mother had debated for weeks whether it had been an act of pity or a joke that would eventually result in Daria's humiliation. They had a better opinion of Tobias, which might prove exactly what was needed at that moment.

"I think, if I had the chance to spend more time with the gentlemen in the Jonquils' and Lancasters' spheres, I would be granted space in those circles. But how am I to claim that chance?"

Oh, he was brilliant. She had so often wished she were as clever and quick as he—as almost anyone, really. If she were, she might manage a tactic other than ignoring her parents' more pointed commentary.

Father turned a stern gaze on Daria. "You spend time in those circles. Surely you must know how to gain Tobias entry."

It was not a demand she'd been expecting. She wasn't certain how to answer.

"Would there be objections if I accompanied you to some of the gatherings the Huntresses are part of?" Tobias asked her.

As quickly as that, she had the thread once more. "You did so in Bath and could certainly do so again, and as often as is needed until you carve out your own place."

"I would be grateful to you," Tobias said.

Mother set aside her needlepoint. "Daria, you must include him in every gathering you possibly can. You mustn't be selfish in this matter."

"But I'm not going—"

Tobias spoke over her. "This Season will be a turning point for me, I am certain." He tossed Daria a quick look of warning, which she felt certain was meant to prevent her from mentioning, as she had been about to, the fact that she was not meant to participate in the Season.

"We will expect a regular reporting," Father said.

"I vow to keep you abreast," Tobias said. "I daresay, by the end of our time in Town, I will have laid claim to a great many very beneficial connections."

He'd planted in their parents' minds the need for Daria to remain in London throughout the family's time there. Tobias truly was brilliant.

"If Daria keeps to those gatherings her friends are at and we do not put her forward, then her being unwed still and with no prospects might not be the gossip fodder it would be otherwise. But she will have to be very circumspect during this final Season." Mother retook her sewing. "Ending her days in London by helping her brother is a fine thing."

This final Season.

Ending her days in London.

Her parents were allowing her to return, it seemed. But only this once. One last Season with the Huntresses. One more adventure in London. One last extraordinary dream to cling to.

She would do well to make the very best of it.

CHAPTER TWO

OLDER BROTHERS RUIN EVERYTHING.

While Thomas Comstock, known to his friends as Toss, had been making that declaration for most of his life, he'd done so with extra conviction the past few months. *His* older brother was wreaking more havoc than usual, which was saying something.

Laurence had been a nuisance when they were children, taunting and harassing Toss at every turn. But their parents had tempered that with kindness and understanding. Toss's little sister, Rosamond, had kept him from dismissing all sibling relationships as a misery.

They'd lost Mother five years earlier and Father a year after that, and upon inheriting the estate, Laurence had begun shifting from a bother to a nightmare. The misery had reached new heights when Laurence had arrived at Cambridge mere weeks earlier to bring Toss home, having decided without warning and without reason that he would no longer fund Toss's education. There'd been no arguing with him.

"Do stop sulking, Thomas." Laurence descended the stairs of their London house with that encouraging declaration. "It isn't as though you never slipped away from Cambridge to attend London events. You did so this time last year."

"I was away from Cambridge *temporarily* and of my own choosing. Neither of those things is true now."

"You were wasting your time and my money." Laurence tugged at the wrists of his gloves as he crossed the entryway. "I put an end to both." He set his hat atop his head. "Your time is better spent here establishing yourself in the circles you ought to occupy."

Laurence had always been overbearing. The current situation had but one twinkling light of hope. "Were you in earnest about this Season being mine to do with as I choose?"

He nodded. "Within reason. Every gentleman should have at least one bachelor Season. This is yours. Don't squander it."

On that declaration, Laurence stepped to the front door but, after the footman opened it, paused. "I still need to stand you for membership at my club." He uttered the realization in much the way one would acknowledge an obligation to empty the chamber pots.

"Don't torture yourself for my sake," Toss said dryly.

"A gentleman has to belong to a club. You'd be a laughingstock otherwise."

It was a shame Laurence was the sibling he would be required to spend the next few weeks with. Rosamond was actually pleasant company.

From the other side of the open door, a familiar voice said, "Mr. Comstock, what a great honor it is to be in your presence." Toss could only just make out the figure of his very good friend, Charlie Jonquil, at the door, bowing so deeply and formally to Laurence that one would assume Charlie was in the presence of royalty. "To think, if I'd been a mere minute or two delayed in my arrival, I would not have crossed paths with you. What a blank my life would have been without this chance encounter."

Laurence sighed almost silently and looked sidelong at Toss. "Why are all of your friends utterly ridiculous?"

"He isn't wrong," Charlie said, grinning affably as he stepped inside the house.

"Ridiculous, they may be, but this one is the son of an earl," Toss said to his brother.

"The *seventh* son of an earl. That makes him little better than absolutely nobody."

"He isn't wrong." Charlie's smile still hadn't slipped. Few people had his knack for enjoying the absurdities of life. Fortunately, one of those few was Toss himself.

Laurence, as always, looked unamused. "Do spend some time this Season, Thomas, filling your social circle with people I need not be ashamed to interact with."

Charlie assumed a look of confused concern. "Does this mean I need to stop picking my teeth in ballrooms?"

"Not if you use a golden toothpick," Toss said in mock-serious tones. "And make certain you identify any bits of particularly fine food you discover in your digging so all within earshot will know how refined your meals are."

Muttering something indiscernible, Laurence quitted the house, and not a moment too soon.

"He is still a ray of sunshine," Charlie said.

"Watch yourself, there, Charlie. If you don't stop being so ridiculous, I'll be forced to stop spending time with you next Season."

Charlie chuckled. "I have a brother-in-law who is very fond of the word *ridiculous*. Perhaps we ought to introduce Laurence to him."

Toss knew precisely which brother-in-law Charlie referred to. "His Grace would likely pummel my brother within five minutes of being forced into his company."

"I am not unaware of the likely outcome." Charlie shrugged, raising an eyebrow. "Might even be one of the reasons I suggested it."

They walked together to the library, small when compared to most, but as the room was mostly for show, where Laurence was concerned, it didn't need to be enormous.

"Do you think your brother will keep his word and allow you to spend this Season however you choose?"

"'Within reason.'" Toss repeated the caveat Laurence was certain to include every time the topic was raised.

"What do you mean to do with your brief bit of freedom?" Charlie asked, dropping onto an obliging chair.

"If I thought my brief bit of freedom could possibly include returning to Cambridge, I'd commandeer some unsuspecting person's carriage and make the journey in a heartbeat."

"That was badly done of Laurence. You ought to have been permitted to finish your studies." Charlie spoke with utmost empathy. He, too, had been forced to leave university before he'd planned to. Charlie had previously held the goal of being a don, lecturing in theoretical mathematics, but circumstances hadn't allowed it.

"I had one term left." Toss leaned against the mantel, knowing his audience wouldn't begrudge him the expression of frustration. "One. There was no reason Laurence couldn't have allowed me that."

"No reason other than him being a starched-up rip of a fellow."

"A starched-up rip who despises music," Toss added. "Music connected in any way to his brother, especially."

"Does he have any idea how talented you are?" Charlie asked.

"He has heard me play often enough, and I've told him which compositions were my own." Toss shrugged, making his way to a chair and dropping inelegantly onto it. "He was unimpressed."

"Meaning he's pudding-headed, to boot." Charlie scratched at his chin. "Are you certain the two of you are related?"

"I wish I could say we weren't." Toss crossed his legs at the ankles and set his hands behind his head. "Still, I've been given leave to not be entirely miserable for this one Season. Seems I ought to prove myself *not* pudding-headed and make the most of that."

"Then consider me your temporary social secretary," Charlie said with a smirk.

"You've come with a suggestion?"

"An exceptional one, in fact." Charlie sat up straight once more. "Tonight is the Debenhams' ball, the annual event at which the Huntresses make their entrance into the social whirl each Season. It is quite a sight to behold. You don't want to miss it."

Though Toss had been present for about a week of the previous Season's activities, he hadn't experienced what was quickly becoming legendary. "I'd enjoy seeing the moment play out."

"My Artemis certainly knows how to make an entrance." Charlie couldn't have looked more besotted if he'd tried. "And she's taught her Huntresses well."

"I recall a time when you didn't speak so highly of 'your' Artemis's entrances." Toss bit back his amusement. "Repented, have we?"

"I've seen the error of my ways, yes." He didn't even look embarrassed to have been so wrong about his beloved for so long. "And this time, Newton and Scott and I all get to make the entrance with them. You don't want to miss that."

Newton and Scott were friends of theirs who had both married members of Artemis's band.

"Will it be enjoyable enough to be worth Laurence refusing to fund my final term at Cambridge?"

"No," Charlie said without hesitation. "But it'll be loads better than whatever your brother would suggest you do instead."

"And unlike years to come, this Season, I don't have to listen to his suggestions."

Charlie's gaze narrowed a little. "You are a grown man who has reached his legal majority. You don't truly have to listen to Laurence after this Season has ended."

"Except he has complete control over my income, and the roof over my head is his. Unless I find a means of making my music compositions profitable, which is unlikely without having completed my time at Cambridge to give me cachet enough to receive endorsements and assistance from influential people in the world of music, then I do have to listen to my rip of a brother."

"Have you considered simply being a vagabond?" Charlie shrugged. "You'd likely be a dab hand at it."

"We tried that once, you will recall. Didn't last long."

"In our defense, it was raining, and there was to be pork pie for supper that night."

"In our further defense," Toss added, "Eton during exam week was probably not the best place to attempt our dissolute life."

"Could you perhaps attempt it when you've returned to your family's country estate?"

"Rosamond would likely insist on joining me," Toss said. "And that would land me in her governess's black books, and I am terrified of that woman."

"Seems to me you're in a quandary, my friend. You'll have to listen to Laurence the Lout next Season regardless of his pudding-headedness."

"That's a problem for next Season. This year, I believe I will fill my time specifically with things that my brother will never permit once he is dictating my comings and goings."

"Within reason," Charlie said in a perfect imitation of Laurence.

Toss laughed, deeply and fully. "I hope you'll have a few suggestions as the Season goes on."

Charlie grinned once more. "What are friends for?"

CHAPTER THREE

Early in the Season every year, Lord and Lady Debenham hosted a ball that fell somewhere between a chaotic crush and a fashionably attired horde. The Huntresses never missed it.

It was at this annual gathering that they made what Artemis termed their "strategic entrance" into the social whirl. They always stepped into the ballroom with Artemis at their head, walking with the poise and confidence their fearless leader had taken great pains to teach them.

From that moment on each year, Society was their oyster, or so Daria had been told. She wasn't entirely certain what that metaphor meant, but she suspected it indicated that the *ton* decided each year to welcome the Huntresses in large part because they'd made such an unshakable impression.

The annual arrival always made Daria a little nervous, but it was also a highlight for her. She never felt more valued and important than she did during that walk through the tall doors of the stately London ballroom.

This year felt different. Perhaps it was that she knew it would be her last. Perhaps it was that three of their band were now married and the dynamic among them all had changed. Likely, it was a little bit of both.

Daria was not the first of the Huntresses to arrive, which was just as well. She'd not have entirely known what to do otherwise. Her parents abandoned her in the entryway, as they always did. Tobias left her reluctantly, likely only willing to do so because Eve and Nia O'Doyle, two of the Huntresses, reassured him they would look after her.

"Does it not seem odd to you, Eve, that we've known Daria as long as we have, yet we're not overly well acquainted with her brother?" Nia tapped her lip, her expression one of overdone pondering.

"Seems Miss Daria doesn't wish any of us to whisk him away and claim him for our own."

There was no mistaking their Irish heritage during the most mundane of conversations, but when the two of them were teasing, which happened quite often, the flavor of their homeland filled every syllable.

"My parents are insisting I make certain Tobias is made more a part of our group," Daria said. "Tobias tricked them into it."

"He's a crafty sort, then, is he?" Eve asked with a twinkle in her eye.

"I like him better already," Nia added.

Society struggled to tell the sisters apart. When Daria had first met the sisters, she had wondered if that bothered them. She'd quickly discovered that they not only seemed to be accepting of the situation, but they also seemed to perpetuate it. They fashioned their hair the same and shared gowns, though the latter was a financial necessity, from what Daria understood. And they often undertook conversations this way, with the two seeming to have precisely the same thoughts at precisely the same time and, thus, finishing the thought the other one began. Coming to know them these past years, Daria had reached the firm conclusion that she would have liked to have had a sister.

"We are well met!" Ellie Hughes, another of their band, rushed to greet them after she, too, arrived in the Debenhams' entryway. She and her husband, Newton, had arrived with his parents, a very formidable and important couple in Society.

Newton offered the present Huntresses a bow and kind words of greeting, and the Huntresses each embraced Ellie. They nearly always greeted each other this way.

"We missed you at the house party," Daria said. "It simply wasn't the same without you."

"Hold the next one in London, and I will make certain to be there." Ellie was one of the most genuinely content people Daria had ever met. Life had not been easy for this member of the Huntresses' band—it hadn't been for any of them, really—but Ellie had navigated her difficult upbringing and claimed a future with Newton that clearly pleased her quite perfectly.

"That gown is gorgeous on you, Ellie," Nia said.

"From Miss Martinette's?" Eve made the observation as if it were a guess, though all the Huntresses knew a Miss Martinette's gown when they saw one.

Ellie swished the dress skirt a little. "Isn't it lovely? I'd not have believed only two years ago that a gown existed that looked good on me. My mother quite insisted such a thing was impossible."

"That's because your mother hasn't the least understanding of fashion," Eve declared firmly. Her stern expression quickly melted into the trademark grin she and her sister were known for, and the lot of them dissolved into quiet laughter.

It was in this joyful moment that Artemis—their fearless leader—and her beloved Charlie arrived in company with Gillian Sarvol and her husband, Scott.

Daria's smile turned to one of absolute joy. Gillian was her dearest friend among the Huntresses, and Daria had missed her these past months. They had done absolutely everything together since the Season three years ago when Artemis had taken them under her wing.

They quickly embraced.

"We're both in London," Daria said, realizing in the next moment how utterly obvious the observation was. But Gillian never mocked her for that, never laughed at her.

"Fate is, at last, choosing to be kind."

Gillian's attention returned to Scott, who was gabbing with Charlie and Newton. Daria loved Scott almost like a brother, and she refused to feel sorry for herself that he had so much of Gillian's time. She refused, but her aching heart did not always obey orders.

The other Huntresses also greeted Daria warmly each time they saw her, a welcome reminder that she had an entire group of friends, not merely one. She would not be completely alone even if Gillian did not spend as much time with her as she used to.

"Is Lisette not in London yet?" Daria asked Artemis. Lisette was the youngest of their group.

"She is not. And there is reason to believe she won't be leaving France to join the whirl this Season."

"No." Daria's heart dropped. "She'll be so miserable at home." Lisette didn't talk a great deal about life with her family, but she said enough for all the Huntresses to know full well that leaving France behind when she had the chance was a source of relief for their dear friend.

The gentlemen broke off their conversation, moving to stand beside their wives, who all took their usual positions in the Huntresses' V formation they assumed when making this annual entrance. Artemis stood at the front. Gillian stood to Artemis's right, and Daria always stood in the V after Gillian, trailing a few steps behind.

The group's arrangement was adjusting, though, making room for the husbands who had become part of their circle. Scott stood directly beside Gillian now, her arm through his.

"I am prepared to be amazed," Scott said to his wife. His American accent made his voice easy to distinguish even in a crowd.

"That is a very good thing," was Gillian's reply, "because we are inarguably amazing."

It was the sort of repartee that Daria and her dearest friend had once exchanged together. Daria wasn't part of it now.

Do not feel sorry for yourself, Daria. Be grateful you are in London at all.

The band of Huntresses moved with confidence into the ballroom. Everything and everyone came to a halt, watching with awe this now-familiar entrance.

Artemis had explained it as starting the story of each Season the way they wished it to be told. Every year Daria prayed *her* story didn't prove to be a tragedy.

Once Artemis was satisfied with the impression they had made, the Huntresses began to disperse, something that didn't used to happen so quickly or so entirely. But half of their present number was married and became rather distracted. Eve and Nia, the only others of the present Huntresses who were unattached, kept close to each other.

Just as Daria began to feel she would be spending the evening alone, Tobias stepped up beside her. Bless him for that.

"I, for one, cannot imagine how it is Father and Mother aren't so overawed by your group of friends that they feel that alone is worth continuing to bring you to London." He slipped her arm through his. "Could it be our parents are insufferably stupid?"

"No." She shook her head. "That's *me*."

"Just in case you actually believe that, I will say yet again that it is not the least bit true, Daria."

She appreciated her brother's kindness but knew he was wrong. She often said rather stupid things and struggled to remember information. She could read but not as quickly as most, and she stumbled over her words when reading aloud.

Her governess had declared her a lost cause and had simply stopped trying, and Daria had been grateful when her daily lessons had been abandoned; they'd only ever made her feel more thickheaded than she already had.

"Now, dearest sister, our parents are watching. Let us make a point of you providing me with the very beginnings of a foot in the door to Mr. Charlie Jonquil's circle of impressive friends, one that will, of course, require many more meetings in the coming weeks."

She smiled conspiratorially; they'd decided to make measured progress so as to stretch out Tobias's need for her in these introductions. "Mr. Seymour and Mr. Kendrick are still at Cambridge, I believe. And you met Mr. Hughes in Bath. But I don't think you know Mr. Comstock. He's here tonight."

"All the more reason to introduce me to him."

Of course. She shook her head at her silliness. "You didn't need me to restate all of that. I could simply have moved directly to undertaking the introductions."

"Do not castigate yourself," Tobias insisted. "Thinking out loud is not a failing."

It *was*, though, when a person's thoughts weren't overly intelligent. Daria walked with Tobias to where Charlie and Artemis stood, flanked by admirers and would-be associates. Their approval and presence was quickly becoming sought after in Society.

As Daria and her brother approached, Toss Comstock saw her and smiled. Charlie's friends and the Huntresses had attended a house party together several months earlier and had ended the gathering on a first-name basis, though they all knew better than to use them out loud in public.

"Miss Mullins. A pleasure to see you again." Toss bounced a little as he offered the greeting, and even as he executed an otherwise proper bow. Daria smiled broadly and easily at the sight. He always felt so very alive.

That was a rather ridiculous way to think about a person. Everyone she knew was alive. Well, everyone she knew *had been* alive when she'd met them, though not all still were. Toss certainly was.

Her mind seemed to forever be spinning itself in unending circles.

Both Toss and Tobias were watching her, amused and expectant.

"Oh crumpets," she muttered, realizing she'd been so lost in her thoughts that she'd left the group in a very awkward situation. "Tobias, this is Mr. Thomas Comstock. Mr. Comstock, my brother, Mr. Tobias Mullins."

Bows and words of pleasure were exchanged. Tobias was teasing and comfortable with her, but she'd noticed a tendency toward bashfulness when around others. That held true here as well. Thank the heavens Toss had shown himself well able to put people at ease. He'd done so for her at the house party, treating her with kindness and smiling comfortingly at her when she'd felt overwhelmed. He'd seemed to understand without being told that she was struggling, and she had deeply appreciated that.

"The last I heard, Miss Mullins, your presence here in London was in question. The Huntresses must be delighted to have you among them after all."

"Our entrance would have been lopsided otherwise."

"I am certain they are pleased for more reasons than that." Tobias offered the response in kind tones but with a sharp look at Toss.

With hands held up in a show of innocence, Toss said, "I hadn't given even a moment's thought to the potential asymmetry of the Huntresses's formation. It is for the joy of your company, Miss Mullins, that I believe they are pleased to have you in London."

She had made a mull of the introduction so quickly. If only Gillian weren't so very married; she had always rescued Daria when she'd bungled things like this.

"I would introduce you to Scott," she told her brother, "but he is leading Gillian out to dance."

"Another time," Tobias said. "In fact, I am engaged for this set as well and must abandon you both."

"For a waltz?" Daria asked, recognizing the tune being played.

"The lady's parents agreed to let me walk about with her," Tobias said. "Waltzes aren't entirely scandalous any longer, but none of us wishes to give any unintentional impressions."

"I will see your sister returned to your parents," Toss offered.

With bows between the gentlemen, Tobias went off in search of his partner, and Toss walked beside Daria along the edge of the ballroom.

"You really needn't go out of your way," Daria assured him. "My parents don't wish me to hover around them all evening."

"Most parents prefer that their daughters stay close by," Toss said.

"*Mine* are very particular that I not cause them too much bother. I often do rather silly things, and my father finds that tedious." Seeing surprise register on Toss's face, Daria realized she'd said aloud something she likely shouldn't have. Speaking ill of one's parents was considered quite a breach of etiquette. "He is only teasing me," she insisted. "He teases like that a lot."

"Does he?" Toss didn't sound amused.

She supposed it wasn't actually very funny. But *teasing* was the only way she'd thought of to explain the things her father said that weren't as kind as they ought to be. She didn't want people to think badly of her family, but neither did she want them to think of her as tedious or slow-witted or any of the other things that her father sometimes called her. And she certainly didn't want whispers about her unflattering comments getting back to her parents. She endured them mostly in silence for the sake of maintaining the peace. That peace would vanish should they think she wasn't being loyal enough to the family.

"Will he 'tease' you the entire time you're in London?" Toss asked.

Their circuit of the room was slow, as the size of the crush made navigating difficult. Daria didn't mind; she liked Toss's company. She suspected most everyone did.

"We don't interact overly much during the Season," Daria said. "Father is very busy with his club, and Mother has friends she spends time with when she's not planning whatever gathering she chooses to host that year."

"Does the nature of that gathering change from year to year?"

Daria nodded. "She hasn't yet found one variety that she is good at planning." Merciful heavens, she'd done it again. "I shouldn't speak unflatteringly of my mother."

"I know you didn't mean it unkindly."

Relief settled on her comfortingly. "I hope whatever she chooses this year proves a success. She'll be in better spirits if it does, and I would prefer to end my final Season on a positive note."

"Your *final* Season?"

She nodded. "I mean to try very hard to have a wonderful last time in London."

The smile returned to his face. "You and I are in very similar situations, then. I am here for what is, in many ways, my *last* Season in London, and I have vowed to enjoy *my* time here."

"I thought this was your first Season." She was almost certain of it. He'd come to London for Newton and Ellie's betrothal ball the previous year but hadn't been in Town for more than a week.

"It is both," Toss said. "My brother insisted I be in London this Season and has declared that it is mine to do with as I choose because next Season I will be required to live by his dictates in pursuit of a match that meets with his approval."

"And you can do whatever you want?"

Toss laughed lightly, quietly. "'Within reason.' He keeps adding that caveat."

Daria smiled broadly. "Does he think you're going to run about causing scandals?"

"I suppose that has crossed his mind."

She bent around a gathering standing a bit in their way, though she kept her arm through Toss's. A few in the group offered him a word of greeting. A couple of people did the same with her. He was probably liked for himself. For her part, she knew she was accepted mostly because of her association with the Huntresses, because Artemis had snatched her out of obscurity. Society's notice she could take or leave. It was the escape from isolation that she cherished most.

Isolation. It was both fitting and sad to have that word echoing in her thoughts in the same moment she spied Gillian spinning about the dance floor with Scott. Daria was, in a way, being left behind as her dearest friend moved forward with her new life. But, then, Daria wouldn't be coming to London in the years to come. She was going to be lonely either way.

Toss guided her around two ladies standing in their path. Thank the heavens for him. He was lovely company, kind and thoughtful. He didn't make her feel silly or burdensome. And in that moment, he was keeping many of her worries at bay.

"I think my parents feel much the same as your brother," she said "They likely don't overly care what I do this Season, so long as I don't cause them any inconvenience. I do need to introduce Tobias to Charlie's various friends—that is the reason I was allowed to come to London. But outside of that, I can do what I wish this Season. Since it is the last I will ever have, I would like for it to be memorable."

"Charlie suggested I pick things my brother would never choose for me; that way, I'll have a chance to do those things at least once."

"Within reason," Daria added, repeating his rule.

"Precisely."

She looked up at him as they walked on. "I ought to do the same: choose things my parents wouldn't think of or choose for me. That would certainly make my last Season something I won't ever forget."

"Within reason." Toss spoke very properly, with an ostentatious posture. She couldn't help laughing at the picture he made, though she managed to keep the sound quiet enough to not draw undue notice.

"How many things do you suppose we could do in a single Season?" She was warming to the idea more by the moment.

"Loads, I imagine." His mouth formed a sudden *O*. "I've just had a delightful idea."

"What is it?"

"A competition, between the two of us. We receive a point for each thing we do that our respective families would not have chosen for us—though truly scandalous things are strictly off limits." He looked more and more excited. "On whatever day we choose between us, whoever has accumulated the most points is declared the winner."

Oh, she did like this idea. "And is there a prize for the one who wins?"

"There ought to be, though I don't know what." He shook his head as if trying to dismiss the thought. "Put your mind to it. We'll stumble upon something."

"My mind is not the best to set on questions," she warned him. "You'll have to think hard enough for both of us."

They'd nearly reached her parents. Father and Mother wouldn't care in the least whether she was there or not, but it was where she was expected to be when the Huntresses were all dancing or away and Tobias was not near at hand. For her part, Daria rather dreaded the time she had to spend near them; it was never a truly pleasant experience.

"Beginning in the morning, Daria." Toss spoke quietly enough that no one would overhear his use of her given name. "No scandals, no crimes, nothing hurtful to anyone, just a Season filled with adventures we'd never otherwise have."

"And a mystery prize at the end," she added, smiling from her very heart.

"Brilliant."

Long after he left her to her parents' indifference, her mind remained on that final word of farewell. *Brilliant.* No one had ever said that about her.

Not ever.

CHAPTER FOUR

Miss Martinette's modiste shop was relatively new to London, having opened late in the previous Season. Yet it was already considered *the* place for fashionable ladies to obtain their gowns. Artemis and a woman the Huntresses thought of as an older sister or favorite aunt, Rose Narang, ran it. In the back of that shop, in a private room, the day after the Debenhams' ball, the Huntresses all gathered to select the details of new day dresses.

"The shop appears to be an unparalleled success," Gillian said as she flipped through a pile of fabric samples.

"We've hired a second woman to work the front," Rose said. "And we've added six seamstresses."

"That is a lot of people who know your secret," Daria said. "Aren't you worried they'll tell someone?"

If anyone knew the identity of the shop's actual owners, the scandal would be volcanic. Artemis would struggle to not be ruined socially. Rose's participation would not be looked on with kindness by an unfortunately large portion of London Society. No matter that India had long ago been forcibly made part of the United Kingdom, those who hailed from there were too often treated as if they had no place in that kingdom.

"Only the original woman we hired, Mrs. Beckett, knows that Artemis and I run the business," Rose said. "The rest are told that Mrs. Beckett is the sole proprietress."

"Oh, that was wise," Daria said.

"I thought so." Rose allowed a little smile.

Daria had inadvertently said something that could have been construed as an insult. Fortunately, Rose didn't appear to have taken any offense.

Artemis had created this group of friends, but Rose made them feel like a family.

"You ought to consider this one, Daria." Gillian held up a swatch of blue fabric with small white flowers.

"My parents do prefer that I wear shades of blue," she acknowledged. But that caught her up short. "Except, this Season I'm meant to choose things my parents wouldn't, so perhaps I oughtn't choose a blue fabric."

Six pairs of eyes were quite suddenly on her, confusion in them all.

Artemis was the first to speak. "What do you mean you are meant to choose things your parents wouldn't?"

"Toss said at the ball last night that his brother has said that Toss can do what he chooses this Season and enjoy himself in London, but next Season, he will have to fall in line with whatever his brother insists he do. That will, I'm certain, prove a misery, but at least he gets to return to London. I do so wish I could."

"You won't be returning to London next year?" Artemis looked and sounded horrified.

Daria shook her head. "I'm to put on caps and remain at home."

"And what's all this to do with you doing things they'd not choose for you to do?" Eve, the older of the O'Doyle sisters, always sounded more Irish when she was put out about something.

Perhaps Daria had agreed to something she oughtn't have. Perhaps what had seemed like a harmless lark was, in fact, very inappropriate. She hesitantly explained, "Charlie suggested to Toss at some point that he ought to do things this Season that his brother was unlikely to choose for him next Season."

"That sounds like something my Charlie would suggest," Artemis said, eyes twinkling with amusement.

"Toss suggested I could do the same," Daria continued, "but with regard to my parents' preferences. Nothing scandalous or inappropriate or truly terrible. Little things. Silly things, really. Things like . . ." Oh, why did her mind always empty itself so entirely in precisely the moment she needed it to offer up information?

"Like choosing a dress in a color other than blue?" Ellie suggested.

"Yes, precisely." With one example provided, Daria was able to think of others. "I'd thought of having an ice at Gunter's. That isn't a scandalous thing, but my parents always said I ought not do it because it was an unnecessary indulgence. They also disapprove when I offer greetings to the dogs being walked in the green outside our London house because it makes me seem dim-witted."

"I, for one, think you should do all of those things," Gillian said firmly. "Not despite the reasons your parents gave but because those reasons are utter poppycock."

Firm nods of agreement filled the room. Daria would like to do all those things, and it seemed that none of them were truly shocking.

"I would have three points, then." She pressed her lips together to hold back her grin of delight.

"Points?" Artemis pressed.

"We're making a game of it, Toss and I. We'll each receive a point for everything we do that our respective families would not choose for us, and at the end of the Season, the one of us with the most points will be the champion." It really was a fun game, the more she thought on it. And spending her last Season in London doing something truly enjoyable was a lovely prospect. Toss really was a dear to have given her a means of finding extra delight in her last trip to London. "We don't have a prize chosen, but there is something to be said for simply emerging victorious. I'm so seldom the victor in any sort of contest, excepting the little wagers Tobias and I undertake from time to time. He won our most recent one and will buy me a ribbon for my hair that I have to wear when he says so because I lost. I do win sometimes, but not often." Her mouth always did run away with itself when she was excited or worried. This time, it was the former. "Toss will likely recruit Charlie to help him, so I'm unlikely to think of as many things that would earn me points as they will together. But it will be lovely to try. And I will get to greet dogs and eat ices and do other enjoyable things. That will be well worth doing, don't you think? Even if I don't win."

"Charlie is helping Toss?" A smile began to bloom on Artemis's face.

"I assume he is. He's likely been thinking about it ever since he and Toss first discussed it."

"How fortunate for you, Daria, that you now have all the Huntresses, aside from our much-missed Lisette, thinking about it too."

She looked around at them all, excitement bubbling. "Would you help me?"

"I haven't the least doubt Toss will recruit his and Charlie's friends to the cause. It seems only fair that the ladies do the same for our competitor."

"It is to be the ladies against the gentlemen?" Ellie seemed to very much like the idea.

"Oh yes." Artemis rose to her full height. "And *we* are going to win."

"If I might make a suggestion," Rose said, pulling all their attention to her, "there is a swatch in that pile that is deep plum printed with tiny yellow Welsh poppies. It would make a very lovely day dress."

"And 'tis decidedly not blue," Nia said.

Daria smiled broadly. "I pick that one."

"Your first point," Gillian said. "The first on the road to victory, I predict."

"You'll help too?" Daria didn't actually doubt it. Gillian was distracted lately but not dismissive. Why, then, had Daria felt compelled to ask? Sometimes her brain gave her mouth instructions that made very little sense.

"I will help for as long as I am in Town."

She'd forgotten Gillian and Scott would not be staying in London long. Their funds were quite limited, and they'd only been able to come at all because of the generosity of a family friend. Daria's very best friend and their final London Season together would be cut horribly short. She realized that London was not the only place where two friends could spend time together, but she doubted her parents would be willing to expend the effort and money needed for her to journey to other counties to spend time at the homes of her friends. This really was, in so many ways, her last time with any of them.

"It will be a fine diversion attempting to best the gentlemen at this game they invented. And Toss showed himself to be a tremendous amount of fun throughout the various diversions we all undertook during the house party," Daria said. "This will make our time in London all the more enjoyable."

"And to make it even more so," Artemis said, "I mean to propose a prize to the gentlemen."

That perked up the entire room.

"What prize?" Daria asked.

"If we win, the gentlemen will be charged with planning our next house party. Planning it *and* making certain everyone is able to attend."

"Everyone?" Daria held her breath.

Artemis reached over and squeezed her hand. "Absolutely everyone."

"And what if the gentlemen are victorious?" Ellie asked. "It cannot simply be the reverse of the prize because the house party is likely to be planned by one of us as it is."

Ladies did tend to carry the responsibility for such things. But it wasn't the planning part that Daria wished to place on the shoulders of Toss's friends; it was the responsibility for gathering everyone. Other than perhaps Artemis, none of the Huntresses was in a financial position to fund the travel of another person. Lisette had money enough, but being in France and having rather overbearing parents, she'd not be able to do it.

"It seems only fair," Rose said, "that if the ladies choose the prize they would win for being victorious, the gentlemen should be granted that same ability."

Rose always had been a voice of reason among them.

"Never you fear, Huntresses," Artemis said in conspiratorial tones. "I'll make certain Charlie's friends choose a prize we will be perfectly happy with."

With a look of amused pseudo-annoyance, Rose jumped in. "*I* will liaison with the gentlemen, as something of a neutral third party."

"Secure us something wonderful, Rose," Eve said. "We're depending on you."

CHAPTER FIVE

Toss SAT IN A SITTING room at Falstone House with Charlie, Newton, and Scott, enjoying tea and ridiculous conversation, both of which they'd indulged in far more times than they could possibly count. It felt almost like being back at Cambridge again, almost like Toss hadn't been dragged away by a brother who had never bothered to understand him and was unlikely to even try.

"I feel like you should get a point in your game for this plum of a gathering," Scott said. "From everything I know of your brother, he'll not allow this when he's in charge of your social calendar."

"I *should* get a point," Toss said firmly. "And that would mean I would have the lead, at least for the moment. I have no doubt Daria would be both happy for me and insistent that my lead would not last long."

Charlie laughed lightly. "She's a good gun, as my brother would say."

"She most certainly is." Toss had liked Daria from the very first moment he'd met her. She was sweet-natured, funny, and so wonderfully genuine. Perhaps it was his exhaustion with Laurence, who put such store in appearances and placed very little value on sincerity, that made Toss appreciate it all the more.

He'd thought about Daria often when he'd returned to Cambridge after the house party, often enough to know he was experiencing a bit of calf love. As with all fleeting infatuations, he'd expected it to pass as the months had passed. When he had spotted her participating in the Huntress's entrance at the Debenham ball, his heart had hiccupped a bit. Not such a fleeting infatuation after all, it seemed.

"You should commandeer a traveling coach and return to Cambridge no matter Laurence the Lout's feelings on the matter," Newton said. "That would be worth a dozen points at least."

"Especially since I haven't any means of paying for the journey, let alone the schooling." Toss laughed. "Would I lose points, do you suppose, for doing something utterly foolhardy?"

"Let us hope not," Charlie said. "Most everything any of us will dream up is destined to be foolhardy."

Scott snorted. "Speak for yourself, Jonquil. I'm an American, and we are known for making very reasoned and practical decisions."

That set the lot of them laughing, Scott included.

"As an American," Charlie said, eyeing Scott far too seriously to actually be in earnest, "what is your opinion on Mr. Thomas Comstock earning significant points by riding a horse through Hyde Park?"

Toss met Newton's eye and saw as much confused amusement there as he felt. "My brother wouldn't object to that. He'll likely insist I do precisely that many times next year."

In tones of utter innocence, Charlie said, "Did I forget to mention you'd be making your circuit of the park entirely naked?"

"You did forget that." Toss chuckled.

"As the resident future man of the law," Newton said, "I feel I must point out that your agreement with Daria was that neither of you would do anything scandalous or illegal, and riding nude through Hyde Park is both."

"I suspect our future man of the law would suggest instead that you sit in on Mr. Finley's inheritance trial," Scott said. "It's due to begin soon."

"I would win points for that, but I'd be bored out of my mind."

"Actually, it promises to be fascinating," Newton said. "And the whispers I'm hearing about what is necessitating the trial make me think it'll be shocking in a lot of ways. It isn't every day someone's claim to an inheritance is challenged years after the fact with enough credibility to lead to a trial. I—"

Toss made a loud snoring noise and assumed a posture of being bored into a deep sleep. His eyes were closed, so he didn't know precisely what was thrown at him, though it felt like a crumpled bit of paper. "My apologies," he said in hasty tones of sleepiness, "that was all just so fascinating."

"It truly will be," Newton insisted, though he was clearly not offended by the teasing.

"Gillian and I are attending a concert tomorrow evening," Scott said. "Charlie's mother has invited us to join her. We are to be guests of a member of the *prestigious Jonquil family*." Scott uttered the last three words in tones of overdone importance. They liked to tease Charlie about how important and significant his family was, something he'd appreciated over the years when he'd not felt particularly important or significant himself. Laughing about that perceived chasm had made it less daunting.

"My brother would consider that a waste of an evening," Toss acknowledged. "Which actually makes it a perfect choice. I would earn a point in this competition I've entered into, and I'd enjoy some wonderful music at the same time."

"Someday, Toss," Charlie said, "we'll be enjoying *your* wonderful music at just such an event."

Charlie had always believed in him in a way no one else did, a trait he had, from Toss's experience, inherited from his mother. The dowager Lady Lampton had taken many of her sons' friends under her wing and offered them kindness and encouragement. Mater, as the dowager was known to those fortunate enough to have been embraced by her, had been a balm to Toss's soul many times since he'd lost his own mother.

"If only Laurence hadn't insisted I leave university." Toss tried not to be constantly angry about that, but he couldn't entirely shake his frustration.

"There must be other means of learning what remains to be learned." Scott had known them for only a short time, yet he was as dedicated to their various causes and needs as the rest of the group. "Could not Duke or Fennel send you information from the dons you would have been learning from had you remained?" Duke and Fennel were the two members of their group still attending that venerable institution.

"I suppose I could ask." But if Laurence knew he'd done so, the miserable rip of a fellow would ring such a peal over Toss's head. And while it might earn him some points in the delightful diversion he and Daria had invented, it would make life miserable overall. He could only be at war with his brother over so many things at once.

A quick knock at the door preceded it opening and a maid stepping inside and dipping a curtsy. "Miss Narang to see you, Mr. Jonquil." She stepped back outside, and Rose stepped inside. All the gentlemen stood.

In any other household, the arrival of a woman, one who had worked as a ladies' maid, calling on a gentleman so boldly would be looked at askance, and the gentleman she was calling on would be eyed with some degree of suspicion. But Rose was well-known and well-liked at Falstone House, and Artemis and Charlie were far too significant to the Duke and Duchess of Kielder, whose house this was, for their staff to have any interest in so much as thinking unflattering things about Rose or Charlie.

"Sit back down," Rose instructed the four of them. "I've been sent to parley with you, and I suspect doing so will take some time. We'd do well to all be comfortable."

"Oh dear," Newton said in a theatrical whisper, "what is Charlie in trouble for this time?"

"Shockingly enough, he is on firm footing at the moment. That, however, is not what I have been sent here to discuss." Rose smoothed the front of her sapphire-blue dress, her posture one of a person who'd come to see to a matter of business and was unlikely to be distracted. "The Huntresses have decided to assist Daria in the contest she and Mr. Comstock have invented and are doing so with the likely correct assumption that you gentlemen have already decided to do the same for him."

"We have," Charlie said quite matter-of-factly.

"Further, since no specific ending date was chosen, they would like to propose that the final tally be made on the last evening the O'Doyle sisters will be in London. The O'Doyles are the first scheduled to depart Town, aside from Gillian and Scott, who are leaving too soon for the contest to truly be undertaken."

Toss exchanged looks with his friends and saw no objections. "I can agree to that."

Rose dipped her head in acknowledgment. "Since no prize for the winner was decided upon, they have identified the forfeit they wish to receive should Daria emerge victorious. I am sent to deliver their request and hear what you would ask 'in the unlikely event that Toss proves the victor.'"

"Not exactly a neutral negotiator, are you?" Scott asked with a laugh.

"I assure you, Mr. Sarvol, I am quoting them."

"I don't doubt that." Charlie's grin only grew wider. "What is it they are asking for?"

"They are asking that another house party be held with the Huntresses and 'that group of gentlemen who are so lacking in creativity that they have not managed to fashion a name for themselves despite having been an established group for years.'"

"Quoting them?" Newton guessed aloud.

"Naturally." She returned to the topic without batting an eye. "In the event of Daria's victory, the unnamed group of gentlemen will be charged with planning and carrying out this house party and will be further charged with making certain *all* members of both groups are in attendance."

"I'd say that was a simple enough ask, and one we'd enjoy as well," Scott said, "but three of the Huntresses do not live in Great Britain. And we'd have to schedule it with the Cambridge terms in mind. And Newton and Ellie are not in a position to leave London for any length of time. And Gillian and I haven't the funds yet to trek across counties."

"Neither have I," Toss added, "unless Laurence suffers a blow to the head and suddenly decides I ought to be permitted a bit of happiness." If Daria was not returning to London and Toss was not given the means of traveling outside of his brother's preferences, he didn't know when he would see her again after this Season ended. A heavy disappointment settled over him at the realization.

"The complications are the reason it is a prize worth striving for," Rose pointed out. "And they are well aware you are likely to choose a forfeit that will not be easily managed either."

"This is a rare opportunity, my friends," Charlie said. "We dare not squander it."

"You may have your work cut out for you, Miss Narang," Scott said. "This group of very distinguished gentlemen has a penchant for increasingly ridiculous suggestions."

"I am painfully aware of that." She did not, however, seem upset at that aspect of their collective behavior. "And while I do hope you think of something that will motivate both groups to dedicate themselves all the more to this very welcome distraction from difficulties, I also intend to make certain your forfeit is something reasonable."

"Something complicated and difficult to arrange but also motivating for our competitor." Charlie assumed an amusing expression of pondering. "Could the ladies arrange for Mr. Laurence Comstock to suddenly absent himself from London for weeks on end?"

"And Miss Rosamond Comstock to just as suddenly arrive in London for those same weeks on end," Newton added.

"I would love to have Rosamond here." Toss turned to Rose. "She is my twelve-year-old sister."

"Ah." Rose gave a single nod.

"What if the ladies are charged with leaving Laurence where he is but somehow arranging for Toss to be returned to Cambridge to finish his studies." Scott's suggestion was equally sincere and teasing, a sure sign that he understood how perfect that would be and how impossible.

"We know he cannot return to Cambridge," Charlie acknowledged, "but there must be another way of furthering his education. Informally if need be."

"Is there the equivalent of the Inns of Court in the study of music?" Newton asked.

"Not exactly." Toss shrugged. "The Royal Society of Musicians provides opportunities for its members to learn from and support one another. And sometimes, outside of that society, aspiring musicians are mentored by more established ones, helping them find more opportunities for their works to be performed and income to be obtained. But I don't know any well enough to arrange for anything like that."

Rose's expression had turned ponderous, her deep brown eyes studying him. Charlie wore a look very similar. Truth be told, so did Newton and Scott.

It was Charlie, though, who spoke first. "What if that was our forfeit? Should you emerge victorious, the Huntresses will have to introduce you to an established musician who is willing to assist you in filling the gaps in your knowledge and connections that your early departure from Cambridge has created."

"They can't possibly know any such musicians," he objected.

"And we have not the first idea how to arrange a house party." Charlie shrugged.

Rose nodded slowly. "Both forfeits are complicated, not easily accomplished, and deeply motivating to those who would be the beneficiaries."

A mentorship at the feet of an established musician. Toss didn't dare get his hopes up, and yet . . .

"Are you, the neutral negotiator, agreeing to these terms?" Toss asked Rose.

"I believe I am." She rose, and they all did as well. "Gentlemen, I leave you with two bits of wisdom. The first: fashion a name for yourselves; you will simplify so many things if you do. And second: pour yourselves into this effort, but be advised that Miss Daria Mullins is more easily wounded than she generally lets on; do not cause her any actual misery."

"I never would," Toss insisted and, despite not being the sort of person who wished misery on others, was surprised at the earnestness with which he meant the declaration.

"See that you don't." It was not a request. If Toss wasn't mistaken, it was a warning.

CHAPTER SIX

"Your time would be far better served at a gathering of the *ton* than sitting in a likely half-empty venue waiting for interminable music to come to an end." Laurence's parting declaration repeated in Toss's mind for the umpteenth time, the one his brother had laid out as Toss had left the London house bound for the chamber orchestra performance. That denouncement, no doubt intended to convince him to change plans, had only further solidified them. After all, Laurence had made it perfectly clear that an evening listening to a symphony was *not* something he would choose for Toss to do.

His very first point! He could hardly wait to tell Daria.

He had, at first, thought to purchase a subscription to the Argyll Rooms and attend the concerts held there by the Royal Philharmonic Society, but he'd learned upon his arrival in Town that the venue was closed and undergoing extensive renovations. Considering how the past weeks had gone, it seemed rather fitting.

The venue chosen that night for the symphony performance was not so large nor so crowded as the various opera houses and dramatic theaters of London, making Scott, Gillian, and the dowager Lady Lampton easy to find upon his arrival there. Mater, as he would likely always call the dowager countess, greeted him as warmly as she always did, offering genuine words of delight at his presence.

"Not everyone appreciates chamber orchestras," Mater said after everyone had expressed their delight at being in company. "I am so pleased to know that all three of you do." She looked at Toss with an expression of mischief he had seen in Charlie's eyes on more than one occasion. "I trust your brother expressed his rejection of your choice of entertainment this evening?"

"You trust?"

She shrugged a little. "How else are you to earn a point in your competition?"

He ought to have known she would be aware of the game. Few things escaped Mater's notice. "I am happy to report that I have earned an indisputable point by being here this evening."

"Excellent," Scott said, earning a teasing look of disapproval from his wife.

"Do not grow too confident, you two," Gillian said. "I happen to know the invitation was extended elsewhere as well."

It was in that very moment that Daria and her brother entered.

"Do you think for even a moment that Mr. and Mrs. Mullins would have chosen for their daughter to spend her evening listening to a chamber orchestra in so unremarkable a venue?" Gillian answered her own question with a quick shake of her head.

"Hmm. It seems you are at one point all." Mater looked ever more mischievous.

"Whose side are you on?" Toss whispered in tones of mock offense. Truth be told, he was pleased Daria had also secured a point in their competition. And based on the bubble of excitement forming in his chest, he was perhaps even more pleased simply to see her again.

Mater laughed as she turned to greet the newest arrival. Mater was the only person he knew who could exude cheerfulness and joy whilst always wearing black. It was not *unrelieved* black but enough that on anyone else the effect would have been somber.

"Mr. Comstock!" Toss had discovered, to his delight, during the house party that Daria legitimately spoke in exclamation points. She hadn't adopted the *ton's* preference for ennui and indifference. "I have earned a point."

"Your parents were not enthusiastic about tonight's entertainment?" he guessed aloud.

"Not at all." She smiled brightly. "And as a chamber orchestra concert in a respectable place is not scandalous nor criminal, I believe this qualifies for a point." Her brows shot low. "Except, I did agree to bring Tobias so he could be introduced to Mr. Sarvol, which *did* meet with my parents' approval. Do you suppose that means I lose the point?"

He resisted the urge to reach out and take her hand, unsure where the inclination had come from. "I do not think so, and as I am one of the inventors of the game, I think that opinion holds some weight."

Her smile returned on the instant. "I am the *other* inventor, and I agree with you."

"Well then, we have a consensus."

"For two people locked in a contest with such significant forfeits, you are being very friendly," Scott said.

"Ooh, Mr. Sarvol." Daria pulled her brother forward. Toss had noticed her brother did not always seem overly eager to receive these introductions. "Mr. Sarvol, this is my brother, Mr. Tobias Mullins. Tobias, this is Mr. Scott Sarvol of Sarvol House in Nottinghamshire and before that, of America in . . . America." She winced. "I should have thought through that before I started speaking. It ended all wrong, I'm afraid."

Gillian sent every one of them a look of dire warning; she was very protective of her friend. But the warning was, in actuality, unnecessary. Not a person among them would mistreat Daria. Indeed, Toss couldn't imagine anyone not thinking she was delightful.

"Your timing is perfect," Mater said. "I do believe the concert is to begin shortly. We'd best take our seats."

The space was too small to be called a concert hall but was larger than those more intimate locations where chamber music was often played. Still, there were a half dozen boxes, which provided a bit of privacy for those fortunate enough to have use of them, which the dowager had secured. It was into one of these spaces that they retreated, finding exactly six chairs. Either the space usually held that number or Mater had known Daria would bring her brother and had planned accordingly.

Because Scott wished to sit with his wife and Mater wished to sit beside Scott and no one would countenance Mater being relegated to the second row of seats, Toss and Tobias sat in the row behind with Daria between them.

The concert-master cued the other musicians, and the performance began. Toss didn't recognize the piece but heard in it the influence of Beethoven's early work, itself influenced by Haydn and Mozart. This piece, though, did not have quite the dynamic of Beethoven's compositions.

"Why is there not a person standing in front of the musicians waving his arms about?" Daria asked him in a whisper.

"Chamber orchestras are smaller and do not utilize a conductor. They play by listening to and reacting to each other."

"They must be very talented." She even looked impressed. Not many who weren't versed in the complexities of music making truly appreciated the skill required.

"The man playing the violin who is seated nearest the audience, he is the concert-master. The other musicians look to him for cues to begin each piece."

"Then he is like their conductor," she said, "except he can't wave his arms about on account of his currently playing his violin."

"Wouldn't that be quite a sight to see though?" Toss chuckled silently.

She smiled at him, so sweetly and so sincerely. Toss couldn't remember the last time someone had fallen so easily into conversation with him on the topic of music. His friends were very supportive, but they tended to tease him about the boredom of such a topic in the same way they all teased Newton about the law.

"The concert-master just nodded his head," Daria said. "Only a little, but I did see it. Do you suppose that means something to the other musicians?"

"Most certainly. He was likely telling them to adjust their tempo or move to a new section or stop holding out a particular note. They will have worked all that out during their many rehearsals."

Something pleading entered her eyes. "Then I sorted that out correctly? I noticed something, and I wasn't wrong about it?"

"You were, in fact, brilliantly perceptive." He set his hand very briefly on hers and squeezed it reassuringly. "Not everyone recognizes the cues amongst the musicians unless they have studied such things."

Relief passed over her features, followed immediately by curiosity. "Have you studied such things?"

"Again, brilliantly perceptive."

He didn't think he'd ever seen anyone so sincerely pleased to have received a compliment as she looked in that moment. She turned toward her brother and whispered something to him.

Out of the corner of his eyes, he saw Tobias look in his direction. He let his own gaze shift that way. An almost imperceptible nod passed between Tobias and him, one even more subtle than that employed by the concert-master.

Though Toss couldn't be certain, he thought it was a thank-you. A sincere and casually offered bit of praise was, it seemed, much appreciated.

Throughout the first piece, Daria continually glanced at him, smiling every time she spotted a cue from the concert-master to the other musicians. Toss didn't think he'd ever sat with someone during a concert who took such delight in that small, usually unnoticed aspect of the performance. Daria had been that way during the house party as well, of a curious mind and a pleasantly delighted disposition. It certainly made sense that he'd grown so fond of her.

"Why are they called a chamber orchestra and not . . . an ordinary orchestra?" she whispered. "I know other orchestras aren't called *ordinary*, but I don't know what they are called. I likely shouldn't guess. You'll think me an absolute featherhead."

"Not knowing something you've not yet had the chance to learn is not a poor reflection on you," he insisted, whispering as well. "Chamber orchestras are thus called because they are small and usually perform in chambers or rooms rather than in grand concert halls or theaters."

"Oh, that does make sense." Her gaze studied the musicians as the next selection began. "Do you like chamber orchestras better than concert-hall orchestras?"

"I like them both," he said.

She smiled at him once more. "So do I."

Daria was delightful company throughout the evening, asking questions, expressing sincere enjoyment of the music. So many who attended performances either affected the ennui Society expected or made an effort to portray themselves as being an expert in music or to possess such lofty taste as to find the evening dissatisfying. Daria was wonderfully and charmingly herself, and Toss, who would have enjoyed the evening regardless, found himself entirely enchanted. The Daria he had thought back on so often in the months since he'd last seen her was every bit as lovely as his heart and mind remembered her being.

CHAPTER SEVEN

Daria's parents had no opinion on the matter of her being fitted for the gown Artemis and Rose were providing her, and therefore, she would not be receiving any points for the *time* she spent at Miss Martinette's Dress Shop. She was pleased to be there, though, and not merely on account of the beautiful dress she was receiving, which she would be earning a point for.

She was in the back room, where the Huntresses always gathered when visiting the establishment, but this time only she and Rose were there. Daria didn't often have time alone with the woman she'd come to think of, in many ways, as the older sister she did not have. All the Huntresses felt like sisters to her, but there was something unique in her connection with Rose, something more protective, more comforting.

The Huntresses gave her confidence and helped her feel less alone in the world. Rose made her feel safe.

"I think the purple was an excellent choice." Rose eyed the fit of the gown, walking in a slow circle around Daria as she spoke. "It is flattering in a way that feels intentional, a selection made by one who knows what she's about."

Daria laughed. "Then everyone will know at a glance I had help. I can't think of a single person who believes for a moment that I know anything at all about anything."

"I can state with confidence that any number of people know perfectly well that you are not so featherheaded as you too often believe you are." Rose crossed to the wall of drawers where fabric, buttons, trimmings, and such were stored.

"I suppose you're right. The Huntresses don't think I'm entirely mutton witted."

"They don't at all." Rose pulled a drawer open.

"And my brother, at least, pretends he doesn't, though I cannot say for certain if he does actually believe it."

"Though I do not know Mr. Mullins well, I do not think he is a talented enough actor to have fooled all of us on that matter."

Daria laughed a little. "I suspect he isn't." She looked at herself once more in the tall mirror placed in the room specifically for fittings. The purple was rather flattering. How delightful to have earned a point for obtaining a dress she liked so very much. The reminder of the game brought Toss to mind once more. "Toss has twice said that I am brilliant. And he answered all my questions about music at the concert two evenings ago. And he didn't seem to think I was stupid for not already knowing the answers."

"Not knowing something does not make a person unintelligent," Rose said. "Every person who knows anything learned it at some point."

"He said something very similar."

"And sometimes people who know a lot of things are the most thickheaded of all." Rose returned to where Daria stood, a folded length of soft fabric in her hands. "I think we should fashion for you a shawl of this material. It will complement this dress quite nicely but would also be a lovely addition to any number of ensembles."

She draped a bit of it over Daria's shoulder, eyeing the combination with what looked to be satisfaction.

The fabric itself was a light cream, soft and flowing and printed with tiny sprigs of poppies in a rainbow of colors. "I do love poppies," she said.

"The very reason I thought of you when I saw the fabric at the drapers." Rose nodded. "I like this as a shawl for you."

"I do have some pin money," Daria said. "If it is enough, I would like to have the shawl."

But Rose waved that off. "I am not *selling* it to you, Daria. I am giving it to you because I believe you ought to have it."

"But you have already gifted me two dresses this Season."

"And if your parents make good on their current plans, I will not have an opportunity to give you anything next Season."

That was true. "They may leave me behind simply because they forget about me. I know the Huntresses generally think of my parents as being rather harsh toward me, but I think they are more indifferent than actively disapproving."

"Should they forget about you," Rose said, "what do you mean to do?"

Daria looked away from the poppy-patterned fabric and at Rose once more. "I don't understand."

Rose moved to stand directly beside her and took her hands in her own, a kind, sisterly gesture she didn't often employ but which all the Huntresses cherished. "Your parents' indifference has taught you some inaccurate lessons, Daria. It has led you to believe that you are unimportant and forgettable. After this Season, you are to be left behind to do whatever it is you choose to do. Thus, my question for you is, *what* do you mean to do?"

"I'll be a spinster daughter living in the country." Daria swallowed against the lump of disappointment that formed at the admission. "What can I do? What choice do I really have but to put on my caps and dawdle about the estate?"

With a squeeze of Daria's hands, Rose said, "You always have a choice. Maybe not all the choices you would like to have, but there is always a choice of one kind or another. You either make it yourself or fate makes it for you. And she is not always kind."

A quick knock at the door pulled Rose's attention away. She crossed to the door, having a low conversation with the person on the other side, most likely the woman hired to run the shop.

There is always a choice of one kind or another.

But what choices did Daria really have? There was so little she was permitted to do. So little she had any ability to do.

You either make it yourself or fate makes it for you.

That would actually not be terribly different from how her life had gone thus far. Someone else was always making her decisions for her.

"Mr. Layton is here to consult for a bit," Rose said, having closed the door once more. "I'll unbutton your dress in the back, then you slip into the dressing room and change back into the dress you wore here."

That was accomplished relatively quickly. Rose saw Daria fastened into her own dress and set fully to rights by the time another knock at the door announced the new arrival.

Mr. Digby Layton was something of a legend in Society. He was an arbiter of fashion, a man of impeccable taste and significant standing. He was that odd combination of tastefully elegant and somewhat extravagant. A friend of the Jonquil family since the days of the late earl, he was also privy to the true ownership of Miss Martinette's.

"Miss Narang." He greeted Rose with a bow. "And Miss Mullins." He offered the same to Daria. "A delight to see you both."

"I thought you would be at the trial today." Rose could be abrupt in her conversation at times, but those who knew her did not mistake that tendency for rudeness.

"It has been adjourned for the day, leaving me time to acquaint you with a very significant bit of news." He spoke in tones of secrecy but so theatrically that

Daria felt certain he had come to either tell Rose something that was, in actuality, insignificant or something that was otherwise unattainable. "Lambeth Drapers has received a new bolt of silk that has the precise shimmer and texture of the sapphire silk you made your rather stunning gown from, but this shipment is in a sumptuous shade of emerald. As I know India silk is sometimes difficult to come by, I thought I'd drop a word in your ear before it is snatched up."

"It will certainly sell fast." Rose's brow pulled in thought. "Daria's maid is waiting for her, but I had intended to hail a hackney to see them returned home."

Mr. Layton dipped his head. "With Miss Mullins's approval, I will happily see her and her maid returned home in my carriage."

"I would be most grateful," Daria said. Her parents had spoken well of Mr. Layton in the past and, therefore, would not disapprove of the arrangement. That meant she couldn't claim a point for the journey. If Toss were there, and she found she very much wished he were, he would have teased her about that, but not in the hurtful way some people teased her. His variety of teasing made her feel special and wanted. Outside of the Huntresses and Tobias, few people did that for her.

Rose disappeared upstairs, no doubt to fetch her pelisse and other things she might need to make the journey to the drapers.

Mr. Layton, with his flawless manners and knack for putting people at ease, motioned for Daria to slip from the room ahead of him. As she did, he said quietly, "Have Mrs. Beckett send for your maid to meet you at the front of the shop. I will call up my carriage."

It was the perfect way to accomplish it all. What must that be like? To be presented with a situation or a complication and be able to sort it out quickly and in just the right way?

Daria was still pondering that when Mr. Layton stepped inside the shop from the street outside and ushered her and her maid—one of the chambermaids her parents had agreed to let accompany her—to his waiting carriage, a very elegant one, well suited to its very elegant owner. He must have been in his sixties, but he moved with every bit of the agility of the youngest of Town bucks. Her own father was only in his forties, yet he moved slowly and with an obvious air of one who preferred sitting to almost any other activity.

"Thank you for your kindness, Mr. Layton," Daria said. "I did manage a journey with only myself and my maid last autumn when leaving a house party but only because Artemis made all the arrangements and gave the driver very specific instructions. If left to me, I likely would have bungled the entire thing."

"I suspect you are overstating the situation." He was as gracious as he was fashionable. The two characteristics did not always go hand in hand. "But I am pleased to be of service just now."

Jenny, the maid who sat beside Daria, watched the older gentleman with a look that could be interpreted as nothing other than absolute awe. Mr. Layton *was* quite well regarded. Mother and Father would no doubt consider his acquaintance quite a feather in their caps. And to make Tobias acquainted with him would be seen as further proof that bringing Daria to London had been a good decision.

"Would you—" She hesitated. But the thought of her parents deciding she had done all she could for Tobias and sending her home gave her the nudge she needed. "If it would not be asking too much, would you be willing to step inside for a moment when we arrive at my family home and allow me to introduce my parents and brother to you?" With the request now made, she felt rather too bold for having made it. "I likely shouldn't ask that, and you are no doubt wondering what could have convinced me to do so. It's only that my parents were reluctant to bring me to Town, and my brother told them that doing so would be a good idea since I could make him known to some important people on account of my being friends with Artemis and Charlie. And you are an important person. Not that I think you are only worth knowing because you are important. I certainly don't mean that."

"I would be happy to meet your brother, Miss Mullins. And if your parents are present, I would not object to an introduction to them." The response was gracious, but there was something in the wording that told her the introduction, to her parents at least, was not entirely to his liking.

"You don't have to, of course. I don't wish to cause you any distress or discomfort."

"No distress or discomfort, I assure you, and I am sorry to have given you any impression otherwise."

Daria leaned forward, a little closer to him, and lowered her voice. "I have no expectation of you choosing to make my parents your friends or even people you seek out. I am not the cleverest of people, but I do know they are not always pleasant to spend significant amounts of time with."

He leaned forward as well and dropped his volume to match hers. "Why is it you are so certain you are not clever?"

She smiled and shrugged a bit. "There is ample evidence. Likely more than I even realize or remember. My father has pointed out that I've a mind like a sieve. If even I can recall enough proof of my featherheadedness, then it is clearly true."

"Do you know, Miss Mullins, I find myself increasingly inclined to make your parents' acquaintance." Mr. Layton leaned back once more. "Is your brother of the same opinion as they on the matter of your . . . featherheadedness?"

"He has a brother's bias." Daria couldn't help but smile when thinking of Tobias. "He treats me quite as if I weren't stupid in the least."

"I suspect your dear Huntresses treat you as he does."

She nodded. "They do. I feel more clever when I'm with them. That is a lovely thing, don't you think? To have friends who make you feel like a better version of yourself?"

"It is a rare and wonderful thing. I am blessed to have friends just like that."

"Charlie's friends are very kind to me as well. His friend Mr. Comstock is having his first Season in London, and next Season, his brother will be dictating all he does. And my parents have already said they won't bring me to London in the future since I have not had any success in the Marriage Mart. So Mr. Comstock and I devised the most wonderful game to make this Season better than it would otherwise be. He is also very kind to me, and he tells me I'm brilliant, which I think is a wonderful thing."

Mr. Layton smiled. "What is this game?"

"We will try to think of things our families would not choose for us to do during the Season, and we will do those things. Whoever does the most things by the end of the Season will be the winner." She quickly added, "But we, of course, wouldn't do anything wrong or inappropriate or illegal."

"I could not think otherwise." He smiled kindly. "Who is currently in the lead?"

"I don't know. I earned a point by attending a chamber orchestra performance last night and a point for choosing purple fabric for my dress. I don't know how many points he has."

Mr. Layton's kind and avuncular smile slowly shifted to something a little mischievous. "Once we have accomplished the introductions to your family, *I* have an idea, Miss Mullins, that I believe will earn you a point in your competition with Mr. Comstock."

"Is it something I will enjoy?"

"I can confidently say that you will."

"And it is not wrong or inappropriate or illegal?"

"I would never suggest anything that could be described in any of those terms."

She nodded and smiled broadly, anticipating the joy of telling Toss that she had earned another point. "I cannot wait to hear what it might be."

CHAPTER EIGHT

Daria could hear Father and Mother's talking as she walked with Mr. Layton toward the sitting room. She could not entirely prevent her steps from slowing.

"We cannot continue to delay," Father said. "The situation will only grow worse."

"But we must see Tobias well-established," Mother said. "Everything depends upon that."

"Even that will fall to pieces should we not move forward as we are supposed to."

Daria was too embarrassed to look at Mr. Layton. She had already confessed to him that her presence in London was contingent upon helping her brother become a social success. Hearing her parents speak of it so plainly was a little humiliating.

She and Mr. Layton stepped into the sitting room. Though he was meant to do so upon the entrance of any lady, Father didn't rise. He only glanced at her before reaching for a book to read. But an almost immediate second glance brought him immediately to his feet. It was not a sudden remembrance of the gentlemen's code, she suspected, but the realization that someone other than his daughter had also arrived.

"Mr. Layton," Daria said, "might I make known to you my parents, Mr. and Mrs. Mullins."

Mr. Layton offered a small bow.

"Father, Mother, this is Mr. Layton of Pledwick Manor in Yorkshire."

"We know where he is from," her mother muttered to her under her breath. Daria ought to have realized they would know of him and where his home was.

Mother indicated Mr. Layton should be seated. He did so after Daria and her mother were seated once more. No one could fault his manners.

"To what do we owe the honor of this visit?" Father asked.

"Mr. Layton was kind enough to see that Jenny and I returned home after my appointment at Miss Martinette's."

"He did not ask you," Mother quietly corrected. "Do try to think before you speak, Daria."

She *did* try, though she knew it did not always help. But neither did arguing with her parents. So she kept her objections to herself.

"To what do we owe the honor of your visit, Mr. Layton?" Father repeated his question, making clear to whom he addressed it and from whom he hoped for a response.

"I was fortunate enough to be in a position to see to it your daughter and Jenny returned home after Miss Mullins's appointment at Miss Martinette's." Though his tone was utterly benign, there was a pointedness to his answer. "As your daughter said."

"She sometimes speaks out of turn," Father said. "And her hamfistedness in making your introduction must not be held against the entire family."

Heat stole over Daria's cheeks.

"I thought her introductions were well made and charmingly executed." Mr. Layton's eyes narrowed on Father even as one of his white eyebrows arched ever so slightly. "In what way do you consider *my* evaluation of her efforts to be incorrect or lacking?"

"I didn't—wasn't—" Father was almost never at a loss for words.

"We consider you to be quite an undisputed arbiter of all good taste." Mother's words emerged almost as a plea.

"Yet, you corrected your daughter's introduction, in contrast to my feeling that she managed it very well indeed." His posture was somehow casual and unwaveringly alert at the same time. "Either that correction was warranted, *or* I am 'an undisputed arbiter of all good taste.' I am deeply curious to know which is actually true."

Oh, that was clever. Were Toss there, he would, without question, declare Mr. Layton brilliant as well, though Daria knew she was not the older gentleman's equal. Still, she would have enjoyed seeing how impressed Toss would be and how broadly he would smile to have witnessed the well-delivered retort.

And how would her parents answer Mr. Layton's question? Either they insulted him by insisting their disapproval of Daria's introduction was warranted, or they admitted to being wrong in order to not contradict their previous compliment of him.

Father sputtered a little. Mother simply blushed deeply.

Mr. Layton continued without looking the least uncomfortable. Here was a gentleman who was entirely comfortable in his place among all of Society. "Your daughter had hoped to make me acquainted with your son. As she assured me he is above reproach, I had looked forward to the introduction."

"Oh, our Tobias is a perfectly lovely young gentleman." Mother found her voice once more. "I do wish he were here so he could make your acquaintance."

"If he and your daughter do not have other plans this evening," Mr. Layton said, "I would extend to them an invitation to attend a small gathering at the home of Lord and Lady Aldric Benick this evening."

"The uncle and aunt of the Duke of Hartley?" Father's words filled with awe as he asked the question.

"Do you truly not know who they are, or was the question rhetorical?" Mr. Layton asked.

Again, the sputtering and blushing. Oh, it was a fortunate thing Toss *was not* present just then. She suspected his eyes would have danced with amusement at Mr. Layton's expert navigation of the situation, and she would have been hard-pressed to keep hidden how much she enjoyed his company. Mother and Father were likely to interpret that as Daria taking delight at their embarrassment.

With her thoughts wandering, she'd not realized Mr. Layton was speaking to her. "I hope to see you and your brother there at eight o'clock this evening."

There? Oh, yes. The home of the Duke of Hartley's uncle. "Will not Lord and Lady Aldric be upset to find themselves with additional guests they were not expecting?"

"They will be delighted, I assure you."

This was, then, the event that Mr. Layton suspected would earn her a point in her competition with Toss. But her parents seemed to approve. She wasn't certain how to reconcile those contradictory facts.

He rose, and she and her parents followed suit. Quick words of farewell were exchanged as they walked with him to the entryway. In the moment before stepping out, Mr. Layton looked back to Daria and asked, "How fond of poetry are your parents?"

"I can't say they have any taste for it."

A slow, small, conspiratorial smile spread over his face. "Excellent."

"You are certain Mr. Layton's invitation included me?" Tobias looked as uncertain as he sounded. He had ever since they'd left their home to journey to the sophisticated residence of Lord and Lady Aldric. Now that they had arrived, his obvious worry grew enormously.

"Mother and Father also understood it to include you," she said. "I think that decreases the chances that I am wrong."

"I hadn't meant to imply that you were thickheaded. I've simply never met Mr. Layton, and I don't wish to make a nuisance of myself in such exalted company as he keeps."

"He *did* invite you. I swear to it." She was certain of that much, but she'd not yet managed to sort out why Mr. Layton thought she would earn a point for that evening's entertainment. Her parents were quite pleased that their children had received such a distinguished invitation.

And why had Mr. Layton asked her about poetry of all things?

Daria was beginning to suspect she wasn't clever enough for the game she was playing.

They were ushered into a stately entryway by a statelier butler, whom they followed all the way to an *even* statelier drawing room. Mr. Layton was nearest the door and smiled when he saw them, which set Daria's mind more at ease.

"Welcome," he said, bending a bit of a bow toward them. "Please allow me to make introductions."

A quick glance around the room showed her she didn't know anyone but him, and only one person in the room was of her generation.

"Friends," he said, "I am pleased to make known to you Mr. Tobias Mullins and Miss Mullins." He motioned Daria and her brother toward the nearest couple. "This is Lord and Lady Aldric Benick." The next couple. "Mr. and Mrs. Barrington." The next. "Mr. and Mrs. Greenberry." And the next. "Mr. and Mrs. Fortier."

"Oh." Daria had a sudden realization upon hearing their name. "You invested in Thimbleby." That was a holding of Scott's, one he and Gillian were working very hard to make profitable, something far more likely thanks to the investments of a few people, including, apparently, this couple.

The beautiful Mrs. Fortier smiled. "We have, *oui*."

"Gillian is so baffled by your kindness toward her, and she swears she doesn't know you at all. She's grateful but . . . baffled. As are we all. Grateful and baffled, I mean."

The woman's gaze turned a bit searching, as if piecing together some mystery. "You are one of the Huntresses?"

Daria nodded.

"Then we are doubly pleased to meet you, Miss Mullins." Her English was impeccable, and her French accent, while obvious, was not difficult to decipher.

"Because I am one of the Huntresses?"

Mrs. Fortier nodded but offered no explanation.

"Why should that make you additionally grateful to know me?" Daria realized Mr. Layton and Tobias were watching her, Tobias with a look of quiet admonition. "Oh dear. I wasn't meant to interrupt the introductions. I am always doing these things wrong."

"No harm done, Miss Mullins, I assure you." Mr. Layton motioned to the final person in the room; a gentleman likely eight or nine years older than she was and stunningly handsome. "Mr. and Miss Mullins, this is Mr. Colm Greenberry."

Daria glanced back at the couples she'd just been introduced to. "And those are your parents?"

"They are." He smiled in the very moment she looked back at him. The man had dimples, which she thought terribly unfair. He was handsome enough already. She would have some difficulty not staring at him. Fortunately for her composure, he turned to Tobias. "Mr. Mullins, it is nice to meet you. I've heard you spoken of the past couple of days and had hoped to make your acquaintance."

Tobias took a quick look around the room, his expression of confusion growing. "Who has spoken of me?"

"The dowager Countess of Lampton."

At that, the two young gentlemen launched into a discussion of acquaintances they had in common and their various interests. Daria felt hopeful that Tobias had found a new friend.

"I thought the two of them might get on well," Mr. Layton said to her.

"My parents would certainly approve. They brought me to London specifically to help Tobias make friends, but that means I won't earn a point for tonight."

Mr. Layton smiled very kindly. "Have faith, Miss Mullins."

"Is this to do with your question about poetry?"

He nodded, looking almost as if he were a little proud of her. "It is. You indicated your parents' indifference to poetry, and tonight's gathering is an annual one dedicated entirely to extremely entertaining poetry."

The butler announced another arrival. "The dowager Countess of Lampton." Then a second unexpected name. "Mr. Thomas Comstock."

Her heart swelled on the instant, beating a rhythm of eager anticipation. She enjoyed his company and thought of him often when they were apart, but she'd not expected this feeling of bone-deep delight at seeing him again.

Upon seeing Daria, Toss burst out laughing, his eyes twinkling with enjoyment. Mater looked at Mr. Layton and shook her head with a silent laugh of her own.

"It seems, Digby," Mater said, "we had the same idea this evening."

"Apparently."

Toss crossed to Daria. "Are you here to earn a point in our competition?"

"I am, though it seems it won't profit me much, as you are receiving one as well."

"At the rate we are proceeding, we will end the Season with precisely the same number of points, and no one will be the winner."

"Oh, but I have one more than you do." She took hold of his arm, squeezing it in her excitement. "I will earn a point for a purple dress. My parents prefer my dresses to be blue, but the one I ordered from Miss Martinette's is going to be purple."

"I should choose a book on music composition from the lending library. My brother would certainly never choose that for me."

She still had hold of his arm, enjoying his easy enthusiasm and lack of disapproval. Her parents never had appreciated her inability to hide her eagerness. "You would enjoy the book, which makes the point all the more meaningful."

"Does that mean you would give me an additional point?"

She laughed, not overly worrying that she would be condemned for it. "No additional points. I mean to be an ogre about this."

"Shall we begin?" Lord Aldric asked the room, claiming all their attention.

Everyone was quickly situated.

Mr. Fortier led the discussion after that, his French accent more subtle than his wife's. "As we have new participants joining us, I will quickly review the evening's challenge. We will, this evening, work as teams to extemporize short poetry and do so based on prompts drawn from hats. At the end of the evening, we will recognize those who composed the best, most unique, most entertaining, and most ridiculous poem."

Oh dear. Daria was not particularly adept at games that required intellect and cleverness.

"You don't seem overly enthusiastic," Toss whispered, having taken the seat beside her.

"You witnessed my struggle with the games at the house party. I haven't the quick-wittedness that pastimes such as this require."

"I thought you did marvelously well at all the games," he said. "I have no recollection of your being utter rubbish."

"Your memory is being kind to me."

"Or perhaps your anxious thoughts are being *un*kind to you."

"We will create three teams," Mr. Fortier continued. "One will have only four members compared to the others' five."

"You'd best make that *your* team," Mr. Greenberry said.

In explanation, Mater leaned closer to Toss and Daria. "Mr. Fortier is quite adept at crafting poetry."

Then Daria would look even more foolish.

Something in her thoughts must have shown in her expression. Toss took hold of her hand. "I have learned of this group of ladies and gentlemen, both from Charlie and from Mater, and I do not think you need to worry that any of them will be unkind."

"I'm certain they won't say anything, but . . . they'll *know.*"

"Know what?" he asked quietly.

"I've always been a bit stupid. It is such a miserable thing watching people realize that about me."

"I spent a fortnight in your company at the house party," Toss said, "and a few evenings thus far this Season, and I have not yet 'realized' that about you. You should know that I am well able to judge such things, as I attended Cambridge with some shockingly thickheaded people."

She smiled a bit at that, grateful for his kindness. Grateful for *him.* "Do you have a knack for poetry?"

"Not at all. But I have my suspicions that *good* poetry is not the aim of this evening." He leaned forward enough to talk past her and address Mater. "Are we meant to create *impressive* poetry?"

Amusement dancing in her face, Mater said, "Absolutely not."

Toss turned to Daria once more and laughed. The sound wrapped itself like a wonderfully warm blanket around her heart.

CHAPTER NINE

Lord and Lady Aldric both held hats out to Mr. Fortier, who drew a slip of parchment from each. "A meal," he read from the first slip. The second read, "Harrowing." He folded the papers together and slipped them into the watch pocket of his waistcoat. "Best of luck."

Toss turned toward the others on his team—Mater, Mr. Layton, Daria, and Mr. Greenberry—eager to begin.

"A harrowing meal." Mater tapped her fingers together as her unfocused gaze turned ponderous.

"Meals can be harrowing for many reasons," Daria said. "The food served or the location or the people participating in the meal." She bit her lips closed for a moment. "You all likely thought of that already."

She was clearly convinced of her own thickheadedness, which was baffling. She was perhaps not academically inclined, but she was hardly bacon-brained.

"Making a list is always helpful when working as a group," Mr. Layton said with every indication of sincerity. "Which ought we to pursue," he asked them all, "a meal that is harrowing on account of the food, the location, or the guests?"

"I suspect our competitors will choose the guests or the location or event," Mr. Greenberry said. "We ought to choose food."

"What about the food makes the meal harrowing?" Mater asked. "The taste, the presentation?"

An idea formed immediately in Toss's mind. "Every meal must be harrowing *for the food*, seeing as it is about to be eaten."

"Oooh." Daria bounced a bit, something Toss tended to do as well. "I like that idea. No one else will think of it."

They began suggesting different ways of applying the idea, each suggestion more absurd than the previous. Laughter was plenteous and universal among their team. Daria's suggestions were met with compliments and laughter, as was appropriate.

After one particularly funny suggestion, Daria turned toward him, smiling so broadly she was likely to fill the entire room with figurative sunshine. "I think I'm doing well."

"You are doing brilliantly," he said.

She clasped her hands together. "My parents would hate this."

"No surer way to win a point, Daria."

She laughed lightly, the twinkle in her eyes rendering them even lovelier. With her smile still in place, she began to turn toward the others in their group but stopped partway, her eyes fixed on something.

Toss followed her gaze directly to Mr. Colm Greenberry watching her from his own group with a soft smile of his own. She blushed a bit. There was nothing untoward, nothing objectionable in the younger Mr. Greenberry's expression or notice of her. Toss ought to have been happy that a lady he considered a friend was being treated kindly.

Why, then, did he feel the urge to place himself between the two of them and put an end to all the smiles and blushes and attention?

"Time to share, *mes amis*," Mr. Fortier announced. "Let us begin with Lord Aldric's team."

Mr. Colm Greenberry rose to read their offering.

> "'Twas at a gathering near Aberdeen I had my first taste of haggis.
> In the days and weeks to follow, alas, I learnt what it was to gag-is."

The room erupted in laughter.

"Tobias had a hand in that effort, I am certain of it." Daria's voice lilted with a laugh of her own. Utter delight filled her expression, pulling a smile to Toss's lips as well. He particularly liked seeing her happy.

Mrs. Fortier rose to recite their team's composition.

> "The food was expertly prepared.
> The company was charming.
> But a table balanced upon a cliff
> Proved, above all else, alarming."

Applause followed that offering, with ample commentary on the dual meaning of the phrase "above all else" when paired with the imagery of being on a cliff. It was a lighthearted poem but the composition was quite good. Mr. Fortier was, as Mater had said, quite talented at poetry; his team's entries would almost definitely be of a higher quality than the rest.

When Mr. Layton rose to read their team's verse, he was met with calls of "A royal reading" and "The King wishes to be heard" and "What an honor, Your Majesty." This was a group of long-acquainted friends, and Toss didn't doubt these were long-established teases among them.

> "'Woe is me,' the carrot cried.
> The card players eagerly farro-ing.
> The chef's knife sharp and ready
> For vegetable narrowing.
> When one is on the menu, you see,
> *Every* meal is harrowing."

More laughter and applause followed. Daria looked pleased. She'd often spent their games at the house party the previous autumn with a vague look of embarrassment. He'd wondered at the time what had inspired that particular response. Their conversations of late had illuminated that: she considered herself humiliatingly lacking in cleverness, a misjudgment of herself he wished he knew how to counter.

"*Gag-is* and *farro-ing*." Mrs. Fortier shook her head in amusement. "It seems *invented* words are the order of the day today."

"We may have some difficulty awarding the honorific of Most Creative this time," Mrs. Greenberry said. "Creating new words certainly qualifies as creative." She sounded vaguely Irish. The story of how this group came to know each other, hailing from such different places, was likely an interesting one.

"We might win the Most Creative prize," Daria said to him in a hopeful whisper. "I never win any games like this, the kind that require a person to be clever."

Again, that unflattering view of herself. "It was your suggestion that we not wax poetic about location or company or the experience of those eating a meal that led to such a creative poem. That was quite clever."

Though she didn't argue, he didn't think she believed him.

The game continued on, with the teams fluctuating between humorous offerings and more impressive ones, though the tone of the evening never stopped being lighthearted and convivial. Daria grew more and more at ease and delighted with the undertaking. Seeing the transformation, Toss told himself he would make absolutely certain their friends found opportunities this

Season to undertake similar evenings. Daria ought to have every chance to be as happy as she was then.

When had that begun to matter so much to him? He could not, with any degree of honesty, deny that it did.

Mr. Fortier pulled slips of paper from the two hats in what was to be the final round of poetry composition for the evening. "Judgmental," he read from one paper. Then from the other, "Pianoforte."

Daria grasped his arm as she addressed the rest of their team. "*We* will have the advantage with this poem. Toss plays the pianoforte masterfully. I've heard him."

Toss wasn't often put to the blush, but her unlooked-for compliment sent heat across his face. "I don't know about *masterfully*."

"You do though." Her earnest gaze held his. "You play wonderfully and beautifully. I listened to you play during the house party, and I have not forgotten a single note. I could not. It was, as I have insisted, masterful."

He set his hand atop hers, still on his arm. "Everyone should have someone like you in their life, Daria Mullins. I am certainly fortunate that I do."

At that, she blushed as much as he could feel he was. The sweet smile that she gave him and the pink warming her cheeks further convinced Toss that Daria was one of the most charmingly pretty ladies he had ever—perhaps *would* ever—meet.

"You should consider playing at a musical evening, Mr. Comstock," Mr. Layton said. "I have been to plenty that featured some whose confidence far outpaced their actual abilities. Someone with true talent would be deeply appreciated."

"But not by my brother." Toss knew that without having to ponder; Laurence had made his thoughts well-known on the matter.

"Which would earn you another point in this game of yours," Mater said.

Mr. Layton grinned at her. "If you mean to forward Mr. Comstock's cause in this competition, then I will have no choice but to further Miss Mullins's."

Mater sat up quite straight, eyeing him with theatrical confidence. "Challenge accepted, Digby."

"May the best co-conspirator win, Julia."

Daria giggled, the sound not the least silly or childish. There was such sincere delight in her participation in these things, such joyful enjoyment in her company. Did she realize that about herself? Did she realize what an admirable trait that was?

Mr. Greenberry—father, not son—was very quiet, and until he spoke in the next moment, Toss had all but forgotten he was there. "Do you suppose the pianoforte is meant to be the recipient of the judgment or the giver of it?"

They all began laughing once more.

"What's it to be, then?" Mater asked the team. "A pianoforte *treated with* judgment? Or a pianoforte *casting* judgment?"

Daria looked at Toss. "Which do you think is most fitting?"

It was a decidedly odd thing to have someone consider his musical inclination an asset. The past weeks with Laurence had nearly convinced him his abilities and interest were shameful. "I can say I often feel as though the instrument judges me for the sour notes I play."

"Then that must be how we proceed." Daria didn't often speak with such firmness and confidence. "No one would know better than you would."

Another quarter-hour passed before all three teams were ready to share.

Mrs. Fortier once again read for her team, the soft cadence of her French accent adding something soothing to their offering.

> "Music, its magical melody smoothing the wrinkles of disappointment,
> Floats upon waves of memory, offering glimpses of yesteryear.
> Those who reminisce through tinted lenses and broken recollections
> Do not the dissonant notes recall nor the discordant melody hear."

Fervent applause met the poignant verse. Toss, for a moment, couldn't even manage that. A very evocative poem, the imagery powerful. And composed so quickly.

"That one has Henri's mark on it," Mr. Layton said, his expression inarguably proud.

"These evenings began many years ago as a way to help Mr. Fortier flex his poetic muscles and seek out ideas for new poems," Mater explained to both Toss and Daria.

"He writes poetry in earnest, then?" Toss asked.

Mater, Mr. Layton, and Mr. Greenberry all nodded.

"Professionally?" Toss further pressed.

"It is a well-known secret that he has published poetry for decades under a nom de plume," Mr. Layton explained. "His family was very much opposed to the idea in the early years, and hiding his activities was crucial."

That was familiar. It was also deeply, deeply intriguing. A man of birth and standing, still embraced by Society, who pursued the arts professionally.

Mr. Colm Greenberry rose on behalf of their team. Daria watched him with pink-tinged cheeks, the same blush that *Toss* had inspired earlier. The one that had inspired a return of the "heart hiccups" he'd been experiencing since he'd first met her. *His* blush.

He knew his response for what it was: jealousy. But he wasn't yet ready to explore why he was feeling it so acutely.

Having secured Daria's gaze and likely oblivious to Toss's disapproval, the younger Mr. Greenberry began his recitation.

"The harp, the trumpet, the lyre, and horn
Sometimes sound a misplayed note.
But only the pianoforte, when all goes awry,
Takes the time to gloat."

While he was embarrassingly reluctant to associate the young gentleman he had only just met with anything worthy of approval, Toss couldn't deny he appreciated the poem. He'd often felt the pianoforte took notice when he played something wrong. The way the note hung in the air for moments after being played did, at times, feel like the pianoforte was gloating. Still, he didn't have to give Colm Greenberry credit for the poem. Toss was wallowing in jealousy, after all. It stood to reason he would feel a bit petulant.

But it was his team's turn, and Toss had been chosen to read on their behalf for this final round. It had been suggested Daria do the honors, but her response had been more panic than hesitation, and Toss had quickly volunteered himself in her stead. He could set aside this sudden one-sided rivalry for the sake of saving her from misery.

"I fill it with my doubts, played in chords and trills.
It reveals each sour note, and all my secrets spills.
The notes become words, each tune a story,
Revealing what my life has been, the failures and the glory."

Only when he finished the recitation did he realize how much of himself had been poured into the verse, how much he had influenced its tone and reflections. Music felt that way to him: powerful, sometimes unforgiving, always revelatory.

The entire gathering praised the poem. Mr. Fortier looked impressed. But it was Daria's gaze, tender and pleased and—he was quite certain—entirely aware of how personal that moment had proven to be, that touched him most.

What he had come to describe as hiccups transformed into hopeful flutters. There was little point denying what he had unexpectedly discovered that evening.

He, whose brother had snatched away his ability to choose his own future, had lost a not insignificant bit of his heart to Daria Mullins, and he didn't know what to do about it.

CHAPTER TEN

Laurence controlled far too many aspects of Toss's life for Toss to afford unmitigated familial warfare. Thus, the next evening, he went with his brother to the home of family friends, Mr. and Mrs. Brinley, for a small dinner gathering rather than spending the evening with his own friends. And away from Daria.

He would have enjoyed her company, but it was likely for the best that he was spending time away. He needed to sort out how he meant to move forward, knowing what he now did of his feelings for her.

At dinner, Laurence was seated beside Miss Midgley, whose family were of good *ton*, from the West of Yorkshire, and had provided their daughters, of whom this Miss Midgley was the second oldest, with generous dowries.

By the end of the first course, it was clear Laurence had more than a passing interest in his table partner. And by the end of the second, it was clear Miss Midgley had absolutely no interest in hers. Still, Laurence persisted: monopolizing her attention with ceaseless conversation, leaning close to her no matter that she did her utmost to lean away without imposing upon the gentleman on her other side. Toss would have been embarrassed for Laurence if he weren't so horrified for Miss Midgley.

When the ladies departed the dining room, leaving the gentlemen to their port, Miss Midgley looked very much as if she would like to run rather than walk with decorum.

After only a quarter hour, the gentlemen followed the ladies' path.

"You made a good choice tonight, Thomas," Laurence said as they walked with the other gentlemen. "These are connections worth solidifying."

"I've known Mr. Brinley since the two of you were at school," Toss said. "It's been good seeing him again."

A nod of actual approval. A decidedly rare thing.

"Miss Midgley is a promising prospect," Laurence said. "She's being aloof, but ladies are expected to act a bit elusive when being courted."

"I don't think I would describe her response to you as 'elusive.'" Toss leaned more toward *panicked.*

"You have too little experience in Society," Laurence said, annoyance dripping from his words. "Even if she is hesitant now, she will not always be. I am a highly eligible gentleman with an impressive estate and income. Now that your musical obsession has been dealt with and Rosamond is quite decidedly out of the nursery, no lady of sense would find any reason to object to being courted by me."

"I hope you phrase your eventual proposal in just that way."

Laurence seemed as though he couldn't decide if Toss was offering the advice sarcastically, which he was. His brother might be willing to run roughshod over a lady's feelings and preferences, but Toss was not.

Once everyone was seated in the music room, Mrs. Brinley addressed the audience. "We would be so delighted to fill this evening with music. We have all tuned and at your disposal a violin, a harp, and a pianoforte, as well as a wide selection of printed music. Please, delight us if you are willing."

Toss could feel his brother's eyes boring into him from behind, a warning not to take up the invitation. And for some time, Toss didn't. He listened as others provided music, both instrumental and vocal. Some were quite adept, others had more enthusiasm than technical prowess. All in all, it was lovely.

You should consider playing at a musical evening . . . Someone with true talent would be deeply appreciated. Mr. Layton's words returned to his mind, echoing louder with each new musician's offering.

Toss wasn't likely to claim his dream of composing music and pursuing that interest, but did it follow that he must forever abandon any and all indulgence in his love for music? Surely not.

You play wonderfully and beautifully . . . I have not forgotten a single note. I could not. It was, as I have insisted, masterful. Daria's words proved even more persuasive.

A lull in the performances offered him an opportunity he chose not to ignore. He rose and crossed to the pianoforte. To Mrs. Brinley's raised brow, he offered a dip of his head. With curiosity, she motioned for him to proceed.

He didn't require any printed music. He had countless pieces memorized, many of which he'd written himself, but though he didn't think of himself as cowardly, he hadn't the nerve to debut an original composition. Not yet.

He chose an early piece by Beethoven, one he knew note-for-note without needing to search his memory. A deep breath before beginning helped him keep his focus, something he sometimes struggled with. But music helped. It always did.

And he played flawlessly, right until the moment he made the mistake of glancing in his brother's direction. Laurence's disapproval could hardly have been more apparent. Had this been a misstep?

The lapse of focus caused him to misplay two notes. Then two more.

Laurence's disapproval turned to something far more like embarrassment.

Toss misplayed a few more notes before forcing himself to put all his attention on his playing. He completed the rest of the piece flawlessly, but the damage was done.

The polite applause he received rang with more pity than approval. Even Mrs. Brinley's words of gratitude for his offering were given with a look of condolence.

As Toss retook his seat, he knew two things with utter surety: he'd hurt his cause with Laurence, and he had just earned a point in his game with Daria. A point he was not terribly happy about.

Daria came to a very important conclusion during the poetry evening at Lord and Lady Aldric's home: she wanted to host a gathering of *her* friends. And she was determined to do so before Gillian left London, which afforded her only a matter of days.

Her parents were unlikely to be enthusiastic about her request to hold the soiree at their home. Neither did she expect them to be easily persuaded to allow her to dictate the details of the evening she wished to plan. She would not ordinarily suggest something so likely to annoy them, especially since her presence in London had already caused them bother. Indeed, she usually avoided time with her parents as much as possible. But she wanted so badly to host a gathering. And doing so meant she would earn a point. She might actually earn *two*: one for hosting the gathering and the other for bothering her parents with the details of it. She had not expected when she and Toss had devised this game that it would give her courage in moments when she needed it.

Toss was such a wonderful friend. He'd been so kind to her from the very beginning of their acquaintance. And he never treated her like she was dimwitted, no matter that she often provided evidence to the contrary. She would miss the Huntresses when she was not in London in the years to come, but she would also miss *him*.

The thought stopped her in the corridor as she approached the drawing room. She wouldn't get to see Toss when she was relegated to the family's country estate. An acute ache radiated through her heart. She might not ever see him again. Daria swallowed the lump that swelled in her throat. How could she bear years on end without being able to laugh with him, never again inventing delightfully absurd games?

No. She would win their current competition, and the gentlemen would be required to make certain she attended the next house party they planned with the Huntresses. She had that promise, that hope to lean on. But that meant earning as many points as she could.

Her parents were in the sitting room, each engaged in quiet and separate pursuits: Father reading a newspaper and Mother focused on her embroidery. They did not like being interrupted, and she usually took pains not to do so. Some people enjoyed spending time with her parents. Daria couldn't remember a time when she had. Being away from them was usually a relief rather than a reason for sadness.

She stepped into the sitting room. "Father? Mother?"

"Is this likely to take long, Daria?" Father asked, slowly flipping a page of his newspaper.

"Not long at all," she said. "Might I be permitted to have the Huntresses come to the house tomorrow evening for a little gathering?"

"We are engaged elsewhere tomorrow evening," Mother said, then, with an air of explaining something to a child, she added, "It would be impossible to be here and where we have already committed ourselves to be."

"You needn't remain here. Gillian, Ellie, and Artemis are all married and would be considered more than adequate chaperones for the unmarried people." She could see Mother grow more tense with each word and quickly moved forward with the reassurance she suspected was needed. "I will make all the arrangements for the evening myself. Neither of you would need to expend any effort."

"Planning an evening is not a simple thing." Mother spoke as if she were offering Daria a brand-new piece of information.

Never mind that Daria had, in fact, done a great deal of work salvaging Mother's soiree the Season before when so much of Mother's planning had fallen through.

"I'll ask Artemis to help me. She has planned ever so many gatherings." Daria didn't think she would actually have struggled to organize such a simple thing. The Huntresses and Toss's friends required so little to enjoy their time together. Rather than belabor the point, she shifted the approach that had convinced her parents on such matters in the past. "Tobias can be the host of the evening. That is certain to boost his standing amongst the young gentlemen. But he wouldn't need to do any of the work, which would leave him time to continue building important connections."

"Is Tobias interested in such an evening?" Mother asked.

"I think he would thoroughly enjoy himself."

Father raised his paper once more, apparently having lost interest in the topic.

"I suppose it is not a terrible idea," Mother said. "And there will be no soirees at your aunt Theodosia's home, so allowing you an additional one while you're here would be a kindness."

"Are we visiting Great-Aunt Theodosia?" She lived in the wilds of Anglesey.

"No, Daria," Father said from behind his paper. "*We* are not visiting. *You* are going to live there after this Season. Theodosia is getting older and needs looking after, and with the two of you being spinsters, the arrangement makes perfect sense."

Live there? In Anglesey? She had heard nothing of this. Surely they wouldn't send her so far away. Surely they could be convinced otherwise. "I am not a spinster. Not truly. I am only twenty-one."

"With no prospects." Mother shook her head. "And though you have had a dowry to tempt gentlemen with, there has been no interest for three Seasons now, no matter the high connections of your friends."

Daria bit back the observation that Mr. Colm Greenberry had seemed to like her well enough, and that Toss had called her brilliant and had been impressed with her contributions to their poems and smiled sweetly at her. Mother and Father would certainly have a dismissive response to that, and she'd not be able to think of a counterargument quickly enough. And if she weren't very careful, they would manage to confuse her enough that she might inadvertently agree with their scheme regarding Great-Aunt Theodosia or convince them to send her away now instead of at the end of the Season.

"A soiree with your friends, if Tobias's newest acquaintances are included to make it helpful for him, can be permitted," Father said. "But do not expect us to twist ourselves in accommodating knots for the remainder of the Season."

"I won't. And thank you." Daria offered an abbreviated curtsy before spinning and speeding from the room, determined to make her exit before her parents changed their minds.

In the corridor, she allowed herself to breathe, though she struggled a little to do so. Her parents weren't likely to jest about sending her away. They did intend to relegate her to Wales and Great-Aunt Theodosia's imperious company. And Daria had very little time in which to thwart those plans.

Rose had told her she had choices, that she needed to decide what she wanted to do and be. She'd made one of those choices—to ask for permission to host a soiree—and it had proven successful. That gave her hope that her next choice—to avoid Anglesey—could be successful as well.

She would tell Rose the next time she saw her that she'd taken her advice to heart and had emerged victorious. But it was the thought of sharing her success with Toss that made her heart swell.

CHAPTER ELEVEN

DARIA WOULD HAVE JOURNEYED TO Gunter's Tea Shop that afternoon even if doing so wouldn't have earned her any points in her game with Toss, and not merely because she looked forward to enjoying an almond biscuit. She had asked the Huntresses to meet her there to plan the soiree her parents had permitted her to host, and she was excited.

The Huntresses were seated at a table together when Daria arrived. It was odd not having Lisette among them, no matter that she'd spent only one Season and the house party as one of their group.

"I am so pleased that your parents agreed to allow you to hold a soiree," Gillian said after greeting Daria with a hug.

Daria sat at the table with them. "They took a little convincing."

"Good for you for being willing to convince them," Artemis said.

"I simply reminded myself that Toss would have to award me a point for it, perhaps more than one, and that was motivation enough." She couldn't wait to tell him. "The guest list for the soiree won't be extensive. All of us. And as I told my parents I was doing so for Tobias's benefit, I have also extended the invitation to the gentlemen. *Our* gentlemen, I mean. Well not *ours*, but the ones we are associated with. Friends with." Daria shook her head in frustration.

"They really need to think of a name for themselves if we are ever to efficiently gossip about them." Artemis made the declaration with a theatrical degree of annoyance. "It is terribly inconsiderate of them to do otherwise."

Her teasing commentary eased some of Daria's embarrassment at being unable to easily explain herself.

"Tobias also made a new friend two evenings ago at a gathering Mr. Layton invited us to. Mr. Greenberry—the son, not the father, obviously." She shook her head. "I suppose that isn't actually obvious. It's entirely possible to make friends outside one's generation. But in this instance, it is the son rather than the father. Though we did come to know his father, but it's not the father I meant to be talking about."

Gillian reached over and set a hand atop Daria's. They had employed that gesture for three years now, Gillian's way of helping ease the anxiety that tended to send Daria's mouth running in an attempt to fix misspoken words.

"Toss also met him at the same gathering. It was a lovely evening and ever so much fun. That was where I got the idea for our own evening party." She couldn't hide her excitement and didn't try to. "I didn't get to speak overly much with Mr. Greenberry, but Toss and I were on the same team for the evening's game, and I spoke with him all night. It was delightful. I want all of us to have a wonderful evening together to look back on."

"I think we would all like that," Ellie said.

Daria had a difficulty to overcome first. "With Mother's soiree last Season, our cook had weeks to plan and arrange for the food that was served. With tonight's gathering, I couldn't decide if the smaller numbers meant less preparation time was needed. But I dithered for so long that I imagine there isn't time left even for simple things. That was a mistake." She couldn't help a sigh of frustration with herself. "My mother had doubts I was equal to the task of planning this small event. I insisted I could manage it, but perhaps she was correct after all." She shook off the heavy thought, not wishing to focus on her mother in that moment. "Oh, do say you will all come even if there isn't any food to be had. I want only for us all to be together before Gillian and Scott leave London. And I enjoy gatherings so much, I was certain I could manage to host one entirely of my own planning. Please promise you'll come." Daria had expected some disappointment at her admission that there might not be any food at her soiree, but she hadn't expected the looks of bewilderment the Huntresses displayed.

"Do you truly think our attendance is contingent on food?" Gillian asked. "Time with each other and, more particularly, with you is the draw of the evening, Daria."

Daria felt a little relieved. The bewilderment arose from her worries that a lack of food options would keep them away. She ought never to have doubted them. "I do wish there were a means of making certain we have a delicacy or two to enjoy this evening," she said. "It is my fault for being too intimidated to speak to our cook sooner. I won't delay next time."

But she didn't know if there would be a "next time." If her parents did send her to live with Great-Aunt Theodosia, there would be nothing resembling gatherings with her friends in the future.

"Approach your gathering the way they do in the countryside of Ireland," Eve said. "Not those of the finer families but of the farmers and country people. When they gather together, they take it in turns to bring things to share with each other."

Daria looked to Artemis. "I've not heard of this being done in the *ton.*"

Artemis shrugged a little. "One doesn't hear of it happening in London. But I suspect, especially at country gatherings, which are a little less formal, neighbors have been known to bring a specialty of their household to complement what is offered."

None of the Huntresses was wealthy. Ellie and Newton had his income from his family to sustain them while he continued his training to become a barrister, but it could not stretch overly far. Charlie had an inheritance from his father, and Artemis had the ever-increasing income of her secret dress business, yet they'd needed to spend the Season living in the London home of Artemis's oldest sister because they hadn't money enough for securing their own lodgings. Gillian and Scott hardly had two pennies to rub together, the reason they were not remaining long in London. The O'Doyle sisters had a single wardrobe among them, as the family could not afford two sets of gowns and dresses and shoes and such.

Daria's family did not lack funds; she should be more grateful for that than she too often was.

Artemis, as was her usual approach, jumped in and addressed the issue head on. "As the soiree will be limited to the Huntresses and the unnamed group of gentlemen, it is more than sufficiently informal for a countrified approach to be entirely acceptable. What any of us is able to contribute, we will, and no one will think anything of it."

"I can bring scones," Eve said.

"Won't your family want them?" Daria didn't like the idea of taking food away from a family in more strained straits than she.

"I've not the first idea how to answer that." Eve spoke seriously, but her eyes were laughing. "If I say my family won't want them, you'll think I am offering to bring horrible scones. If I say they would like them, you'll argue that I ought to allow my family to eat them."

"Tell her the entire family throws a rash every time they eat scones," Nia suggested, her expression nearly identical to her sister's, "but these are so temptingly delicious that they can't help themselves, thus we must find a means of removing the delicious but dangerous delicacy from the house."

The O'Doyles tended more toward teasing than seriousness, but they were also very quick witted. Indeed, all the Huntresses were quite clever. It was an extraordinary thing that they welcomed and liked Daria when she hadn't that same claim.

"If you bring scones," Artemis said, "I can bring something else to accompany tea. Surely your cook is able to manage a tea service without needing weeks of warning."

Daria nodded. That was not very much to ask on short notice.

"What else can we do to help with your plans?" Artemis asked.

"I think it would be a wonderful thing to have some new games to play." Daria had given some thought to that. "What if all of us came with a game in mind? That would allow us to be entertained throughout the evening."

"An excellent idea," Gillian said.

"Do you really think so?" Daria pressed.

All the Huntresses added their agreement, and Daria felt instantly more confident in her plans. More than their enjoyment rested on her success, though they didn't realize as much. Daria didn't want to live with her great-aunt. And her lack of prospects had been given as the primary reason she was not to return to London. If she could show that she was useful, even as a spinster daughter, she would have an argument in favor of remaining.

"Now that we've sorted that," Artemis said, "time for a Gunter's indulgence." She grinned at Daria. "What is something your parents would absolutely not choose for you to enjoy here?"

"An ice." It was such a simple thing, so frequently chosen that Gunter's was particularly known for the treat Daria's parents had allowed her the indulgence only once before.

Artemis nodded. "An ice it is."

"And a point in your competition," Gillian added.

Daria and Toss had devised the game to make the Season more enjoyable. How grateful she was that they had; her sojourn in London—the last one she might ever have—was already the better for it.

CHAPTER TWELVE

DARIA WAS NERVOUS AS THE time approached for her soiree. She was also extremely excited.

Many aspects of interacting with Society were difficult for her. Those gatherings at which conversation grew deep and complex often made her feel stupid. When time spent among the *ton* involved reading aloud, she was sent nearly into a panic. But evenings like the one she had planned, when no one was jostling for importance or trying to prove their worth to anyone, were among her favorite things. She looked forward to them, deeply and thoroughly enjoyed them.

Now that she'd taken Rose's advice to heart and had chosen to do something she looked forward to, she found herself eagerly wishing there were a way for her to do this again. It was what her father often labeled as counting the chickens before the eggs were done, or something like that. When he spoke in metaphors, he often did so very quickly, too fast for her mind to sort out what he'd said and what he'd meant before he moved on to something else. She didn't always hear every word, and that would confuse anyone.

At least that was what she always told herself.

Eve and Nia were the first to arrive that evening, Eve with her arm hooked through the handle of the basket. Beneath the cloth was, most likely, the scones she'd agreed to bring.

"I can see you drooling already," Eve said, her amused grin firmly in place. "Prepare yourself for the very best lemon and bilberry scones you have ever eaten." Stepping inside, she held the basket out to the housekeeper. In imperious terms Daria didn't think she'd ever heard the usually jovial Irish woman use, Eve said to the housekeeper, "These are to be served with the tea this evening."

Mrs. Key dipped a fast curtsy and rushed from the entryway.

"That was impressive," Daria said.

"I simply did my best impression of a particularly memorable neighbor of ours back home. She has the most delightful way of taking charge of any situation." Then, in a conspiratorial tone, she added, "I wanted to stave off any objections that might be made about guests bringing food in case your cook proved as temperamental, as those of her profession sometimes do."

"Have you ever considered a career on the stage?" Daria asked, somehow light-spirited enough to tease even with the weight of the evening still on her. "That was a masterful performance."

"If she was going to take up a profession not open to ladies, 'twouldn't be the stage." Nia lowered her voice. "Eve would likely move to Paris and open a bakery."

Daria laughed a little, walking with the two sisters into the drawing room. "And would your specialty be scones?"

"Eve's scones are wonderful," Nia said. "And yet, they are not the most impressive thing she bakes."

"*You* baked the scones?" She'd assumed the O'Doyles' cook had done so.

"Out of necessity," Eve said quickly and quietly as her eyes spotted Tobias across the drawing room. "The daughters of the house doing the baking is not always looked on with acceptance, let alone approval. I don't generally admit to it."

That was an understatement. Daria had known the O'Doyle sisters for two years and considered them close friends, yet she'd had no idea Eve possessed this talent.

"It seems your friends arrived before any of mine," Tobias said, offering a somewhat awkward bow to the sisters.

"I understand from Daria that you invited Mr. Colm Greenberry to tonight's festivities," Eve said. "I don't know him, though I am aware of him and have heard good things of him."

"He was a lieutenant in the army during the war with Napoleon. I don't mean to imply that being in the army automatically makes him a good person." His eyes darted from one sister to the other, his posture a bit rigid. "He is, though. A good person."

Why was it Tobias always grew noticeably uncomfortable around others? He did tend to grow a little less stiff during games and diversions. She was counting on it that night. She wanted her friends to come to know Tobias, to see the wonderful person he was. Perhaps he might even become particularly good friends with Toss.

She'd let herself imagine that over the last few hours and had taken comfort in the possibility. Toss wouldn't become a stranger to her. She would see him, hear of him. She wouldn't have to miss him for the rest of her life.

She did fear she was destined to miss him *that evening.* All the guests arrived in quick succession, except for Toss. Why hadn't he come?

Daria did her best to hide her continual glances toward the drawing room windows, searching for a glimpse of him. She didn't want everyone else to think she was displeased to have them there or that their attendance didn't matter to her. She was happy they were there, but her disappointment at Toss's absence was proving impossible to ignore.

She mingled among her guests, making certain everyone was comfortable and happy, all while her heart broke a little. Her path took her past Mr. Greenberry. He offered her a smile quite like the one she had received from him during the poetry evening. And once again, it made her blush. She imagined he had that effect on a lot of people, being quite handsome and friendly.

"I'm so pleased you were able to join us," she said. "Tobias had hoped you would be able to."

"I haven't spent any Seasons in London since leaving the army, so I haven't many friends outside of those I had whilst at war."

Then perhaps her soiree was proving beneficial for him. He could gain friends and find his footing in Society. "Mingling with people in drawing rooms and ballrooms must be different from doing so on battlefields."

"Yes, decidedly so."

Once again, she'd managed to make an observation so obvious that a person of sense would have realized how unnecessary it was to speak aloud. She'd simply meant to acknowledge that he'd likely needed to do so much adjusting that having been slow to make friends wasn't a poor reflection on him. Why was it she could never say things the way she felt?

"I hadn't intended to upset you." Mr. Greenberry watched her with concern. "But I can see that I have."

She managed to give that impression more often than she wished. She would twist herself into mental knots thinking through some misstep or another only to realize the person she had been conversing with thought they had caused her distress.

"You haven't upset me," she said. "I didn't relay my initial thoughts very well, and I was trying to decide how to better explain that I thought it entirely understandable that you were still adjusting to life away from the army. It is quite different from life amongst the *ton.* I am assuming, of course. I have never been in the army. Which you most certainly would realize." She was making a mull of things again.

But Mr. Greenberry didn't seem to be laughing at her.

Tobias waved Mr. Greenberry over to join the conversation he was having with Scott. Just as Mr. Greenberry stepped away, Gillian took his place.

"How are you holding up?" Gillian asked, her voice pitched low. "You've seemed a little . . . disappointed, I suppose."

Daria hadn't managed to hide that. "I'm surprised Toss didn't come. I was so certain he would. I think he would enjoy being part of the gathering. And I could have told him that I've earned more points."

"The Huntresses will make absolutely certain he knows of your points," Gillian said.

It was more than that though. She was proud of herself for what she'd accomplished, and she'd wanted to share that with him, knowing he would appreciate it. And she'd wanted to see him again. The highlights of her London Season had always been the Huntresses. How was it her happiness in this, her final one, was intertwined so entirely with Thomas Comstock? "I'm enjoying the evening so far," Daria insisted, feeling a smile pull at her mouth. "These kinds of gatherings are always my favorite. To actually execute one is proving rather fun."

Gillian smiled broadly. "Don't let the gentlemen overhear you say that, else, when we inevitably prove victorious in your game with Toss, they will attempt to convince you to plan the house party for them."

"Are you certain you and Scott have to leave London in only three days' time? It won't be the same without you here." And Daria would be lonely without her.

"We can only live off the charity of Mrs. Brownlow for so long. We need to return home to continue our work in putting it to rights. Once we manage that, we'll be able to stay in London as long as we'd like."

"But I won't be here then."

Gillian's expression shifted to one of determination. "We will find a means of making sure you are," she said. "Mark my words. We'll find a way."

Daria hadn't yet told the Huntresses of her parents' plan to send her to Anglesey. She needed to, as it was proving such a weight on her mind, but she didn't want the evening to be ruined by such heavy thoughts. And she wanted to believe there was a solution, but there was only so much an unmarried lady could accomplish when her father determined a different future for her.

She had choices, yes, as Rose had acknowledged, but she didn't have all the choices she wished she did.

"After I've left for Nottinghamshire," Gillian said, "I will fully expect you to write to me to tell me what has become of Mr. Greenberry's very obvious interest in you."

"His what?" She barely kept her question quiet.

"I'm not saying he's pining away. But he clearly finds you intriguing."

Daria shook her head. "Gentlemen like him are hardly going to be interested in someone like me."

"That is where you are wrong, my friend. He is intrigued, and if you cannot keep me updated on the progress of that intrigue, I shall be forced to send out spies."

"How many of those spies bear the surname O'Doyle?" Daria asked.

Gillian laughed, slipping away to rejoin the others.

Daria watched Mr. Greenberry a moment, wondering if Gillian was correct. He was kind, certainly. And he hadn't laughed at her when she'd not expressed herself well. She had seen nothing in it but friendliness. And as she pondered it, she realized she felt curious about the possibility but not hopeful, not anxious for it to be true. Her heart was more tugged by Toss's absence than by the potential for Mr. Greenberry's interest.

She glanced at the windows once more, thinking she'd seen movement on the street only to be disappointed once more. Why hadn't Toss come?

Tobias set his hand on her arm, pulling her attention into the room once more. "We likely should start the evening's festivities."

Her nervousness returned with added intensity. "You could do that."

But he shook his head. "This is your evening, Daria. You not only ought to be the one holding the reins, but I think you need to see for yourself that you are fully capable of doing so."

Daria let her lungs empty, then nodded. She could do this. Certainly, she could. Not everyone had come, but those who had deserved to enjoy themselves.

The housekeeper appeared in the doorway of the drawing room in the very next moment and announced, "Mr. Thomas Comstock."

Hearing him announced and seeing him step inside after having watched for him with waning hope, Daria didn't know whether she felt more like smiling or crying. It was an odd contradiction, one she didn't quite know how to reconcile.

The gentlemen greeted him jovially and teased him rather mercilessly for his late arrival. He took it in stride, as he always did. As much as Daria had missed her dear friend since last being in company with him, she found herself unexpectedly reluctant to approach him herself. Something almost like bashfulness was tiptoeing over her, and she was at a loss to explain it.

Deciding her best course was to move forward with her duties as hostess, she addressed the group. "I thought it might be fun to play games this evening. All the Huntresses have come with a game in mind. We would have asked the gentlemen to do the same, but as they lack the creativity to even fashion a group name, it seemed unlikely to work out."

Laughter and quips flew about the group at that bit of humor. She'd made them laugh, which felt good. Tobias offered her a subtle but undeniable nod, one she knew was meant to acknowledge that she was doing quite well at the job she'd attempted to fob off on him.

"I thought we might begin tonight with a few rounds of Musical Magic," Daria said.

Enthusiastic agreement met her suggestion.

The game was a simple one, really. Someone was chosen to leave the room. Those who remained decided upon a particular task or performance the absent person was meant to undertake using something in the room. Among some gatherings, those tasks might be embarrassing. Daria hadn't the least worry on that score tonight. Once a thing was decided upon, the participant was invited back into the room. He or she would move about, drawing closer to the item they were meant to interact with. The onlookers would hum a previously chosen tune, growing louder if the person moved farther and softer as the person grew nearer. Upon discovering the chosen item, the humming began again as the person attempted to stumble upon what they were meant to do with that thing. The evening could get ridiculous very quickly and was always vastly entertaining.

Charlie was chosen to be the first charged with leaving the room, which meant the game would begin on a tone of delightful absurdity. Only Toss was likely to be as entertainingly ridiculous.

Once Charlie was out of the room, they decided upon "An English Garden" for their hummed tune. It was then decided that he was to pick up a particular book and make a show of reading it, but he was to hold it upside down. It was a complicated task, but they were all quite convinced that Charlie was equal to it.

The humming was discordant, and Charlie's guesses grew more and more entertaining. At more than one point, laughter was so all-encompassing that the tune grew impossible to identify. He did eventually stumble on the book he was meant to pick up and did so. After several misdirections, he realized he was meant to pretend to read it upside down.

Whilst the group applauded his eventual solving of the riddle, Daria looked at Toss, fully expecting to see him grinning and laughing along. While he seemed to be enjoying himself, there was an unusual heaviness in his eyes, a hint of soberness that he was clearly doing his best to hide. She had not known him as long as his friends had, but she felt she knew him well enough to recognize that all was not entirely well.

When Gillian, upon having her turn, realized she was meant to attempt to play the pianoforte with her nose, something Daria was certain would amuse Toss in particular, Daria's worry grew sharper to see that he was struggling to keep his heavy thoughts hidden. She couldn't think of anything particularly objectionable about this game. And Gillian's task did not belittle the actual playing of the instrument.

Had Daria done something wrong and not realized it? Had she made a particularly grave error? As the game continued on, she found herself wholly distracted by her growing doubts. This was an evening meant to be enjoyed. If the most delightfully happy person she knew was displeased, she must have done something amiss.

Why was it she so often made a mull of things? It was little wonder her parents had wanted to leave her behind. *A mind like a sieve,* just as Father always said.

Needing a moment to regain her composure, she made a quick excuse between rounds and slipped from the room. The sitting room, where her parents usually sat reading and embroidering, dimly lit by the candle sconces in the entryway, sat empty. She found her parents' absence to be an absolute mercy.

Where had she gone wrong? Toss couldn't have been disappointed in the food, as it had not yet been served. He liked music, which should have endeared the game to him. She'd not greeted him personally. Perhaps he was offended. But then, he *had* been greeted by so many of the others upon his arrival.

"Daria?"

She spun about at the sound of Toss's voice, having expected no one to follow her here, let alone him. "I didn't mean to pull you away from the game."

"I suspect I ought to be the one saying that to you. It did not escape my notice that you recognized my low spirits this evening. And I suspect, because I've come to realize you worry a great deal about whether or not you have done something in error, that you are likely convinced my poor mood is owing to a misstep on your part."

It was precisely what she'd feared. "Have I neglected something this evening? What ought I to have done differently so you could enjoy yourself?"

He shook his head as he crossed to her. "I'm afraid I arrived here already in somewhat sour spirits. It is a poor reflection on me that I've not been able to shake that mood despite the delightful evening we are all having."

Her eyes darted to the open door behind him, in the direction of the drawing room. "Do you think everyone's enjoying themselves? I've never been the hostess of an evening, and I don't know truly what I'm doing. I want it to be wonderful." She met his eye once more. "This kind of evening is my favorite: friendly interactions, enjoyable games. To know I could plan one and give that kind of enjoyment to other people would be a dream come true."

He took her hand in his, the gesture friendly and, on the surface at least, brotherly. Yet when her actual brother took her hand, her heart didn't flutter as it was doing then.

"It's been a wonderful evening. Please do not take my poor mood as a reflection on your soiree." He was reassuring her with his words, but the weight in his eyes was undoing it.

"What's happened?" she asked. "What has you so weighed down?"

"Nothing of consequence." He released her hand once more and appeared to try very hard to look his usual bouncy self.

She was not fooled.

"Please tell me what, Toss. I am a good listener. Even my father has said that I am, and he doesn't offer me many compliments."

"I don't know your father, Daria, but there are times I find myself sorely tempted to throttle him."

It was a shocking thing to say, and yet, rather than feel horrified, she burst out laughing. And her laughter seemed to lighten him. He even chuckled.

She set her hand on his arm. "Tell me what happened," she requested again. "I might even be willing to grant you a point in our competition if you do."

"I'll take that point." He set his hand on hers, setting her heart fluttering again. "I had dinner last evening with friends of my brother. It was a smaller gathering than this one, and they ended the evening with musical performances. I took Mr. Layton's advice and sat myself down at the pianoforte to add my offering to the mix."

She could feel her eyes pull wide with excitement.

"Before you get your hopes up, remember that the ending to this story has me at a perfectly delightful soiree feeling terribly sorry for myself."

She hadn't fully thought it through. "Oh dear."

"Oh dear, indeed." He sighed a little. "Things were going perfectly well until I caught sight of my brother glaring at me with a particularly disapproving gaze. Suddenly my brain and my fingers stopped communicating. A couple of poorly played notes changed his disapproval to a look that I can only say indicated to all who glanced at him—and plenty did—that he was terribly ashamed at that moment to claim any connection to me. Which upset my equilibrium even more. I haven't played that poorly in years. My first time doing so in a public setting did not go well."

The poor man looked ready to sink into the floor. No wonder the musical references and Gillian playing the pianoforte in a ridiculous manner had seemed to sink his spirits further. She had bombarded him with unintended reminders of what must have been a terribly difficult experience.

"I've heard you play, Toss. You have a remarkable talent. One attempt that didn't go as you wished doesn't change that."

"But it might very well have ended any hope of convincing my brother to relent on the matter. I had entertained some hope of having a bit of my music in my life once he takes over next year."

"You could always go to the wilds of Wales to see if my great-aunt Theodosia has a pianoforte you could play. There would be no one there to overhear a sour note."

"Are you attempting to banish me to some isolated corner of the kingdom?" A little bit of his teasing tone had returned. "I don't know whether to be offended or rise to the occasion."

She would say "rise to the occasion" if it meant he would actually go to Anglesey. She sighed a little as she reluctantly stepped past him, knowing she'd been away from the others for too long. Wales would be so very lonely. She simply had to find a means of convincing her parents not to send her there.

She walked back to the drawing room, knowing Toss was directly behind her. She worried a little that she would return and find everyone watching her with disappointment because her departure had ruined their fun. They were all gathered together and laughing, though Rose watched her return with curiosity and, it seemed to Daria, a bit of concern.

Artemis waved Daria over. "We are attempting to determine who is winning in the contest between you and Toss."

"Oh." Daria sat among them. "Toss did just win a point."

The looks she got were amused, intrigued, and, in Tobias's case, pointedly glaring at Toss.

"That needs a clarification," Toss was quick to say, holding his hands up in a show of innocence.

Daria clasped her hands over her mouth, suddenly realizing that she had unintentionally implied that Toss had been misbehaving.

"I admitted to an embarrassing moment," Toss said, "one my brother would absolutely not wish to be widely known. Daria kindly suggested that my confession warranted a point."

Rose was the only one in the group whose eyes didn't leave Daria. Rose watched her with a very motherly concern. How fortunate they all were to have Rose.

The tallying of points continued. They both received points for the chamber orchestra performance and the poetry night. Toss received points for playing the pianoforte at the gathering the night before, though he did tell them how badly it went. Daria received a point for her purple dress, for asking her parents to allow the soiree, and for procuring food by means more common to the country, which her parents were likely to think uncouth.

"You had an ice at Gunter's yesterday," Ellie said. "You were meant to receive a point for that."

"I'd forgotten." Daria motioned to the paper on which Charlie was keeping score. "Give me a point for that as well."

Charlie looked back to Toss. "At the moment, she is winning this competition."

"I visited a lending library this morning, which my brother says ought to be reserved for boring and scholarly gentlemen, as well as blue stockings."

Charlie added a point to Toss's total.

"My brother suggested I ride in Hyde Park at the fashionable hour today," Toss said, "and I didn't do so. I'm not certain that counts though: choosing *not* to do something because my brother would wish me to rather than choosing *to do* something he wouldn't choose."

"I think it should count," Daria said.

She did want to win the competition, as it would mean knowing for certain she would get to attend the next house party. She wanted to know that should she be required to live with Great-Aunt Theodosia, she would have something to look forward to.

But should Toss win, all the Huntresses would put in the effort needed to help him find a musical mentor, which might mean he wouldn't give up on his music entirely. She wanted that for him as well. She hadn't any connections to facilitate such a thing and couldn't accomplish it on her own. But it would be managed one way or the other if Toss were the victor, she knew that much.

A few more point-earning events were thought of, and in the end, Daria was ahead by two points.

Toss was subject to some good-natured teasing while she was offered heartfelt congratulations. The evening continued on, pleasant and enjoyable. Toss seemed to regain his spirits, which did Daria's heart a great deal of good. The scones were delicious, prompting Daria to thank Eve profusely when no one else was listening. The fact that she hadn't been the one to tell Daria that she'd baked them, and the further fact that she had never mentioned her ability to the Huntresses, told Daria she might not wish for it to be widely known. At least not yet.

Games were played. Lively conversation was enjoyed by all. By the time the guests began to leave, Daria felt certain the evening could be considered a success.

Toss approached to make his farewell.

Exhausted but unspeakably pleased, Daria said, "I did it, Toss. I planned and hosted an entire evening."

"You did, and it was wonderful."

She couldn't hold back a smile. "I hope this doesn't make me sound unforgivably conceited, but I am so proud of myself."

Toss took her hands in his. Three times he'd done so that night alone. And all three times her heart had trembled in response. "You absolutely should be proud of yourself, Daria. And not just owing to tonight's success."

"I'm not accustomed to feeling proud of myself." She held fast to his hands, not wanting him to let go yet. "It is a nice feeling."

"If ever you need a reminder of all the reasons you should feel exceptionally pleased with the person you are, you need only ask me. I'll give you a list."

She was not merely going to miss him when her time in London came to an end, she was going to be a little lost. "Everyone should have a friend like you, Toss."

He offered her another bow and made his way from the house, taking a bit of her heart with him.

The only guest remaining was Rose. "Your soiree was an inarguable success," she said.

"You told me it was time I begin choosing some things for myself. I chose this."

Rose's gaze hovered a moment on the door still held open after Toss's departure. "Now decide what you mean to choose next." After a brief but pointed look, she, too, slipped from the house.

"The entire evening was brilliantly managed, Daria," Tobias said. "I intend to make certain Mother and Father know as much. If they know what you accomplished with little time to plan, perhaps they'd be willing to allow you to remain at home instead of going to Anglesey and return to London for the Season on the promise that you would help Mother hold successful evenings such as this."

It wouldn't be quite the same as hosting such evenings for herself, to be enjoyed with her particular group of friends, but she would still enjoy it. And it would mean she was in London, which would be wonderful. And when not there for the Season, she wouldn't be relegated to the outer stretches of the kingdom. And she would see the Huntresses.

And Toss. Her heart pleaded with her to do all she could to make certain that happened.

Rose had told her to decide what her next choice would be. Rose had warned her during their previous discussion on the topic that Daria would not always have all the choices she wanted but that she would have some.

Perhaps deciding to ask for this soiree had given Daria a few more precious choices.

CHAPTER THIRTEEN

Toss had nearly ruined Daria's soiree. She had already been struggling with self-directed doubts but had bravely moved forward with a plan she had worried would fail. He ought to have been an unwavering source of encouragement, but he'd let his own disappointments cast a shadow over her evening. Mere days after realizing how much he cared for her and how intricately she had woven herself into his heart, he'd caused her pain.

At least he hadn't compounded that error by mimicking Laurence's behavior toward Miss Midgley at the Brinley's dinner party. Daria had referred to Toss as her friend. He would honor that and defer to her definition of their connection. He was not enough of a cad to impose upon her. She deserved to be treated with compassion and respect.

"You have a remarkable talent. One attempt that didn't go as you wished doesn't change that." Daria's words, kindly and sincerely offered, had given him a means of getting past his disappointment and taking hold of hope once more.

And though she likely didn't realize it, she'd offered him musical inspiration at a moment when he'd been sorely tempted to abandon it altogether. In the midst of their game of Musical Magic, when they'd all been humming "An English Country Garden," Daria had added a bit of a trill and then had wandered her way back toward the tune. That improvisation had stayed in his thoughts, repeating with a tenacity he'd learned not to ignore. Musical refrains that refused to dislodge themselves from his thoughts always proved the seeds of a new composition.

The morning after the soiree, he dressed with more of his usual *joie de vivre*, then hopped down to the breakfast room for a quick bite alone. Laurence likely wouldn't rise from bed for a few hours yet. It was the perfect time to sit at the pianoforte and regain his equilibrium.

After playing a few of his favorite pieces and if Laurence wasn't awake and causing trouble, he'd begin trying a few approaches to building on the brief melody that refused to leave his thoughts.

But when he stepped into the sitting room, the pianoforte wasn't there. The space it usually occupied was entirely empty.

Toss stepped from the room once more, catching the butler just as he made his way down the corridor. "Gibson, do you know where the pianoforte has been moved to?"

"Mr. Comstock ordered it removed from the house."

Removed? What did he mean by that?

In the next instant, Gibson answered the question Toss hadn't spoken out loud. "It has been sold, Mr. Thomas."

Sold. "When did— When—" He took a sharp, stinging breath, his mind refusing to accept what he was being told. "When did this happen?"

"Yesterday afternoon."

No. No, he would have noticed. He would have tried to stop Laurence.

Except, Laurence had sent him away from the house. He'd spent three hours on errands his brother had assigned him, ones that had seemed a bit odd at the time, but in the name of domestic harmony, he'd not objected.

He'd simply gone along, facilitating this catastrophe. Allowing it without realizing.

Toss rubbed at his face, straining his mind for some explanation, some bit of hope. "Did he give a reason?" Perhaps if it were a matter of space or money . . . but that seemed unlikely.

"He offered no explanation, Mr. Thomas."

There'd been a pianoforte in the family's country estate and London home all Toss's life, a presence even more constant than his actual family members. How could Laurence do this? How could he be so cruel? So unfeeling?

But the memory of his brother's expression of shame and revulsion two nights earlier returned with force. Toss had gone against Laurence's wishes and played publicly, and he had done so rather poorly.

Now his pianoforte was gone.

It might have been punishment or a response to embarrassment or determination to prevent a repeat performance. It was likely all three.

"Do you know who it was sold to? Or for how much?" If the amount weren't too steep, Toss might be able to buy it back.

"I don't." Gibson's expression slipped from the very proper but distant one butlers often employed to something far more like empathy. "We were sorry to see it go, Mr. Thomas. All of us know how important it was to you."

Unfortunately, Laurence knew that as well.

Not being able to sit down at the pianoforte and play was a blow, a loss. It was often how he sorted through frustrating and difficult things. But seeing the corner of the room where it had sat now empty and vacant hurt more. He had nowhere else to live but with his brother and no money to obtain another residence or another pianoforte. And because it was Laurence's home, Toss had no voice in it, no true autonomy, and was given very little consideration beyond a bachelor Season that wasn't proving nearly as free of his brother's interference as he'd been promised it would be.

And he hadn't even music to make it bearable.

He needed to get out of this house. Perhaps by the time Laurence the Lout made an appearance, Toss would be composed enough to not throttle the miserable huff.

In short order, he had his hat, coat, and gloves and was stomping his way down the pavement with no actual destination. His only goal was to put distance between himself and his brother. He'd bemoaned not having Rosamond nearby, but Laurence would likely have treated her poorly too. Toss could take some solace in knowing his sister was spared their brother's cruelty for the length of this Season.

And it was a decidedly good thing Daria had not been forced to spend any time with Laurence. From all Toss had heard of Daria's father, Toss felt certain that man was the reason she had such doubts about herself. Toss wasn't in a position to defend her against her father, but he would do all he could to protect her from the unkindness she would likely receive from Laurence.

Which brought him back to his future resting in Laurence's hands. Toss wasn't excited about a match being chosen for him, but he would be heartsick if he was the reason Daria had to endure a lifetime of mistreatment from Laurence.

He realized he was making an enormous leap from having begun to fall in love with her to contemplating the complexity of a marriage between them. He didn't know if his feelings for her were deep and full enough to sustain them for a lifetime. And all she had revealed of her feelings for him did not go beyond friendship. But with his future so fully in his brother's control, even the first inklings of love were doomed. He needed to remember that before he broke his own heart or led Daria to believe things that could never prove to be true.

He was determined to be kinder to her than life was being to him.

Somehow, in the midst of his mental wanderings, his feet had brought him to Falstone House, where Charlie would be. They'd landed themselves in an endless chain of trouble during their years at Cambridge and Eton, yet there were few people Toss depended on more, few people he trusted as fully.

And Charlie once more proved himself as loyal and reliable and good a friend as a man grieving a pianoforte and needing to keep his distance from his own heart could hope for. Well, he proved at home at least, which was a very good start.

Toss was ushered into the elegant book room, where Charlie sat at a table, bent over a stack of very academic books and papers. He looked up as Toss crossed toward him.

"You look about as cheerful as a graveyard in a downpour," Charlie said.

Toss shrugged. "Danced a jig on the way over. Sorry you missed it."

"Have you come to sort out my latest theory to present to the Royal Society?" Charlie motioned at the stack of books and papers on the table in front of him.

"I'll write your 'Euclid was wrong about geometry type things' paper if you'll write out the notations for the tune I can't get out of my head and slip a copy to the Royal Society of Musicians, which I still insist is the apex of Royal Societies."

"Two difficulties with that approach, my friend. Firstly: *my* Royal Society is decidedly superior to *yours.*"

"It's not mine." Toss didn't like the plaintive quality that filled his words as he made that observation.

"It will be." Charlie offered that prediction with the unwavering faith Toss had come to rely on from him. "The other shortcoming in your plan is that were I to take charge of the notations for any tune, the result would be utterly atrocious."

"And what about my efforts to summarize your mathematical theories?" Toss appreciated the ridiculousness of the exchange; it was helping calm his mind.

"That doesn't bear scrutiny, I'm afraid. You'd muddle the whole thing." Charlie leaned back in his chair, a laughing smile on his face. "If you weren't motivated to visit me by a deep love of mathematics, you must've come because you missed me so much."

"Hardly." Toss felt a little less like pummeling someone, which he thought was a good sign. "I came to ask if your brother- and sister-in-law would mind if I spent the morning playing their pianoforte."

"Did your brother start bullyragging you early today?"

Toss shook his head. "He finally abandoned his efforts at harassing me into giving up my music. Instead, he took it away."

Charlie focused more closely on him. "What do you mean?"

"He sold the pianoforte."

Charlie's mouth dropped open the tiniest bit.

"While I was on all those ridiculous errands for him yesterday, he had the instrument removed from the house and taken wherever he'd arranged for it to go. And I have my suspicions he has sent instructions to the country house to have that pianoforte disposed of as well."

"Have you ever noticed that your brother is a shabby dunghill of a fellow?"

"I have, strangely enough." He could actually laugh at that.

"Help me gather up all this." Charlie stood. "We'll wander over to the music room."

"You don't have to interrupt your work for this."

Charlie shook his head. "Artie hums a lot, sings to herself sometimes. I've discovered I actually focus better when the room isn't completely silent."

Toss carefully stacked the various piles of papers into one. "If you'd like, I can play very loudly."

"Only if you promise to also play very well." Charlie carried the books, while Toss carried the papers.

"You're not nearly as generous as Daria," Toss said as they made their way toward the music room. "She said that one poor performance does not negate a person's talent."

"When did you talk to Daria about your music?" Charlie asked.

"At her soiree last night. She thought I wasn't enjoying the evening, so I explained that I was just stewing over my poor showing at the Brinleys'."

"*I* told you that one clumsy performance wasn't the end of the world. Why did you listen to her but not me?"

"Well, you're ugly, and you smell bad, neither of which can be said about her."

"Artie likes the way I smell."

"Now you're making me want to vomit, also something that can't be said about Daria."

They stepped into the music room.

"I do have a pianoforte at my disposal though." Charlie motioned to it. "That must improve my standing at least a little."

Toss set his stack of papers on an obliging table. "I hope you thank His Grace for the pianoforte. Without it, you'd have no friends."

"To quote His Grace, 'Shut up.'" Charlie uttered the last two words in an absolutely perfect imitation of the Dangerous Duke.

The pianoforte was in tune, which Toss chose to see as an indication that fate was smiling on him at last. Charlie was very quickly engrossed in his geometry. It wasn't an indication that Charlie expected to not be entertained by whatever Toss managed to play but was, rather, the result of his friend being the strange sort of fellow who couldn't resist the siren song of mathematics.

"I wish Duke and Poppy were in Town," Toss said as he sat on the stool at the pianoforte.

"They are clever coves," Charlie said. "Might have some ideas of how to adequately torture your brother for being a surly old rustyguts."

"No, I'd like having them here because *they* aren't obsessed with mathematics, which would make them far better company than you." He trilled a few keys.

"Focus on your music, Mozart."

"Focus on your mathematics, . . . Euclid."

Charlie held up a finger. "I am actually actively arguing against some of Euclid's work. You'll have to choose another mathematician."

Toss shook his head. "I don't know any others."

"Pathetic." Charlie flipped a page in one of his books.

Laurence sometimes called Toss "pathetic," but it was different when Charlie said it. Charlie didn't actually mean it.

Toss closed his eyes, his hands hovering above the keyboard. He took a deep, slow breath. Almost of their own accord, his fingers began playing an étude he'd composed his first year at Cambridge. It was often the piece he played at the beginning of his morning practice sessions.

He knew the étude so well he didn't even have to think. Perhaps it was what he ought to have played at the Brinleys'. He likely wouldn't have stumbled over the notes as he had the other song. But playing something *he* had written had seemed like too much of a risk.

He'd done so as part of his studies at Cambridge. His friends had heard his compositions as he'd practiced them in the flat they'd all shared. Laurence had heard them when Toss was at home, though his brother likely hadn't realized the pieces were *his.* And his dear sister, Rosamond, had often requested he specifically play his own works for her. Why had the thought of playing his compositions at the Brinleys' dinner party been so intimidating?

His time at Cambridge had been dedicated to becoming a composer, to writing music that would be played for far more people than had been present two nights earlier. Maybe it was a good thing Laurence had brought that to an end.

It was with that depressing thought echoing in his mind that he reached the end of the étude without his spirits lifting at all.

And in the silence that followed, the Duke of Kielder himself spoke. "I wondered who was playing."

Toss jumped to his feet, startled and unsure what to think about the interruption, mostly because he wasn't at all certain what the Dangerous Duke's opinion was about Toss absconding with his pianoforte. Not knowing what a man as powerful and fearsome as the duke was thinking was dangerous. Literally. "Charlie said I could."

From his mathematics-laden table, Charlie laughed. "You are such a lily-livered traitor."

His Grace didn't appear surprised by the comment. He stepped closer to the pianoforte, watching Toss with a focus that had, Toss knew for a fact, turned lesser men into quivering jellies of fear. His powerful presence had, if the legend was true, once resulted in the Prince Regent himself bowing to the Duke of Kielder.

"You play very well." The duke's compliment was clearly sincere yet still intimidating.

"Thank you, Your Grace."

"He wrote the piece he was playing," Charlie said.

Toss's attention shifted immediately to his friend. "You recognized it?"

"You played it at least 475,000 times while we were at Cambridge. Of course I recognized it."

"Just as you mentioned Euclid 575,000 times, which is why I can remember his name despite his being shockingly boring."

Charlie leaned back in his chair. "Clearly we both received a very well-rounded education."

The duke had not been distracted from his purpose in the least. "You are a composer?"

"I had hoped to be, Your Grace. But I was not permitted to complete my education on account of . . ."

"On account of his brother being a shabby dunghill of a fellow," Charlie supplied.

"You know I don't care for cant," the Duke said.

Charlie sighed as if it were a great tragedy. "And I, sadly, *can't* help myself."

Nothing in the duke's expression changed, yet Toss thought he detected amusement there. Best offer his explanation while the duke's mood wasn't too black. "And I came here today to make use of your pianoforte because my brother disapproves of my musical interest and, to punish me for continuing to pursue it, sold our pianoforte yesterday without giving me any chance to save it."

The duke nodded slowly. "He really is a shabby dunghill of a fellow."

Charlie grinned. "He really is."

"I can't argue with that." Toss kept the duke's gaze. "Do you mind if I continue playing? I will bow to your preferences."

"You're supposed to bow to his face," Charlie said.

"Charlie is even more ridiculous when he is with you," the duke said, "which I wouldn't have thought possible." But there was a laugh in those terrifying eyes and very real brotherly affection. Most people wouldn't believe it possible of His Grace. "You are welcome to come here and play the pianoforte whenever you'd like."

"Thank you, Your Grace."

The duke watched him a moment longer. "Have you ever met Mr. Henri Fortier?"

"I have," Toss said.

"If you have the opportunity, you ought to speak with him about your situation. He, too, pursued an interest at Cambridge that his brother didn't approve of, and that disagreement between them continued for some time afterward. He'd understand. He might even have some advice."

"I could certainly use all the good advice I can get."

The duke nodded. "Charlie's mother has a knack for giving a person back his foundation when he's lost it." He spoke as one who knew. "I would suggest you allow her to help you reclaim yours."

"Thank you, Your Grace."

Even that small bit of sentimentality disappeared almost instantly. "And return to your playing. My daughter was enjoying it."

And it was that last sentence of all that His Grace had said that lifted Toss's spirits the most. *My daughter was enjoying it.*

CHAPTER FOURTEEN

Falstone House was not merely considered one of the most elegant homes in London, it was also one of the most exclusive. The Dangerous Duke was not overly fond of people in general, but he was known to be quite fond of his wife and, for her sake, permitted gatherings to be held now and then. While the duchess did receive callers on her at-home day, it was not a place where many people spent much time, which added to the mystique of both the house and its owner.

Yet Daria was there, in the guest room being used by the duchess's own sister, passing a casual and friendly morning in a way most people could only dream of. Because she knew Artemis as a friend first and foremost, it still sometimes caught her off guard to remember just how well-connected and significant she was in Society. And when Daria would remember that, she inevitably found herself overflowing with gratitude that Artemis had seen fit to rescue her all those years earlier.

They'd both been present at the same at-home, Daria's first ever. Her mother had been deeply worried from the moment they'd arrived in London that Daria would prove a failure in Society, and all that worry had rendered Daria utterly terrified. She'd been overawed at how beautiful and elegant and entirely at ease Miss Artemis Lancaster had been. Daria was not one to envy the good fortune of others, but she'd seen in Artemis what she herself wished she were, what she longed to be: good enough.

The society column was being passed around, the various ladies present discussing its contents and conjecturing as to the truthfulness of it all. Daria watched Artemis, wondering if she was one to speak ill of people or further the often cruel whispers one heard. Somehow, this Diamond of Society was above even that pettiness. When someone would attempt to pull Artemis into a bit of speculation, she would offer a little smile, one that was clearly not approval but which also did not give offense, and make some neutral observation.

Daria silently repeated those very useful phrases, hoping to remember them should she have need of them. "One never quite knows what to think when something is heard third- or fourth-hand." Or, "I would not wish to speculate, knowing I might be wrong," or, "I did hear the most wonderful thing about Mrs. . . ." And she would move to a very kind observation about some person or another.

It was then Daria realized that Artemis Jonquil, as she was known now, was a good person.

When one of the twattlers handed Daria a section of the gossip column, insisting she read a particular bit out loud, Daria panicked. It wasn't merely that she didn't care to engage in the unkind gossip swirling about, but she was also a very poor reader. She was literate, and she could comprehend what she read, but she stumbled a lot, mixing up words and struggling to keep her place. When reading out loud, those struggles were painfully evident.

How well she remembered Mother's immediate look of embarrassment, appearing before Daria had even attempted a single word. Daria had tried to excuse herself from the unwanted assignment, but the older ladies had ignored her objections.

"I did hear the most wonderful thing about Mrs. . . ." Her mind had emptied. She couldn't think of a single person she knew.

Artemis had risen and crossed to her, holding out a hand of friendship. "I know precisely whom you're speaking of. I believe I see my friend, Miss Phelps, arriving. Let us go see if she has heard what we have."

She'd spared Daria painful humiliation and had brought her into the Huntresses' circle. That friendship had changed Daria's life for the better. And though she wasn't certain how to go about it, she was determined not to abandon that life without making some effort to change her parents' plans for her future.

"I cannot say I like that you are frowning." Artemis's voice cut through her thoughts. "Are you disappointed?"

Daria was quick to shake her head. "The frown was not to do with the dress at all, only my thoughts wondering. I can't imagine anyone not being entirely delighted with this dress." She eyed herself in the tall mirror once more, the purple dress she'd ordered from Miss Martinette's finally finished and managing somehow to surpass even her high hopes for it. "I love it so much that I'm almost willing to forfeit the point I will receive for choosing purple. It seems almost unfair to be so delighted with something I'm also winning a game with."

"We will not be telling the gentlemen that you're willing to let go of the point. We are currently ahead, you'll remember." Artemis moved one of Daria's sleeves, eyeing the lay of it with the same studying gaze Rose always employed.

"I do hope we win," Daria said. "And not only because it is terribly fun to win games but also because that means I won't miss the next house party, no matter what my parents have to say about it. I know the Huntresses would do whatever they could to help me be there, but none of us has income enough at our disposal to fund a trip from the Irish Sea."

Artemis met Daria's eyes in the mirror. "The Irish Sea? Your family doesn't live in that area of the kingdom."

"But my great-aunt does. My parents told me that's where they mean to send me when the Season is over. I'm certain once I'm there, they'll forget about me entirely."

"Is this your great-aunt Theodosia?" Artemis asked.

"I've told you about her?" Daria didn't remember having done so.

"You've mentioned her a few times these past years. From all I can ascertain, she's a rather miserable dragon of a woman who runs roughshod over anyone and everyone."

That was, unfortunately, accurate. "My parents have concocted a story about how she needs someone to look after her and help her, but I don't believe that is actually true." If Great-Aunt Theodosia's health had taken a turn or she had suffered a debilitating injury, it would have been mentioned sooner. That they still hadn't spoken of anything of that sort put the lie to their assertion about Daria's help being needed in Wales.

What she couldn't sort out was the actual reason they intended to send her to Anglesey. It made no sense whatsoever.

"There's that frown again," Artemis said. "It is a difficult thing how many of the Huntresses have families who inspire expressions just like the one you are now wearing."

Daria turned a little to look at Artemis more directly. "We have often wondered among us why it is you've taken under your wing so many with difficult families. Your sisters and brother clearly think the world of you."

"My father didn't. Heavens, he didn't. And when my oldest sister married and began building her life with her husband, I was left behind, as I always was. One by one, they left. I had family who weren't cruel to me, but I know what it is to feel lonely. And I know what it is to be rejected by a parent. But thanks to Charlie's dear departed father, I did learn how much joy comes from knowing there is someone in the world who's happy that you're in it."

"And that is why you adopted all of us? So we would know there was someone who cared about us?"

"Actually, I was amassing an army." Artemis had always had a flair for the dramatic, and she utilized it then, managing to look very much like her fearsome namesake. And yet, there was enough laughter in her expression to bring a smile to Daria's face.

"I don't know what we would all do without you," Daria said. "Without each other."

"For my part," Artemis said, "I don't intend to find out."

"I'm hoping I don't have to either." Daria straightened her shoulders. "I simply need to find a means of convincing my parents that having me with them in London during the Season and at home the rest of the year would be to their benefit. Then they won't send me to Wales."

"There is unlikely to be anything 'simple' about that," Artemis warned.

As true as that was likely to be, she knew she couldn't not try. "I have an idea, but I don't know if it will work. I'm no strategist."

"You've come to the right place," Artemis said. "I am a master strategist."

Though she knew Artemis was not misrepresenting herself, Daria was still nervous to share her admittedly vague plan. What if it proved foolish or doomed to failure? She would not merely be a little embarrassed; she would also be discouraged. But this was her best chance of discovering how to move forward.

"I so enjoyed hosting the soiree, putting it together, seeing it through, making certain people were enjoying themselves. It was precisely the sort of gathering I love to attend. To find I enjoyed planning and executing it was a pleasant discovery. My parents hold gatherings too. I'm hoping that by pointing out to them that I did a fine job of my most recent solo efforts and did so without unnecessary expense or bother, perhaps they would consider allowing me to remain in the household and even return to London if I can be put to work planning such things for them."

"You are offering to become part of your parents' household staff?" Artemis did not appear to like Daria's approach.

"Not precisely. Many spinster daughters take on the role of assisting their mothers in hostessing and household management roles. I would be doing that." It was a comedown from being a daughter with prospects who went about in Society with enthusiasm. But she'd left that behind when she'd come to London this Season. "And this arrangement would allow me to keep returning to Town and to avoid moving to my great-aunt's house. I would get to see the Huntresses and Toss and his friends. I think that would be worth donning a spinster's cap and being put to work."

"Without a great deal of time to ponder this, I can't give you a full and complete assessment of your approach. But I will say this: of the three strategies the Huntresses rely upon, this is not the first, which is a good thing. When one is under threat of forcible relocation, retreat is not usually a good approach."

Daria nodded. *Retreat. Wield a shield. Return fire.* Those were the Huntresses' three strategies that Artemis had taught them for navigating Society and their families. In her difficulties, Daria almost always retreated. Wielding a shield involved redirecting blows and subtly undermining peoples' incorrect or unflattering assumptions. That required a degree of cleverness she didn't feel she could claim. Returning fire required, to some degree, an assertiveness that also was not in her nature.

"I can't imagine which of the other two strategies this is," Daria said. "I never thought myself able to execute either of them."

"Oh, Daria, this is wielding a shield at its best. Your parents lobbed at you the barbed threat of sending you into the wilds of who-knows-where in such circumstances as there is no hope of ever returning. You are finding a way to redirect that threat and give them reason to rethink it. You are finding a way of changing a blow into something else. That is a shield and a promising one."

"Truly?" She wanted to believe that. "I know I'm not the cleverest of the Huntresses, so I've never felt quite able to employ the other methods."

"For one thing," Artemis said very firmly, "cleverness comes in many forms. Planning a gathering like you did on such short notice with so little cooperation from your household staff requires cleverness, make no mistake."

"Toss said the evening was an inarguable success." She couldn't seem to help the hint of heat that stole over her cheeks when she spoke of him. "He has told me a few times that he thinks I am brilliant. He's the only one who has ever said that. With him, I don't feel as stupid as I often do."

"Which brings me to my *secondly.*" Artemis hooked an arm through Daria's and walked with her out of the room. "I am an excellent judge of character, which is why I eventually realized how wonderful my Charlie is, even though he worked very hard to make certain I didn't know that. I have not once thought you stupid. You aren't academic. I can't imagine you sitting down in front of a mountain of books on some dry subject and enjoying it simply for the sake of learning what was in it."

Daria shuddered a little bit dramatically. She couldn't imagine herself doing that either.

"You found ways to navigate your family, which is no small feat. Of all the Huntresses, you managed to form friendships with Charlie's friends the easiest at the house party. And of all the Huntresses, you are the one who understood the quickest my efforts at rescuing you all those years ago. None of those things could be accomplished by someone who was in any way stupid."

"Self-preservation hardly counts as intelligence."

"Only according to those who never had to save themselves. You needn't be a mathematician or orator or academic in order to be intelligent, Daria. And if Thomas Comstock has intelligence enough to recognize your brilliance, then his is an association worth keeping."

"He is very . . ." Daria didn't know how to finish that, but not because she hadn't any good descriptors for him. She had plenty, and the list grew every time she was with him. But ever since watching him leave the night before and feeling something in her heart break a little, she'd come to realize that her feelings for him had grown more tender and personal than she'd realized. This newfound connection felt fragile. *She* felt fragile where this topic was concerned.

"Only tell me this, Daria." Artemis looked absolutely fearsome. "Are you stumbling over your words now because Toss has been unkind and you are hurting?"

"Good heavens, no."

Artemis's expression relaxed once more. "Then I am perfectly willing to wait for you to decide how you mean to finish that sentence. We can wait all day if need be."

"I suppose we will have to return to your room and lock ourselves away while I search for and you wait for an elusive word," Daria said with a little tip of her shoulder.

"You'll think better on your feet." Artemis made a show of tugging Daria to the stairs as if desperate not to be locked away.

"I believe I have discovered the threat most likely to motivate you: captivity."

It was Artemis's turn to shudder dramatically, which set them both laughing. The sound joined with the distant notes of music being played on the pianoforte. Toss's instrument. But Daria forced herself not to grow hopeful.

"Are we bound for somewhere in particular?" Daria asked, avoiding asking if they were *looking* for some*one* in particular.

"I am searching for Charlie," Artemis said.

It was a person they were looking for, after all, just not the person she quietly hoped for.

"He hasn't the first idea what is fashionable and what isn't," Artemis said, "but he thinks I'm a genius, and I never miss an opportunity to hear him say as much."

"We're going to show off the dress?"

Artemis nodded. "Won't that be fun?"

Had it been almost anyone other than Charlie, Daria would likely have felt a little self-conscious, assuming they would likely be evaluating her as much as what she was wearing. Charlie was not unkind or judgmental.

"What I can't sort out," Artemis said, "is who is playing the pianoforte? Charlie doesn't. Neither my niece nor my nephew does. My brother-in-law certainly doesn't. And while Persephone can play, her abilities are, by her own admission, merely average."

Whoever was playing was quite proficient. Those uncooperative hopes of hers were beginning to take wing once more. "Toss plays the pianoforte," she said hesitantly, "and he is very good."

Artemis nodded. "I heard him play a number of times at the house party. I suppose it could be him, come to visit Charlie."

It could be Toss after all. Oh, how she hoped it was. Her mind told her she was pleased because they had come to feel like the best of friends. Her heart, however, loudly declared it was something far more than that. But before she could grow fully excited at the possibility of seeing Toss again, a complication occurred to her. "Toss doesn't know that you and Rose own the dress shop, does he?"

Artemis shook her head. "Charlie has left it to us to determine who knows what and when. And the only members of his band of misfits who are aware of it are Scott, because he needed some reassurance that it was possible to formulate a business plan without losing one's claim to Society. And Newton, because Ellie has helped Rose with a few things when I have been away from London."

"How are you to receive your due praise from Charlie if he's not able to acknowledge that the dress is of your design?"

A sly smile spread across Artemis's face. "My husband is a genius. I look forward to seeing how he navigates this."

They stepped into the music room and discovered Charlie bent over books, which was very common for him, he being decidedly academic. And Toss—her heart leapt—was at the pianoforte, playing something very complicated and impressive. Neither of the gentlemen noticed the ladies' arrival.

Toss was very interesting to watch while he played. When away from the pianoforte, he moved about almost constantly; his feet tapped, or he swayed a bit. But when playing music, he was still. Not rigid or frozen in place. There was a serenity to him, a peacefulness.

She felt the strongest urge to go sit beside him in the hope of feeling a bit of that peace herself. But she suspected that if she did, her heart would be in her eyes. She wasn't ready for anyone to know of these feelings yet. Especially him. There was far too much vulnerability in it, and she had learned over a lifetime of disappointments and embarrassment to tread very lightly in areas where she felt fragile.

The music abruptly stopped. Toss jumped to his feet, and Charlie did the same.

"We wouldn't normally interrupt," Artemis said, "but Daria has a new gown from Miss Martinette's, and I told her we simply had to show it off because it's gorgeous."

Daria twirled the tiniest bit so the dress could be shown to advantage.

"This is the famous purple dress that earned you a point in our game?" Toss asked.

Daria nodded. "I think purple was the right choice."

"It's perfect," Toss said with every indication of sincerity. "You look lovely in purple."

Lovely. Never before had so simple a compliment felt so wonderful.

"What do you think, Mr. Charlie Jonquil?" Artemis asked, walking toward her husband with a very regal air.

"I think it is indeed a very gorgeous dress, and though I'm no expert in such things, it appears to be the very height of fashion."

"You are learning quickly." Artemis held a hand out to him, which he took and raised to his lips.

Daria met Toss's eyes once more.

"They are going to be nauseating for a little while," Toss said in a tone of warning.

"Can you believe that once upon a time, we were all afraid they would murder each other?" Daria asked.

Toss laughed. Daria had heard that poets sometimes described laughs as "musical." But his was the first one that she thought truly fit that description. If anyone should have a musical laugh, a musician should.

She smoothed the bodice of her dress. "Do you *truly* like the dress?"

"I do. More importantly, do *you*?"

Daria turned enough to eye the dress once more. "I really, really do."

He was smiling when she looked at him once more. "That is probably why I like the dress as much as I do: you look so happy wearing it."

"That is one of the kindest things anyone has ever said to me, Toss."

Toss took her hand and held it clasped to his heart. "Your encouraging words at the soiree last night were both a kindness and a much-needed bit of confidence." He raised her hand to his lips and pressed a kiss to her knuckles. "You do my battered heart a great deal of good."

Her oft-battered heart threatened to jump through her ribs in that moment. She realized she'd developed tender feelings for him, but she was beginning to suspect she had fallen more entirely in love with him than she'd previously recognized. She knew he wouldn't laugh at her if he knew of her feelings, but she wasn't at all ready to confess them and risk being rejected.

"It *is* lovely," he said. "And you look stunning in it. Though I've always thought you looked very nice no matter what you were wearing."

Heavens. She might never stop blushing.

"When I win the game and your group of friends are required to make certain everyone attends an upcoming house party," she said, "I'll make certain to wear this dress. Then I can look pretty *and* triumphant."

He smiled ever more broadly. "The game is not over yet, Daria. And I suspect my brother is going to give me ample opportunity for finding things he does not approve of."

"May the best Huntress win," she declared.

He laughed again. "May the best—" He shook his head, but the movement was more dramatic than authentic. "We really do need a name."

"Yes, you do," she said.

Toss tipped his head in the direction of Charlie and Artemis. Charlie had his arms around his wife and was either whispering in her ear or kissing her—it was difficult to tell which. "If I play really loudly, do you think they'll stop sparking?"

"I think it is well worth trying."

Unfortunately, that meant he let go of her hand, which made her heart ache a little. But he did start playing again, and she loved listening to and watching him play. Charlie and Artemis more or less ignored his efforts, though, admittedly, he wasn't playing thunderously as he'd threatened to.

Daria was no expert at music, but she could hear a melody repeating underneath the composition. What was wrapped around it changed, but that tune was there. She didn't recognize it, which didn't mean it was new. But she hoped it was.

He ought to keep playing. And he also ought to keep writing his own music. She wanted him to have that bit of himself and the joy it brought him. He deserved to be happy.

CHAPTER FIFTEEN

If Daria had owned a black dress, she would have worn it the next morning. She was bidding Gillian farewell. She refused to believe it was forever, and yet she had no guarantee that it wasn't. Life was so unfair sometimes.

She held her dearest friend once again and extracted for at least the twentieth time a promise from her to write. Gillian and Scott had been kind enough to come to Daria's house to make their farewells, as there'd been no guarantee she would be granted the use of a carriage or allowed a maid to walk with her to the house where Gillian and Scott had been staying.

"I swear to you that I will be a very faithful correspondent," Gillian said firmly. "Even if your parents make good on their threat and send you to Anglesey. I'll write to you wherever you are. I swear."

"And I'll write to you," Daria promised.

"And you must promise to tell me all the details as Mr. Greenberry becomes more smitten with you."

Daria stepped away enough to give her a very dry look. "You are the only person who has seen anything beyond friendliness in his kind treatment of me."

"Is it that you don't think anyone could feel anything beyond that for you or that you don't wish for *him* to?"

A bit of a nervous bubble expanded in her throat. She did hope that she was able to turn a head now and then. But that head, she knew, wasn't Mr. Greenberry's. Even with her very dearest friend, she wasn't ready to admit to her feelings for Toss. To not share her thoughts, her concerns, her hopes with Gillian was both uncharacteristic and, she feared, a foolish decision. Yet she couldn't force herself to spill the secret. Perhaps she would find the courage to do so in a letter, maybe when she understood her own feelings a little better.

Scott stepped up beside his wife, setting his hand gently at her waist. "Though I am likely to be painted a villain for saying as much, we do have to be on the road." He looked to Daria with an expression of regret. "Once our estate is more stable, we'll be able to be here longer and have you come visit us."

Daria nodded. "Never fear. I will emerge triumphant in the game Toss and I are playing, which means you and the other gentlemen will have to find a means of getting me to an eventual house party."

Scott grinned. "I have full faith in Toss. He has an ample store of ways to annoy his brother."

Gillian reached out and squeezed Daria's hand once more. "Keep your chin up, my friend. I refuse to believe this is your last time in London."

"I'll write to you and tell you if I managed to convince my parents."

"Please do."

"Let us know if Charlie and the others ever decide on a name for the lot of us," Scott added. "I am sorry I will not be here to have a say in what they decide. Without Duke and I taking part in the discussion, I suspect they will decide on something ridiculous."

There was too much truth in that not to laugh at it. Daria had met Duke at the house party. She found him wholly intimidating, though he'd given her no reason to actually be afraid of him. He was solemn and quiet and seemed to notice absolutely everything.

Daria stood on the front step of her family's London house and waved as Scott and Gillian's carriage left.

Farewells had always been difficult for Daria. She'd cried for two months when Tobias had first left for school. And she always felt despondent at the end of the London Season when she returned to Yorkshire. But she didn't cry now, as Gillian's carriage disappeared from view. Instead, she set her shoulders the way she'd seen Artemis do countless times and reminded herself to wield her shield.

She would redirect her parents' efforts. She had spent time practicing her assertions, amassing in her mind a list of evidence that her parents would be wise to allow her to remain in the household. She felt she could be convincing if only given a chance.

And that chance was now.

She turned around and stepped back into the house. Inwardly trembling but with head held high, she walked to the sitting room, where Mother and Father would most likely be. As always, Father was tucked behind his newspaper and Mother was bent over her embroidery. Their predictability, she hoped, would prove helpful. When unexpected things were thrown at her without warning, she struggled to formulate ideas and understand what to do next, but this situation was more predictable, which allowed her to approach it more prepared and more competent.

"During my visit to Falstone House yesterday, I heard a great many positive things about the soiree Tobias and I held two nights ago." She didn't bother attempting to make the observation entirely casually, as she suspected her parents would know she was making the observation for a very specific reason.

She sat in a chair that allowed her to face them both. In perfect unison, they looked up at her, matching expressions of confusion on their faces. Daria gulped a breath, uncomfortable at having them both looking at her at once. But she pushed forward.

"Those who attended spoke highly of the evening, and that praise was repeated. That I was spoken of highly in so grand a household for having planned the evening with so little time feels like quite a triumph."

"Are you certain you didn't misunderstand what was being said at the duke and duchess's residence?" Father asked. "They might have been expressing disbelief rather than praise."

Daria had expected Father to have doubts. "I think the Duke is well able to express himself, enough that I can't imagine suggesting he can't make himself understood."

"Heavens, you didn't say anything to him about not expressing himself well, did you?" Mother asked, looking a little worried at the possibility.

"I certainly did not." Daria pressed forward. "I should very much like to plan another gathering to be held here this Season. It would be a fine thing both for the family name and for Tobias as he's beginning to make a splash in Society, for this house to become known as a place where enjoyable events are held."

"I am quite capable of hosting any number of events." Mother was clearly a bit offended.

Daria had anticipated that objection. "I haven't the least doubt what success I had was owing to your example. I made my suggestion, not because you aren't fully capable but in the hope of taking a burden off your shoulders and freeing up your time for more of the things you enjoy. This is something I am capable of, as evidenced by the praise I received at Their Graces' home." How she hoped they didn't press the question of whether or not the praise she had received there had actually come from the duke. It hadn't, though she had intentionally given her parents that impression. The duke likely hadn't heard a thing about the soiree.

"A gathering of a group of friends is not going to help the family standing or further Tobias's social cachet," Father said. "He has already made the acquaintance of those you are in a position to introduce him to."

"I must agree with your father on this," Mother said. "If we send out invitations to a gathering and promise it will be grand and extraordinary, we would look worse than if we hadn't hosted anything to begin with. Best that we don't risk it."

Daria had long felt her parents were a bit indifferent to her and her happiness, but she couldn't describe them quite that way now. There was an anxiousness, a hint of panic when she so much as suggested she might continue on in Society. That did not seem to be a good sign. But she wouldn't give up. Too much depended on success. Perhaps a slightly different approach would help.

"If the evening goes terribly," Daria said, "you can always point to the failure as the reason why your daughter is no longer attending the Season in years to come."

That shifted her mother's expression from doubt to interest.

"If, however, it goes wonderfully well, I can organize future gatherings," Daria said. "Perhaps even invite a young lady who would be worthy of Tobias's consideration."

"We wish Tobias to meet people this year," Mother acknowledged, "but he is still too young for marriage."

It was the perfect opportunity to at least hint at this as a long-term arrangement. "I would, of course, work hard to plan and organize gatherings for however long is needed to see him appropriately settled."

That clearly set her parents a bit on edge. Why did the possibility of her *not* going to Wales worry them so much?

"I only wish to offer you more freedom to enjoy yourself."

From the doorway of the sitting room, Tobias entered the conversation. "You have said how much you appreciate the time you spend with your friends during the Season, Mother. Daria's evening really was quite a success. Mr. Greenberry has almost as many impressive connections as the youngest Mr. and Mrs. Jonquil, and he spoke of how much he enjoyed his time in this house. I think it's worth seeing if Daria can recreate that success."

At that—a repetition of almost exactly what Daria had said—Father grew very ponderous.

"You make a very good point, Tobias." He even lowered his paper. "And should the evening be disappointing, we would know not to try again." He spoke as if it were his idea and not Daria's. "The evening will need to be something more than people merely mingling, though I don't think something as complicated as a ball ought to be attempted."

Daria agreed with him on that. She didn't feel ready to undertake anything so challenging. "What about a musical evening?" she suggested. "Either a performance by a professional musician or one in which the guests are invited to display their talents."

Mother gave it a moment's thought. "If you think you are equal to the task of organizing it, then a musical evening could be a good choice."

Proving she was equal to the task was the point of the evening. Daria would make certain she was successful.

"How soon would you like the musical evening to be held?" she asked.

"Within a fortnight," Mother said. "That will allow you to plan around significant Society events that are already scheduled and announced."

Daria nodded. "Perhaps in years to come, the events at this house will be considered a 'significant Society event.' That would be a grand thing."

"It would," Mother conceded. "And help planning such important gatherings *would* be nice."

Daria had spoken of years' worth of events, and Mother had acknowledged wanting her help planning them. *Years' worth.* Daria couldn't do that from Anglesey. Here was hope.

"I would like that, Mother."

"We will have to see how this musicale goes before deciding anything."

"I understand." Daria swiftly left the room before her parents had time to second-guess themselves. Tobias followed close on her heels.

Once safely out of earshot of the sitting room and away from the disquiet she always felt when with her parents, she breathed at last. "Thank you for that," she said to Tobias. "They didn't take my suggestion seriously until you echoed it."

"Have I told you often enough how unfair that is?"

She smiled at her brother. "You have. Please don't think that because I choose not to confront them about the things they say and do that I don't realize they are often unfair and unkind. On the few occasions when I have, it has made things worse. I've chosen peace over fair treatment, which I realize is not ideal. It might even be the wrong choice." She shrugged and shook her head. "It's probably the *weak* choice. I'm certain plenty of people would insist that were I truly strong, I would vociferously object every time they treat me that way."

"They would have sent you to Great-Aunt Theodosia's years ago if that had been your tactic," Tobias said.

"Avoiding that fate now is what this musical evening is all about." She threaded her arm through his and walked with him. "I need to ponder whether to make this a professional performance or a participatory one. But I think either will make for a nice evening."

"It will be grand," Tobias said. "I'm certain of it. I'm happy to help in whatever way I can."

"If I do decide to have a professional performer, I would likely need you to undertake those arrangements, as such a thing would, I suspect, be inappropriate for an unmarried lady."

He nodded his agreement with that assessment. "In exchange for doing that favor, I would ask you one in return." There was enough mischief in the request that she knew he wouldn't refuse to help her, regardless of whether or not she agreed to whatever he meant to ask.

"What is this favor?"

With a smile, he said, "Allow me to see the guest list once you've made it?"

"Are you afraid I might include someone you don't want to be there?" she said with a laugh.

"Quite the opposite, in fact."

She eyed him with curiosity. "This is someone you like very much?" She let her tone and her expression turn teasing. "Is it possible that my brother has had his head turned by a lovely young lady?"

"Oh, it's possible. Before you go on, I am not going to tell you who I will be searching your guest list for no matter how much you press." He slipped his hand from hers. "But I do hope you accidentally invite her." He made his way down the corridor, walking with a jaunty step.

She was planning a musical evening that, if successful, would allow her to avoid the doom of Great-Aunt Theodosia's house. Her parents had expressed the tiniest bit of faith in her. And, it seemed, Tobias was a little bit in love with someone.

Daria knew she had a history of getting her hopes up only to have them dashed, but in that moment, she let herself fully, completely, and unabashedly believe there were good things yet to come.

CHAPTER SIXTEEN

Toss HAD ONLY JUST FINISHED working on his composition when Daria bounced into the music room. As had been the case upon her arrival in this very room the day before, his heart thundered like a kettledrum. Warmth radiated through him. And the tune she'd inspired, the one he'd continued expanding on, echoed ever louder in his thoughts, thoughts that had returned to her again and again for days.

"Toss." She smiled at him, speeding up his thunderous pulse. "What brings you here?"

"I am working on my composition still," he said, proud of his composure. "The duke and duchess have kindly continued allowing me use of their pianoforte."

Her lips pursed the way he'd noticed they did when she was puzzling over something. "Does your brother not allow you use of your own pianoforte?"

"No, he does not." Toss didn't think now was the time to explain how truly horrid Laurence was lately.

Daria squared her shoulders. "Well, I am feeling very brave today. Perhaps I will march myself over to your brother's house and tell him just what a loathsome person he is being."

Toss slipped his hand around hers. All felt right again, even if only for that moment. "What has you feeling so brave, Daria?"

"I told my parents that I ought to be permitted to plan another gathering at our house since the soiree was a triumph. At first they objected, but in the end, they agreed. And I can remain in London until it is held. And better still, if I do a good job, I think it will convince them that I ought to remain at home and come to Town for the Season in the future in order to plan such things. I wouldn't be relegated to Great-Aunt Theodosia's house where I'd be all alone."

He pressed a kiss to her hand, which he'd also discovered the day before was very much to his liking. "Congratulations. You were not only brave, but you were also successful."

Her wide smile lit her entire face. "A wise person once told me I was brilliant. I simply decided to believe him."

"Whoever told you that was wise indeed."

She laughed. "It was *you*, Toss."

He laughed as well. "As I said, very, very wise."

Daria moved so she was standing beside him, her hand still in his. "I can tell you are on your way out, and I don't mean to keep you." She walked with him toward the door of the music room. "But I am glad I got to tell you how courageous I was today. I knew you'd be proud of me."

"And deeply happy for you as well. Also relieved to know you'll be here for weeks yet. London wouldn't be the same without you."

She looked up into his eyes, a blush of pleasure pinking her cheeks. London wouldn't be the same without her nearby. But he knew *he* wouldn't be the same either. Yet he needed to be more circumspect. His tender feelings for her would soon be obvious to everyone if he wasn't careful. But he'd already had the horrifying realization of the misery Laurence would cause her, assuming Laurence even proved willing to abandon his plans to choose Toss's eventual match.

Toss could only fight so many battles at once. And he did not wish for Daria to be pulled into any of them.

And that thought remained with him all the way to his club, where he had arranged a meeting with Mr. Fortier, just as the Duke of Kielder had suggested.

He made his way to the reading room and found the tall and elegant Frenchman waiting for him. Mr. Fortier greeted him warmly, and they took adjacent seats in a quiet corner of the room.

"Thank you for granting me a bit of your time," Toss said.

"I would have regardless, but I confess I was particularly intrigued to hear that it was His Grace who suggested you reach out to me."

Toss nodded. "I was not aware the two of you were well acquainted, but he seemed entirely confident that you would prove helpful in a very specific matter."

Mr. Fortier offered a serene and sedate smile, not unlike those Toss had often seen the vicar of his home parish wear over the years. There was a reassuring peacefulness to Mr. Fortier. "The duke and I are not of the same generation, but His Grace has a deep connection to the group of gentlemen you met at Lord

Aldric's home during the poetry night. His Grace's early years and our youthful years are intertwined in rather entertaining ways."

"Mr. Layton indicated you all were friends of very long standing."

"We've known each other since our school days, and I will save you the trouble of stumbling over any attempts to observe how very long ago that must have been without causing offense. It has, indeed, been decades."

Toss liked Mr. Fortier more the longer he knew him. "I've been fortunate enough to gain very close friends myself. I hope that decades from now, I can say that we are all still friends."

"I hope so as well." There was a sincerity in his words that touched Toss. "What is the matter on which His Grace suggested you speak with me?"

Toss had told so few people any details about this aspect of his life that he couldn't help feeling nervous. He wasn't ashamed of his music, nor was he ashamed of his talent and interest, but he'd encountered enough difficulty in this area, especially lately, to give him pause. "Whilst at Cambridge, I studied music composition. I believe I've a knack for it. I know I have a love for it. I'd hoped that at the end of my time at university, I would leave with the tools and contacts and knowledge I needed to pursue a vocation in that area, as much of a vocation as a gentleman is permitted, at least."

Mr. Fortier listened, watching him intently with a look that told Toss in an instant that the man understood the conflicting feelings he was trying to express.

"My brother has never approved of my musical pursuits, and to that end, he refused to pay for my final term at Cambridge and instead exercised the power he has over me and brought me here to London for the Season to begin molding me into the gentleman he wishes I were." It was tempting to get up and pace, but he didn't particularly want the conversation to be spread throughout the entire club. "Without that conclusion to my education, without the connections it would give me, I'm not certain how to proceed. I would very much like to continue my efforts and my compositions and perhaps even earn an income from it. My brother's disapproval is a significant obstacle. My father's will does not guarantee me any income from the estate, and I live quite literally on the charity of my brother. Antagonizing him means being penniless, without a home, which isn't a great option. His animosity toward my music has grown since he pulled me from Cambridge. Despite having told me that I would be permitted to do what I chose and enjoy myself in this, my first Season, he's taken exception to my inclusion of music in my activities."

"In what way has he expressed his disapproval?" Mr. Fortier asked.

"He had my pianoforte removed from the house and sold. I've hidden all my musical notation, as I very much fear he would destroy them if he found them."

"I'm sorry to hear that," Mr. Fortier said with very real understanding. "I spent far too many years of my life hiding my poems and fearing what would happen if my brother discovered them. It is difficult to feel free to create when one also must hide that creation."

Why was it so reassuring to know someone else understood what he was experiencing?

"I don't want to abandon my music. My brother controls so many aspects of my life, and I have already sacrificed so many things in order to keep the peace with him. Losing this, too, would feel like losing my soul."

"In many ways, it would be," Mr. Fortier said. "Art resides in the soul. When we create art, it arises from so deep a place within us that it is, in many ways, part of us. To have your music torn away would not merely feel like losing a part of yourself; it would literally be a loss of self."

"You have no idea how reassuring it is to hear that." Toss released a deep breath. "I've wondered for weeks, years, really, if I was simply being overly dramatic."

"I have had that same conversation with myself, Mr. Comstock. It was the words of someone very wise that helped me realize it was not only permissible for poetry and other creative pursuits to feel deeply personal and important but that it would also be shocking if it were otherwise."

"Who was it that told you that?" Toss asked.

"The lady I eventually married," Henri said. "She was the first person I told that I was actively composing and publishing poetry. The Gents—that is what my group of friends call ourselves—knew I had studied it and knew I still read it, but I'd not even told them that I wrote it. It wasn't that I didn't trust them, nor did I think they would dismiss or laugh at my efforts. I was hesitant to burden them with a secret that came with a great deal of complications. *Ma Nicolette* helped me see that poetry is an important part of who I am and helped me realize how ridiculous it was to not lean upon my friends in my difficulties, to not trust them with something so deeply important to me."

"Mrs. Fortier sounds a great deal like Daria—Miss Mullins," he corrected with a quick shake of his head. The familiarity with which the Huntresses and his group of friends interacted would not meet with Society's approval.

Mr. Fortier did not look shocked. And to Toss's relief, he didn't press the matter of the social faux pas.

"I would suggest you share with your friends the difficulties you are facing."

"I have, to an extent."

Mr. Fortier nodded. "Consider allowing them to know more than just *an extent.* And I would further suggest you ponder for a time how fortunate you are to have someone like Miss Mullins in your life, who is encouraging and sees the value in what you do. That is rarer than you likely think."

"As much as my brother makes me question what I do with my life, her family makes her question her intelligence and judgment."

Mr. Fortier's brows pulled low. For a man who must have been in his sixties, he actually had very little silver mixed in with the gold. "There were a few times during the poetry evening when she spoke of herself in surprisingly unflattering terms but did so without any hint of self-pity. The comments always seemed to be on the matter of her intelligence, which I thought odd because she struck me as being more than capable of participating in a game that does require some intellectual flexibility."

It was Toss's turn to nod with understanding. "Because she's not academic and stumbles over her words sometimes, especially when reading aloud, her family has convinced her that she is, in their words, stupid."

Mr. Fortier's face pulled into a look of disapproval. "No one should be made to feel that way, especially by family."

Toss wanted Daria to see what a remarkable person she was. She'd advocated for herself. Seeing the triumph and pride in her eyes as she'd recounted that moment had done his heart good. And it was proving rather inspiring. Daria had faced her unsupportive family members; surely he could do the same.

"How is it you managed to continue on with your poetry even with your brother's disapproval?"

"For one thing, I did it in secret, which helped. It also somewhat simplified my situation that I was guaranteed a certain income from my late father's estate. My brother did not, at first, give that to me willingly, and he knew I hadn't the funds to press the matter in the French courts. But with the help of my friends, we found a means of claiming some financial freedom from him. That was one of his greatest sources of power over me. Reclaiming that made a difference."

"I don't know how I would do that with Laurence. I have no income outside of what he's willing to give me. I have no home to claim, no means of supporting myself."

"I had no home either. I rented some inexpensive rooms in London during the Season, and moved from the house of one friend to another the rest of the year. It was a lowering and humbling experience, I will admit, but it gave me a bit of independence, which was not a bad thing."

Toss had come directly from Cambridge to London and so had not pondered the possibility of moving about, staying with friends. He knew Charlie and Artemis would let him visit them at Brier Hill for a time. He would ask Scott and Gillian, but he knew their finances were terribly strained. Newton and Ellie had enough generosity that they would offer as well, but he knew that their time was exceedingly limited, with Newton still undertaking his education in the law.

Duke's family likely wouldn't object to Toss's staying with them, but Duke's mentions of them over the years made him think perhaps the Seymours' home would not be the happiest place to stay.

Fennel, the one they laughingly called Poppy, had his own estate, inherited from his father when he was still at Eton. He lived near the coast in Kent, with many acres and a large house to his name. That might be a possibility. As Fennel was still at university, he might not mind having Toss there to look after the place in his absence. Toss knew nothing about breeding horses, which was what the estate did, but he would leave that part to whomever was doing it now.

"I likely could find places to live," Toss acknowledged aloud. "They would not be ideal situations, but my current situation is so far from ideal that almost anything would be an improvement."

Mr. Fortier's smile was as quiet as the ones he'd offered thus far, but this time it held an amused spirit of understanding. He had likely endured a great many less-than-ideal situations whilst at odds with his brother.

"I have a younger sister though," Toss said. "A chasm between myself and my brother might separate me from her."

"I have a younger sister as well and experienced that same fear."

His Grace had not been exaggerating when he'd suggested Mr. Fortier would understand Toss's struggles.

"Did you manage to remain part of her life?" Toss asked.

"A great deal happened in the time leading up to and shortly after I was married, far too much to recount here, but fate intervened in some shocking and, at times, horrifying ways to make certain I did not lose my connection to my sister."

"I would rather keep close to my sister without fate intervening in 'horrifying ways.'"

Mr. Fortier nodded. "Understandably."

"And if I could make my music profitable, I would have some additional freedom, which would help. But I don't know how to make that happen."

"I believe there is a Royal Society of Musicians," Mr. Fortier said. "Their advice and knowledge and support would go a very long way."

"There is," Toss said. "I intended to apply for membership once I completed my education, but I wasn't given the opportunity."

"Not finishing your education would not automatically eliminate your chances of successfully applying to join," Mr. Fortier said. "Many of the great composers did not have formal university training, just as many successful writers did not study the craft at any institution, yet literary societies are open to them."

"You're saying it would be worth trying?"

Mr. Fortier gave a quick and firm nod. "I struggled for quite a long time in my poetry. But twelve or so years ago, the Literary Society was founded here in London by William Wordsworth. I became one of the earliest members, and it has been invaluable. Seek out others of your profession. They will help you learn better your craft, help fill any gaps your untimely removal from Cambridge has left. They will help you discover how to make a success of your ambitions."

This single conversation had done wonders for Toss's peace of mind. He had direction and hope. "I cannot thank you enough, Mr. Fortier. This has been more helpful than I can say."

Mr. Fortier shook Toss's hand. "I'm pleased His Grace sent you my way. Please reach out again. I understand all too well the path you're on. It's one that is easier when walked in company."

They both stood, Mr. Fortier looking elegantly subdued, precisely the sort of gentleman whose arrival made a person feel instantly more at ease.

"I would remain longer," Mr. Fortier said, "but I am testifying at a trial this afternoon."

"Mr. Finley's inheritance trial?" Toss guessed, knowing that had consumed a great deal of interest in the *ton*.

The Frenchman nodded. "The miserable wretch could have avoided all this if he had simply decided to be a decent person. But he crossed a line that Mr. Layton rightly found unforgivable and did so after more than sufficient warning. Now there will be no saving him from his own choices."

Toss walked alongside Mr. Fortier to the front door of their club. "During our evening at Lord Aldric's home, it was Lord Aldric I found the most intimidating. But I'm beginning to suspect the one whom I ought to be afraid of is Mr. Layton." He made the observation laughingly.

But the look Mr. Fortier gave him was serious. "Many people have underestimated him to their cost."

Mr. Fortier went his way, and Toss went the other. Toss had a great deal to think about. Among all of it was the realization that this group of older gentlemen, who had fashioned themselves the Gents, were not entirely unlike his group of friends. They, by all indication, were like brothers. They carried their own secrets and their own weights, yet they helped each other endure them. It was a comfort to one whose actual brother was causing so much misery.

And on the heels of that contemplation came thoughts of Daria. Lately, she was seldom out of his thoughts. And she was always intertwined in the beating of his heart. He'd liked her at the house party. He was in love with her now.

Dear, loving, delightful Daria. She had made this Season, which could have been an utterly miserable disaster, into something enjoyable and light and happy. She gave him reason to smile when the heaviness of life was threatening to crush him. She laughed with him, held his hand, defended him, and praised his music.

She saw him when he felt invisible.

Her family was threatening to send her away, to tear her away from the sources of joy and light in her life. No matter what became of the connection he felt to her, Toss knew one thing for certain: he meant to do all he could to ensure Mr. and Mrs. Mullins did not succeed in hurting her that way.

CHAPTER SEVENTEEN

Toss left the club with a spring in his step that had been missing. He considered himself an optimistic and cheerful sort of person, not easily defeated by life's difficulties. But he'd not realized until Mr. Fortier had given him back a bit of hope just how much he'd been struggling to feel that lately.

Not wanting to ruin the moment, he avoided Laurence's home and made his way, instead, back to Falstone House. He hummed Daria's tune all the way there, anxious to fully immerse himself in the budding composition and looking forward to telling her about his meeting and the hope he felt.

When he arrived at the door and knocked, he wasn't even asked for a calling card. The butler simply showed him in and instructed him to see himself to the music room. With a continued bouncing step, Toss made his way there, grinning as he hadn't in some time.

"Daria!" He was so happily shocked at seeing her in the room that all he could manage was her name.

She rushed to him, looking absolutely delighted, and took his hands, her deep brown eyes shimmering with excitement. "You will never guess!" she said with infectious enthusiasm.

"I suspect you're right," he said, "so I will forgo the guesses and simply tell you how anxious I am to hear whatever it is you're excited to tell me."

"That is because you are the very best of friends," she said.

"I do try to be." It took all his self-control not to pull her into his arms. He hadn't that right. But he could continue to hold her hands, to stand near her, to watch her beautiful smile play across her lips.

Her bright and dancing eyes never left his face. "Artemis sent for Mr. Layton and her sisters—between all of them, they are invited to absolutely everything of any importance in Society—and we found an evening when nothing of tremendous significance is scheduled. That was one of my parents' requirements. I suspect they thought I wouldn't be able to overcome that first obstacle. But I did. And I did it so quickly."

How could anyone not be utterly delighted listening to her recount what might, from anyone else, seem like a simple triumph?

"Artemis's sisters who do not live here have returned to their homes. Mr. Layton is still here. He and Artemis decided that Charlie's green waistcoat would be a better choice with what he is wearing today than the blue one he chose. So the three of them went back upstairs to, as Artemis very seriously put it, *rectify the situation*. That made Charlie laugh, to which Mr. Layton said, 'Fashion is not a laughing matter.' And that made all of them laugh."

Toss laughed a little as well, not necessarily at the story but with delight at how happy Daria was in that moment. He'd seen her weighed down and sorrowful so often of late that his heart couldn't help rejoicing to see this change.

"I'm blathering again, I know." She shook her head at herself. "But I can't help myself. When I'm excited or worried or embarrassed or . . ." The sentence tapered off, though she picked up the thread an instant later. "It's as if my mouth starts running away, and I can't stop it."

He squeezed her hands. "I like listening to you talk. And I like seeing you so happy."

"And I like that you looked so happy when you came into the room. You were bouncing again. You haven't been doing that as much lately."

"We have both had a very good day, as it turns out, and have both received help from very generous people."

Her mouth pulled in an *O*, and her expression shifted to one of someone having a sudden realization. "Artemis said you were meeting with Mr. Fortier on a matter of importance. It went well, then?"

"*Very* well." Toss couldn't remember ever having an ongoing conversation with a lady while holding her hands. If he had his way and if fate suddenly decided to be kind, he'd always talk with her this way: holding her hands, perhaps eventually holding *her*.

"What did you discuss?" She sounded both impatient and amused. He'd apparently been lost enough in visions of a future he could only dream of that he'd noticeably delayed his retelling.

"Mr. Fortier was very encouraging. He endured difficulties very similar to what I am experiencing and, in the end, claimed the life he'd been hoping for."

"Oh, that *is* encouraging."

"And he suggested I apply to join the Royal Society of Musicians, though I'm not certain I actually qualify."

Her expression grew earnest. "But you will at least try? You must. Otherwise, how will they discover how remarkable you are?"

"To be accepted into the Royal Society of Musicians, an applicant must have some irrefutable proof that he is already remarkable. I don't have the sort of proof that they require."

"*I'll* tell them," she said firmly.

"I'm afraid they won't accept that as convincing evidence."

"No, they wouldn't, would they." Splotches of color appeared on her face. "I am usually so good about not putting so much faith in my own evaluation of things." Her eyes took on a pleading quality. "I have always been a little stupid. I sometimes forget not to put so much store by my own judgment."

He slipped a hand free of hers and cupped her face. "I don't think you have ever actually been stupid, Daria Mullins. I think what you've been is lied to."

She shook her head. "I was always horrible at my lessons. And if you ever heard me read out loud, you'd know I'm—" She didn't finish the sentence but dropped her eyes and, to his horror, began to cry.

"Oh heavens, Daria. Please don't cry." He fumbled in his pocket for a handkerchief. "I have heard you read, and nothing in it made me think any less of your intelligence." He set a square of linen in her hand, watching her with concern, wanting to dry her tears himself and hold her to him.

"But I fumble so terribly." She wiped at her trickling tears.

He set a hand on her arm, rubbing it slowly and, he hoped, comfortingly. "Many people stumble when they read. That doesn't mean they aren't clever or intelligent."

"But my struggles with reading are not the only evidence that has been pointed out to me."

By her father, Toss would wager. "I could make a list right now of things you've done that I inarguably believe are brilliant."

For reasons he didn't entirely understand, her tears picked up pace. He brushed one away with his thumb, unsure why his sincere compliment had made things worse.

"I'm not crying now because I'm upset, I promise you," she said. "I swear to it. I don't think it's even just that I'm happy. It's . . . It feels almost like relief." It was all too evident that she had heard too many of her father's lies for too long. She had learned to believe them. "It is a frightening thing to let myself believe someone might think very well of me, because if I discover later on that they don't, it hurts so much more."

"Set your mind at ease on that score, Daria Mullins. The better I know you, the more I think the world of you."

Her cheeks were still damp, and her lashes shimmered with tears, but her smile felt real and sincere. "I really shouldn't be keeping you from the pianoforte." With her free hand, she took hold of his hand once more. The simple touch allowed him to breathe more freely for the first time since inadvertently implying that her judgment was lacking. She pulled him to the pianoforte. "You have a composition to work on."

He laughed. "At the moment, I would very much like to keep talking with you."

She shook her head firmly. "I will not be the reason you do not work toward your goal."

"And you insist I do so right this moment?"

She nodded. "Artemis taught the Huntresses to be very effective at convincing people to do things. We swore to her that we would use the powers she bestowed upon us only for the pursuit of good and not anything evil."

Toss laughed. How good she was for him; how delightful her company was.

He sat on the small round stool in front of the pianoforte and played what he had composed thus far of the piece she had unknowingly inspired. It was very simple and very elementary in its conception, but it was the foundation on which the entire piece would eventually rest.

When he was done playing it, he turned to look at Daria, finding himself eager for her thoughts.

She stood beside him, his handkerchief pressed over her heart, watching him—not the pianoforte, not the keys, not looking off into the distance pondering things—she was watching *him*.

"That was beautiful." It was a simple evaluation but was offered with such sincerity. It was quite possibly the most wonderful praise his music had ever received. She had been his support before he'd even known how much he needed it. She had believed in him.

"Thank you," he said. "I hope I can play it for you when it is finished."

"I would like that."

Toss gave the keys a little trill, a habit he had picked up when he was very young.

"Do you remember at the house party when you played the pianoforte while we all danced?" she asked.

He nodded, plunking out a simplified version of the melody he had just played.

"I remember thinking at the time it was a shame that the one who so generously provided the music never got to participate in the dancing. And I thought how nice it would be if someone could play the pianoforte and dance at the same time." She laughed a little. "I realized quickly how silly that thought was. I'm grateful I didn't say it out loud then."

"Might I say, for the record," Toss said, "that you need never be afraid of saying anything to me, no matter how silly you might think it is. I like talking with you. And it would be rather devastating to discover you were afraid to say things to me because you thought I would laugh at you or belittle you or think less of you."

"You're not like other people," she said quietly. "Not everyone is so generous."

He rose, standing so near to her he could smell the soft, sweet flowery scent of her perfume. "And not everyone is as determined as I am now to discover if one can, in fact, play the pianoforte while dancing."

He set one arm around her waist. His heart responded immediately, beating furiously against his ribs. She set a hand on his arm, smiling so sweetly that everything in his world felt right again, as if that smile alone smoothed over every rough bit, every struggle, every worry.

Remembering what he was meant to be attempting, he plunked at the keys of the pianoforte with his free hand. His attempt at producing anything resembling music failed miserably.

"This might take practice," she said.

"Promise?"

Her lips parted in a tiny, silent "Oh." Her blush returned, this time in what was clearly a moment of pleasure. He couldn't manage to pull his gaze away from her increasingly tempting lips.

Dare he try? Dare he hope she was thinking what he was?

And then, with a sense of timing that might have seemed humorous under other circumstances, Charlie arrived, and the magic of the moment was shattered.

CHAPTER EIGHTEEN

"How many points do you suppose these two should receive for this rendezvous, Artie?" Charlie asked Artemis as the two of them, along with Mr. Layton, stepped into the music room.

Though she knew he was teasing, Daria blushed at his use of the word *rendezvous*.

"Be nice, Charlie," Toss said. There was both laughter and warning in the declaration.

Charlie liked to tease, and Daria sometimes forgot that unlike her father, his teasing wasn't cruel.

"Toss was playing the pianoforte, which I know his brother wouldn't approve of," Daria said. "So that's earned him a point in our competition. And he played a song of his own composing, which should earn him another point. Ooh, and he was in a room alone with a lady, though with the doors wide open for propriety's sake. I still think his brother would not choose that for him, which means another point."

"Don't stop there," Toss said. "I need the points."

"As I have been on Miss Mullins's side of this competition from the beginning," Mr. Layton said, "I feel I need to point out that *she* should also receive a point for being in the empty-with-open-doors room. And she was here speaking of the musical evening she is planning, and though her parents have agreed to it, they would likely not wish for her to be making strides so quickly."

"Another point!" Artemis declared.

"And I accepted a handkerchief from a gentleman without my father's permission," Daria added, excited to have thought of another item so quickly. "That should add a point."

With a chuckle, Charlie said, "Our comfortable lead of only a moment ago has quickly disappeared, Toss."

"Though he did make me cry, and even his brother couldn't approve of that, which would earn Toss a point." She mentioned it to be teasing, but Charlie, Artemis, and Mr. Layton's expressions all turned suddenly thunderous.

It was Charlie who spoke first. "You made her cry?" She had never before heard Charlie Jonquil sound so formidable.

Mr. Layton was glaring at Toss as well. "Explain yourself."

Daria quickly realized her mistake. "They were happy tears, and he didn't actually *cause* them. I was only teasing, trying to make a joke." She pleaded with them all. "I am forever saying things wrong. Please don't hold that against him."

Toss set a hand gently on her arm. "Charlie's father taught all his sons to never tolerate a man mistreating a woman. And as the late earl and Mr. Layton were very good friends, I suspect he feels as strongly on the topic as Charlie's father did."

"I don't want them to think badly of you, Toss." The very possibility sat painfully on her mind.

"If either of them fully believed I had caused you pain, I would likely already be flattened on the floor. That they hesitated enough to allow for an explanation is proving to be one of my proudest moments."

She watched Toss, wanting to make certain she hadn't made tremendous trouble for him.

He took her hand once more. "All is well, Daria. I promise."

The same warmth that had rushed over her as they'd attempted to dance spread through her once more. She'd thought in the moment before Charlie had stepped into the room that Toss might have been considering kissing her. But she had no experience with such things, and her ability to analyze new situations was far from reliable. She would let herself be certain that he had enjoyed dancing with her and that he liked her very much, but she would keep herself from becoming too attached to any possibility beyond that.

As quickly as Toss had taken her hand, he released it once more, then turned to the others in the room. Daria pushed down the feeling of loss.

"I had a very enlightening conversation with a friend of yours, Mr. Layton," he said.

"Which friend?"

"A certain Frenchman with a knack for poetry."

"Ah." Mr. Layton nodded his understanding.

While Toss recounted his conversation, Artemis crossed to Daria and threaded an arm through hers. They walked together to the far windows.

Little louder than a whisper, Artemis said, "I've known you three years now, Daria. I have seen you in moments that would crush most everyone else's soul, and yet I've not seen you truly cry. Please tell me, honestly, without attempting to protect him, did Toss actually bring you to tears?"

"I did grow a little teary, yes. But they truly were tears of happiness."

"Again, I have known you a long time, and I've not ever seen you cry, even when you were happy."

It was odd, now that Daria truly thought about it. She didn't cry, hadn't in years. "He said something very kind. I desperately needed that bit of kindness." She sighed a little. "The Huntresses, of course, are always very kind to me, but there's something different about it when he is. It's also different from when Tobias is." Even as she began babbling yet again, she managed to keep her voice very quiet. The gentlemen would not be able to overhear. "I suppose because Tobias is my brother and the Huntresses feel like my sisters, and kindnesses from him and from all of you are . . ." She shook her head. "Family doesn't always speak kindly. I'm likely making no sense whatsoever. I'm only trying to say that it was special. That *he* is special."

There was studying quality to Artemis's gaze. "Don't feel you have to answer immediately, as you might not have pondered this yet, but is it possible you have developed a bit of a tendre for him?"

The question swirled around in Daria's head and bumped up against her heart, but it didn't cause any foundation-shifting realizations. She already knew he had laid claim to her affections. She already knew a bit of her heart walked about with him. But she'd not ever admitted that to anyone. "I do like him very much," she said. "All the Huntresses do. All his friends do. But I—I think perhaps—" She couldn't manage the denial any longer. She was bungling the effort as it was. She pushed out a breath of frustration. "Oh dear."

Artemis faced her. "Why 'Oh, dear'? Toss is a wonderful person."

"I have been falling in love with him all Season, more every time I see him. But he's my friend."

Artemis shrugged. "Charlie and I developed a friendship before we felt anything beyond. It was the way in which we came to know each other and grew close enough to fall in love."

"I referred to him before you came into the room as my friend, and he seemed completely satisfied with that description." Daria watched Toss a moment as, across the room, he continued his conversation with the other two gentlemen. "I could fall desperately for him; I know I could. But what if all he ever feels for me is friendship?"

"Do you think that is all he feels now?"

Daria wasn't certain how to answer. He'd not obviously indicated anything more than friendship. But she had thought he'd meant to kiss her. At least, that was how she had interpreted things, but she knew better than to place too much reliance on her own evaluative skills.

"I hadn't meant to plunge you into turmoil." Artemis leaned forward and squeezed Daria's hand. "None of these questions have to be answered immediately."

"'Borrowing trouble' is what Gillian always calls it," Daria said. "I do wish she could have stayed in London, at least until Nia and Eve have to return to Ireland."

"Do you get the impression this Season that there is something the two of them aren't telling us?" Artemis asked.

Daria nodded. "Eve in particular has offered some oddly evasive answers, particularly to questions about future gatherings. I haven't been able to make any sense of it."

"I vowed when I began assembling our fearless band that I wouldn't pry into anything any of you didn't wish for me to," Artemis said. "All of you regularly make that a difficult promise to keep." Her look of annoyance held a significant amount of amusement.

"If you want a chance to pry, I could use some help guessing who the young lady is that Tobias is hoping I will include in my guest list for the musicale. He won't tell me who she is but says he means to check to see if her name is there."

Artemis's eyes grew wide, and her smile tugged upward. "Won't that be fun to sort out?"

Daria was feeling a little better. She was clearly not hiding her tender feelings for Toss, and that was a risky thing. He was her friend, regardless of what else she might wish him to be. That was worth safeguarding. She would watch and wait and do her utmost to make sense of it all.

CHAPTER NINETEEN

Toss had played "O, Dear! What Can the Matter Be?" so many times over the course of his life that he no longer had to think about which notes came after which. Indeed, as he sat at the pianoforte at Lampton House, he added flourishes and additional trills to the tune simply to entertain his fingers. Watching his friends attempt a country dance in the sitting room kept the rest of him fully entertained.

Mater had invited the Huntresses and Toss's group of friends, along with Tobias and Colm Greenberry, who both appeared to now be a permanent part of their group, to spend an evening together away from the whirl of Society.

"The elder Mr. Comstock would certainly never suggest such a thing," Mater had added slyly, inspiring laughter from the entire group. She and Mr. Layton had continued helping their chosen participants scheme and plan for eventual triumph, adding a tremendous amount of humor to the undertaking.

Mater sat not far distant, watching Charlie with unmistakable amusement and fondness. He, true to form, had taken the idea of a simple country dance and turned it into a performance worthy of any court jester. It was chaos and hilarity and a sharp reminder to Toss of all he missed about being at Cambridge with his friends.

Yet it wasn't Charlie and his antics that continually drew Toss's eye; it was Daria. The chaos introduced into the dance meant everyone regularly bumped into everyone else. And while they all took it good-naturedly, Daria smiled broadly and laughed with such ease and such delight. The soul-deep joyfulness of her drew him in more every time he saw her, every time he was with her.

I should have kissed her. The less logical part of his mind had insisted on that from almost the moment Charlie had interrupted their attempt at a dance. He was all but certain, when he was thinking clearly, that kissing her would have been a monumental mistake. He didn't know her thoughts and feelings.

He had no future to offer her, which made kissing her the behavior of a cad. It would have been a mistake. A wonderful, heart-stopping mistake.

The weaving and movement of the dance put Daria into partnership with Colm. He danced that portion with Daria, executing every step perfectly and brilliantly even with Charlie's efforts to upend them, and then Colm made an admittedly funny show of being proud of his executed steps, which only encouraged Charlie's antics even more.

Soon enough, everything descended into chaos once more, with laughter plentiful in the room.

"I give up," Daria said, grinning but breathless as she abandoned the dance and sat, to his delight, in the chair next to the pianoforte. "This dance is like being the pins in a game of lawn bowls. I believe I will sit here away from it all."

"I'll not complain," Toss said, not missing a single note.

"Spoil-sport!" Eve O'Doyle declared but so good-naturedly and with such obvious laughter that no one could possibly take offense.

"Artemis says there is always laughter in the homes of the Jonquils," Daria said. "I like that idea very much."

"When I am with Rosamond, there is laughter and happiness," Toss said. "Provided Laurence isn't anywhere nearby," he added dryly.

"And no music when he is anywhere nearby either." Daria shook her head, a clear expression of disapproval in her eyes. "How anyone would want to prevent you from playing the pianoforte, I will never understand. Even playing something very commonplace, you make it special by adding such interesting additional bits to it." She gave him an apologetic look. "I don't know the technical terms for doing that."

"Few people do who haven't studied it, Daria."

She gave a quick nod. "I will not hold that against myself."

"I am pleased to hear that." He gave a quick swirl of ending notes. "For the sake of English cultural heritage, I bring this monstrosity Charlie has created to a close." Toss stood and stepped from the pianoforte, pausing to dip a bow to Mater. "My sincerest condolences that you have such a graceless lump for a son."

"His father's fault," Mater said, looking almost serious.

Charlie, a little out of breath but not out of energy, responded with a smile. "I suspect Father was actually a very good dancer."

"He was, but given the choice between grace and humor, he could not resist indulging in the latter."

Artemis hooked her arm through Charlie's. "That sounds extremely familiar."

"The important question," Toss said, "is do I get a point for enduring that display?"

"If you do, so does Daria." Newton, ever the barrister, gave a serious answer.

Tobias crossed to the pianoforte and held a hand out to his sister. Toss silently pleaded with her to refuse the offer and remain there with him. But she didn't.

"The more important question is," Charlie said, moving with the others to gather the furniture they had moved out of the way for dancing, "How many times can Toss or Daria receive a point for doing something he or she has already done simply because it is *still* something their respective families would not approve of? Because while I certainly want to see Toss win, I'd be embarrassed to know our team was victorious by being boring."

"While I suspect I am not actually losing the game, I do think I need to argue in favor of receiving points for anything I can," Toss said.

"I've been keeping very close score," Charlie said, "and I can tell you that you and Daria currently have the exact same number of points."

Daria was just then sitting in a chair her brother had led her to. "Then I must object to points given for playing the pianoforte."

Her objection, made in a theatrical tone of panic, set the group to laughing once more. Toss stepped away from the pianoforte, unsure where he meant to sit since the seat beside her was occupied by her brother. There was no place he'd rather sit, which somehow made choosing a spot all the more difficult.

Colm was the next to speak. "Does Mr. Comstock the Elder object specifically to 'O, Dear! What Can the Matter Be?'? That might earn the gentlemen's team a point without simply repeating the 'point for playing' claim."

"Laurence the Lout despises asking people what's the matter," Charlie tossed out in a tone that would never be believed to be serious.

Newton joined in the insistence. "The man rages against the very idea of inquiring after a person's state of being. Does so *constantly*."

Artemis looked over at her Huntresses with a dry look of annoyance. "I think it would be best to award them a point for this, or they will never stop."

"And as they cannot even manage to name themselves, I think we need to allow them some intellectual slack," Eve said. She even clicked her tongue as if it were a tremendous shame.

Toss met the eyes of his gentlemen associates. "We really do need to name ourselves. The Huntresses will mock us mercilessly until we do."

"I would suggest corresponding on the matter with Scott and Fennel and Mr. Seymour," Mater said. "Charlie is his father's son and his uncle Stanley's nephew. Leave the matter to him and you'll be known to all and sundry as the Puddingheads or some such thing."

Charlie gave them all a look of growing intrigue and excitement.

"No," Newton said firmly.

"If you finish this Season without having decided what to call yourselves, we likely *will* call you the Puddingheads simply because it will be so fitting," Artemis said.

"Would I get a point for being pathetic?" Toss asked.

The room burst forth in laughter once more. So much about being dragged to London against his preferences had been frustrating and demoralizing. But moments like these gave him hope.

He looked over at Daria and found her smiling back at him. Moments like *this one* gave him more than just hope. They gave him a glimpse of a future worth working for. He felt in his soul a reason, in addition to his passion for it and his independence, to find a place for himself in the world of music. She had inspired more than the underpinnings of a tune. She was inspiring *him.*

But then Daria glanced over at Colm, who smiled back at her, and Toss's heart simply dropped into his stomach, where it most certainly did not belong.

Colm was very new to the group, so Toss hadn't seen him interact much with Daria. And he'd been too distracted or too unobservant to make note of *how* they'd interacted. Was this a budding spark between them? Surely they were simply friends. That was what Daria called her connection to Toss as well. Friends. The best of friends, yes, but friends.

Until he sorted out a future for himself and distance enough from Laurence to protect anyone sharing that future, he needed to remember that friends, best or otherwise, was all he was truly in a position to be for anyone.

"Do you suppose that between all of us, we could gather or borrow enough horses to go for a ride?" Eve asked. "We don't get to ride often when we're in London, and it would be so lovely."

"My family occasionally goes out to Richmond Park," Colm said. "We could all meet there for a ride and perhaps a picnic. There are enough married couples among us and enough siblings to add propriety to the gathering."

"Propriety?" Tobias shook his head. "Anyone who saw that atrocious attempt at dancing would not believe this group capable of any semblance of propriety."

"Or any sense of rhythm," Mater added, to the laughter of them all.

Toss watched Daria, wondering what she thought of the proposed excursion. She didn't always feel comfortable putting forward her preferences. He was ready to eagerly agree with or make an argument against the proposal, depending on her preferences so she wouldn't be alone in whatever she wished for.

"I've not ridden in some time," she said, but not in a way that indicated she didn't want to ride again.

Toss opened his mouth to suggest she seize this opportunity, but Colm spoke first.

"You ought not be denied the privilege any longer, Daria." For that, he received the smile of gratitude Toss would have liked to have had sent his way.

The group was soon engrossed in planning this impromptu outing and determining how quickly they could make arrangements. Toss did not consider himself easily snagged by the green-eyed monster of jealousy, but he couldn't deny that reaction was part of the reason he grew increasingly anxious about the outing.

He could ride, and he enjoyed it. But Colm Greenberry had fought in the war against Napoleon in the Thirteenth Light Dragoons, a mounted regiment. And the Greenberry family were very well-known for the highly prized horses they bred. Toss wouldn't make a fool of himself, but Colm would undoubtedly be shockingly impressive.

A penniless musician whose own family was ashamed of him.

An athletic war hero whose family was well-connected, well-heeled, and well-liked.

Toss *had* asked about getting points for being pathetic. If that were allowed, he suspected he would be about to win mountains of points.

CHAPTER TWENTY

Richmond Park was a lovely spot in the late morning. Toss had visited the expansive parklands on a couple of occasions when in London on term break, though he'd never been among those traversing the grounds on horseback. The park was quiet on this particular day, which was likely a very good thing because the group he had come with was decidedly not quiet. Everyone was present who had been at Lampton House when the excursion had been planned, apart from Mater, who had been replaced in her role of "wise member of the older generation" by Mr. Layton.

The snowy-haired gentleman had provided a few horses, as had the Falstone House and Lampton House stables. Laurence had been unwilling to allow Toss the use of one of his. The O'Doyle sisters had horses in Ireland but none with them in London. They had been provided with very fine-looking animals from the Greenberry family stables.

Tobias and Daria rode horses belonging to their family, but Daria looked a little uncomfortable and unfamiliar with her mount. Was she forbidden from riding, or did she choose not to do so? Her parents had shown themselves too often neglectful of their daughter and indifferent to her happiness.

Toss couldn't understand any parent treating their daughter that way. Did Rosamond remember their parents well enough to know that *she* had been loved by them? Was he doing enough to make certain she knew?

The group intended to enjoy a very friendly and rustic picnic once their riding was over. Sometimes picnics among their class were almost ridiculous in their finery. Entire dining rooms were brought out into nature and set up just as they would be inside, but this groups' version would be of the blankets-cushions-and-hampers-of-food variety. For the moment, though, all were enjoying the cool morning breeze as they rode at a slow and peaceful pace.

Toss knew, theoretically at least, that to be in the dragoons, one had to be an excellent horseman, but as he had predicted during the planning phase of the outing, there was something awe-inspiring in how well Colm rode. Awe- and jealousy-inspiring.

There were certain gentlemanly accomplishments that Society found more significant than others. Composing music was not precisely high on that list. Toss didn't consider himself entirely unathletic, but he knew his skills didn't precisely shine in that area. His fencing was mediocre. He'd learned boxing and was not entirely inept at cricket. He could ride but wasn't the sort to earn gasps of amazement at his skill.

That had never rankled. Until now.

He was seldom in a miserable mood, but it well and truly bothered him that Colm's skills outpaced his so much. And to make things even more frustrating, it bothered him that it bothered him.

He had no understanding with Daria, no declarations of mutual affection to give him reason to be protective of his connection to her. He'd imagined holding her, even kissing her. But he hadn't the right to be jealous over a romance that existed only in his imagination.

"While the park is empty," Eve said to them all, "we should undertake a race."

Mr. Layton didn't seem enthusiastic about the idea. Toss might have thought he disapproved if not for the almost immediate explanation he offered. "The windswept look loses its appeal once a gentleman has a six at the front of his age."

"I've a two at the front of mine, and I am not clamoring for the experience," Ellie said.

Nia slowed her horse enough to be riding beside Ellie. "You and I and Mr. Layton can adopt a more sedate pace."

A great deal of good-natured ribbing passed through the majority of the rest of the group, with most predicting Colm would be the winner. Toss knew he was unlikely to match, let alone best, Colm, but he was determined to at least make a good showing for himself. He was, in fact, determined to.

So, when Mr. Layton gave the signal for the race to begin, Toss urged his horse through its paces to a run.

He was doing well. He wouldn't be last to reach their designated ending point, and as he raced, his thoughts turned, as they so often did, to Daria. He glanced back, hoping she was noticing that he wasn't showing himself to be entirely inept. But all thoughts of being impressive and showing off his skills, such as they were, evaporated. Her horse was tossing its head and champing hard. Daria's frantic expression told him she wasn't entirely sure what to do.

He turned his horse, taking a wider arc than he would have preferred. But at the pace his horse was running, sharp turns weren't safe or likely even possible. He approached, intending to help her soothe the animal, but the horse reared back a little. Daria managed to stay seated, but her look of fear grew.

The horse jumped sideways, tossing its head. Another buck, small but worrying just the same.

Mr. Layton took the reins of Toss's horse, allowing him to quickly dismount. Nia reached Daria's horse in the next instant, taking hold of that horse's reins. Toss moved to its side and reached up for Daria. With her hands on his shoulders and his hands on her waist, Daria soon had her feet on the ground. Toss kept his arm around her as they moved swiftly away from the skittish horse. Nia was keeping the animal surprisingly calm, but it was still being worryingly unpredictable.

Daria wavered as she walked, her strength seeming to give out. Toss held her close, helping her stay on her feet.

"Are you injured?" he asked.

"My heart is racing, but I'm not hurt." She was a little breathless, but her voice was steady.

Relief washed over him. "The horse tossed you about. I imagine your strength is all but spent."

"I am beginning to feel a bit exhausted, I admit."

He slipped his arm behind her and helped her toward an obliging bench not far distant. The sound of approaching hooves told Toss the situation had been observed and the others were coming to be of assistance too. It would likely be most appropriate to seek out one of the Huntresses or Tobias to take his place, but Toss found himself entirely unable—not merely un*willing* but un*able*—to force himself to let go of her.

She sat, and he sat next to her. With a shuddering sigh, she leaned against him. He wrapped his arms around her.

Artemis arrived and instantly took charge of the situation. "Are you injured?"

Daria shook her head, not pulling away.

"Do you need to return home?"

Daria didn't immediately answer. She looked at Toss, a question in her eyes, but he couldn't identify it.

"If you need to return home, we'll make certain you do," he insisted.

"I'd like to stay," she said quietly.

"Then stay you shall," he vowed.

Relief swept over her expression. "Thank you." She spoke softly, little more than a whisper.

"Let's all walk back to the picnic area," Artemis said.

Nia had Daria's now-calm horse firmly in hand, with Colm at her side now as well. Eve and Mr. Layton were looking after Toss's, Nia's, and Colm's mounts as well as their own. The group began walking in the direction of their picnic. Toss and Daria rose from the bench and followed.

Now that the immediate danger had passed, panic was setting in. Toss could see, repeating in his mind, the moment Daria's horse had reared back, could remember the fear in her face.

What if the horse had been running like everyone else's? What if it had jerked in just the wrong way and thrown her to the ground, perhaps directly into a boulder or other dangerous thing on the ground? What if Nia hadn't been so nearby? What if Toss hadn't looked back?

He might have lost her.

He'd noticed her uncertainty before the blasted race had even been proposed, but he'd been so consumed with the desire to make a good showing for himself that he'd not given it a second thought. It was so unlike him to feel threatened by other people's skills and abilities. He'd allowed his insecurities to overcome his judgment, and he'd almost lost her.

"That was terrifying," she said, her words shaking a bit. "I had my suspicions that I wasn't a good enough horsewoman to be with everyone today."

He pressed the lightest of kisses to her temple, shocked at his own boldness but somehow feeling it was the appropriate thing to do. "Horses can be unpredictable, no matter the skill of the rider."

Tobias caught up to them, and Daria was very quickly transferred into her brother's care. Toss bit back his objections. *A romance that exists only in your imagination*, he reminded himself.

"I didn't entirely know what to do, which made the situation more dangerous."

"Yet you managed it." Tobias set an arm around his sister's shoulders, walking with her. "You're whole, and the horse is being seen to."

"And I didn't get thrown," she said.

"You didn't."

"And Toss said horses sometimes misbehave and it isn't the rider's fault."

How he hoped that meant he'd given her some reassurance. The heavens knew he could use some reassurance himself.

"Exactly right," Tobias said. "No reason to blame yourself for any of this. And certainly no reason to decide not to ride again."

"I'll ride again," she said, "given the opportunity. Though probably not today," she offered with a little laugh.

Her brother squeezed her shoulders. "Your only task for today should be eating your fill of sandwiches."

"I believe that is something I could accomplish with near perfection."

Toss followed along behind them, feeling a little unnecessary. Daria was receiving the comfort she needed, and he was deeply grateful for that. But he wanted to be the one with his arm around her, making her laugh, lifting her spirits. It wasn't his place, and he hadn't that right, but propriety didn't change the pull he felt.

He also felt increasingly frustrated with Daria's parents. They gave her so little credit for the strong and brave person she was, but it was so obvious to anyone paying the least attention. Life had done its best to drown her in discouragement, but she continued to rise to the surface.

"I'm so glad Toss was so nearby," Daria said. "I don't know what I'd do without a friend like him."

A friend like him.

A *friend.*

CHAPTER TWENTY-ONE

"Do not think that facilitating this introduction makes me think better of your constant calls at Falstone House." Laurence was in his usual "sunny" mood. "You have, no doubt, made a nuisance of yourself."

"You are welcome to express your suspicions to His Grace, should the duke choose to meet you."

"If he is willing to endure you day after day, he'll likely find me a refreshing change." Laurence stepped out of their carriage on that pronouncement, his calling card already in his hand.

If fate were truly kind, the Dangerous Duke would simply strangle Laurence and put them all out of their misery. But then, if fate were the least kind, Toss would not be spending every waking minute and some of his sleeping ones filled with the memory of Daria declaring him her friend and his breaking heart silently pleading for so much more than that.

Once I have my future secured, and if someone else hasn't captured her heart, I'll have my chance. He simply needed to be patient.

The Falstone House butler, upon answering the door and discovering Laurence standing proudly there, looked to Toss instead, a question in his expression.

"This is Mr. Laurence Comstock," Toss said. "He has come to call on Their Graces, if they are at-home to visitors."

With a nod of understanding, the butler motioned them inside. He fetched a silver salver for Laurence to place his calling card on, which Laurence did with an obnoxious degree of flourish. The butler turned to deliver the card but paused and looked to Toss once more. "Mr. Thomas, you are, of course, welcome to continue on as always."

Doing his utmost to hide his delight at Laurence's look of shock, Toss responded simply with, "Thank you, Gordon."

Toss and Laurence alone remained in the entryway.

Laurence's surprise had turned to annoyance. "I can hardly believe Their Graces employ a butler who is lax in proper behavior."

"They wouldn't," Toss said. "And they don't."

Laurence shot him a look of exasperation. "Inviting a guest to simply wander about? Do you not know anything about how these interactions are supposed to proceed?"

Toss knew from a lifetime of experience that there was little point arguing with Laurence. It was only Toss's respect for the Falstone House resident family and staff that prevented him from abandoning his brother and going straight to the music room.

Laurence eyed the entryway. "This is an elegant home."

"Most in Grosvenor Square are," Toss said dryly.

"Do not lecture me about London, Thomas. I know it better than you ever will." One thing could certainly be said for Laurence: he had a very high opinion of himself. "The home's address is enough to recommend it, but I daresay the opulence within is excessively impressive. I would wager this is a residence that has on more than one occasion boasted a pineapple."

"I have never seen one here." Toss knew perfectly well that pineapples were quite sought-after additions to many fine households. The exotic fruit was rare and expensive; having one testified to a family's wealth as little else could. Yet he couldn't imagine the duke being so gauche as to participate in one of Society's more vain displays. "Perhaps they had a pineapple and served it as an ice or a compote."

"One does not eat the pineapple, Thomas. One displays it. You really do know so little of such things."

A change of topic seemed more than called for. "How have your attempts at courtship been going?" Toss asked.

Laurence tipped his chin at a confident angle. "I am weighing my options."

Toss knew his brother well enough to be able to easily translate that declaration—Laurence had no options.

The butler returned. "If you will follow me, Mr. Comstock, Mr. Thomas."

They did so and were ushered into the drawing room, where they were introduced with no show of enthusiasm. The duke and duchess were present, as were their two children. Toss had met Lord Falstone and Lady Hestia during his many mornings in this house. They were delightful children.

Artemis was present as well, as was Daria. His beloved Daria. It took all his self-control not to immediately abandon his brother and rush to her side.

But if he was not very careful, she would quickly realize that he'd fallen rather unexpectedly in love with her. He couldn't countenance the idea of ruining their friendship by laying his heart bare.

"Your Grace. Your Grace." Laurence's bow was well made, if a bit overdone. He didn't acknowledge the children.

"Mr. Comstock." The duke was not rude but neither did he seem impressed. He turned to Toss. "We wondered if you would be here today. You've not been here for several days now."

Toss dipped his head. "I fear my time has been claimed elsewhere." In truth, he'd been a little nervous about crossing paths with Daria at Falstone House. That concern had proven well-founded; this was the first time he had returned, and she was there.

Lord Falstone approached him, as self-confident as his father even at only six years old. "Will you be playing the pianoforte today?"

Before Toss could answer, Laurence did. "He most certainly will not. He'll not bore all of you with that raucous noise."

The little future duke managed to look down his nose at Laurence. "Raucous noise? That is an insult, I believe."

"Yes, Lord Falstone," Toss answered. "My brother is declaring my music rather horrible."

"Oh." Lord Falstone looked at Laurence once more, disapproval writ on his little face. "You're not very intelligent, are you?"

It was all Toss could do to keep himself from laughing out loud. There was no doubting Lord Falstone was his father's child. The duke's ability to deliver a setdown was legendary.

"Mr. Comstock," the duchess said. Both Toss and his brother turned to look at her. "I mean *our* Mr. Comstock, of course," she specified.

Oh, that would wound Laurence's pride, Toss would wager.

"I am entirely at your service, Your Grace." Toss crossed to her. "What might I do for you?"

"Not for me, but for Lady Hestia. She has been asking these past days why no one is playing music for her." The duchess motioned to the tiny girl, who, other than having her father's blue eyes, was nearly the spitting image of her mother. "I suggest you make your amends."

Toss turned to the little girl. Far from offended, she smiled shyly at him. "Would you like to hear some music?" he asked.

She nodded but didn't speak. He'd been visiting this house nearly every day for well over a fortnight, and he'd seldom heard her speak.

"If you will accompany me, my lady, I will happily play for you whatever and for however long you wish."

Her eyes darted to her father, though whether because she did not understand what Toss had said or because she was bashful he didn't know. Whatever the unspoken plea, her father seemed to understand.

The duke lifted his three-year-old daughter into his arms. "To the music room. She has been disappointed often enough these past days."

The duchess took her son's hand, and she and her husband led their family from the drawing room. Artemis and Daria followed close behind, arms linked. Daria smiled at him as they passed. It was brief, and not a word was spoken between them, yet in that moment, his heart was even more hers.

"And what am I meant to do while you are fumbling over your music?" Laurence grumbled.

"Don't ask me," Toss answered as he walked to the door. "I don't know anything about how these interactions are supposed to proceed, remember?" With a surge of satisfaction, he abandoned Laurence to sort things out on his own.

Toss had to remind himself upon reaching the music room that the pianoforte was not, in fact, his. He'd come to think of it that way of late, and he knew that would lead to a feeling of loss when he inevitably had to stop making these near-daily visits. It was a beautiful instrument, and its tone was rich and full. The room it occupied was equal parts sumptuous and peaceful. He didn't know how the duchess had managed that balance, but he very much appreciated it.

The duke sat beside his wife, taking her hand in his but in a way that if a person weren't looking very closely, he'd not realize it. He was as dangerous as the kingdom believed, but he was, in the privacy of his home, the sort of husband and father every man ought to be.

Toss's gaze shifted to Daria standing with Artemis near the windows. Did she have any idea how often he thought of her? How often his imaginings included a life together and the all-too-distant hope of the sort of familial happiness he witnessed at Falstone House?

Little Lady Hestia, standing at the edge of the sofa where her parents were sitting, was watching Toss expectantly when his eyes returned there.

"What would you like me to play for you, my lady?" he asked.

She didn't blush the way bashful children often did, but neither did she answer. She also didn't look away.

Toss lowered himself to kneel in front of her. It wasn't precisely a dignified and gentlemanly position, but he'd long ago given up on aspiring to unending starchiness. "My little sister and I used to play a game when we were younger.

She would whisper something to me, and then I would tell it to whomever she wished to receive the message. Perhaps if you told Lord Falstone, he could tell me." Hoping to give her ample reason not to be embarrassed by her shyness, he added, "It would be like a game."

The little girl looked to her brother, who moved up very close to her.

"What do you want him to play?" Lord Falstone whispered to his sister, though loudly enough that the entire room must have heard.

The response was much quieter and whispered directly into the little lordling's ear. Toss made absolutely certain his expression communicated nothing but patience and delight at being the children's musical entertainment for the morning.

Lord Falstone stood stiff and straight once more. "Lady Hestia says—" His eyes settled on something behind Toss. "Grandmother!" And he ran toward the door.

"I don't know that tune," Toss said with a laugh.

Hestia had abandoned him as well. Toss, along with the duke and duchess, rose and turned to face the doorway. Mater had arrived and already had her arms around the two children. She was something of an honorary mother to a great many people; it was no surprise that role had expanded to surrogate grandparent.

With both the little ones clinging to her, she offered her greetings to the duchess and duke. Toss did his utmost not to stare when the Dangerous Duke not only accepted a warm embrace from her but a kiss on the cheek as well. And he seemed entirely comfortable with the exchange. Toss knew Mater was on very close terms with the duke and his family, but this was a more revealing moment than he'd expected.

Then, to his further surprise and absolute delight, she turned to him. "Toss, how are you?" She hugged him as well. Until that moment of maternal regard, he hadn't realized how much he missed simply being hugged by his mother. "I saw your brother on his way out of the house, and he looked none too happy. I assumed you were inside somewhere feeling annoyed with him."

"I am usually annoyed with him," Toss said with a laugh. "It is very much a mutual experience."

"Someday, you will have to introduce me to your sister," Mater said.

"I would like that very much."

Artemis arrived at Mater's side and received a hug as well. "I hope you have not called in the hope of seeing your son. Charlie has spent the entire day pacing the book room in stockinged feet, looking quite a sight, while muttering about transitive properties."

"He is enjoying himself, then?"

"Immensely."

Mater's gaze fell next on Daria, who looked a little uncertain of her place in the very familial moment. But Mater, as always, did not withhold her warmth or kindness. She crossed to Daria and embraced her. "How are the preparations for your musicale coming along?"

"Very well, I think."

"Mr. Toss?" The voice was so quiet Toss almost didn't hear it.

And the shock of Lady Hestia inserting herself into a conversation was so great that the entire room grew instantly silent. That, unfortunately, brought nervousness to her face once more, and she clamped her mouth shut.

Poor thing.

Toss knelt again. "Have you thought of the tune you'd like me to play?"

She nodded.

"Is it one I play often when I'm here?"

She nodded again.

Though Lord Falstone could likely tell him the answer, Toss felt in his heart that the little girl would be quite proud of herself if she managed the exchange on her own.

"Is it the one I play first?" He always began his sessions with the same tune, one good for warming his fingers.

"No," she said almost silently.

"Is it the one I play the most?"

She smiled a little, the expression bringing a sparkle to her eyes.

"Ah." He leaned in just a bit closer. "I know which one you mean."

An earnest nod indicated her understanding. "It makes my heart dance."

"I think your heart should get to dance, Lady Hestia." Toss rose once more and crossed to the pianoforte.

As he sat, his gaze fell on Daria once more. This tune was hers, after all. She had inspired it, and he always thought of her when he played it. Having her there in this love-filled home without Laurence to cause misery made playing *her* song all the more fitting.

It also meant his heart was likely in his eyes. He would be wise to focus on fulfilling Lady Hestia's request.

He played what he had composed of "Daria's Melody," improvising a bit in the places he hadn't yet completed. The resident family listened with every indication of delight. Lady Hestia stood at her father's feet, her hand in his, swaying a bit with the tune. Lord Falstone rested against his grandmother's legs, listening. It was a far more pleasant experience than the night he'd played at the dinner party.

Toss might have simply relaxed into the moment if not for the look of intrigue in Mater's expression. She'd pieced something together, and that made him more than a little nervous.

CHAPTER TWENTY-TWO

Toss received the oddest request the next morning: Mater sent a note asking him to join her for a ride in Hyde Park that afternoon, one undertaken in the Lampton landau. She had four sons in London as well as Lord Cavratt, who was known to be as close to a Jonquil brother as one could get without being born into that family. And the duke clearly had a familial bond with her. She might have asked any one of them to ride with her. But she had asked Toss.

She would be fetching *him*, another oddity, from Laurence's home. Toss dressed with care and great curiosity. He also felt a hint of trepidation. Throughout the afternoon at Falstone House the day before, she had watched him with that look people wore when they had pieced together a very intriguing mystery. There was every chance Mater had unearthed his most closely guarded secret.

No sooner was he seated in the Lampton landau on the bench facing her, then Mater launched directly into conversation.

"We have until we reach our next destination to sort you out, Toss."

"Sort me out?"

"Well, sort out the mess you are making of your life, at least," Mater said.

"Which mess would that be?"

She leaned a little closer. "How long have you been in love with Daria?"

Such blunt talk from anyone else would likely have felt like gossip. But, coming from Mater, the observation was unmistakably reassuring and maternal.

"I felt the very first, vague stirrings during the house party last autumn. But as I've come to know her better this Season, those 'vague stirrings' have become undeniable affection."

Mater nodded. "So why do you treat her so much like one of your friends?"

"She *is* my friend," he insisted.

"Is that all she is?"

"She has described us as 'the best of friends,'" he said. "I do not intend to make a nuisance of myself by disregarding her definition of our relationship. Too many gentlemen do that, insisting they are being charmingly persistent when what they are really being is a pest."

"You are not wrong about that, Toss, and I would never suggest you act dismissive or disrespectful of a lady's wishes."

Toss eyed her more closely. "Why, then, do you not seem to agree with my position in this instance?"

Mater's gaze narrowed a bit on him. "Because I watched Daria the evening all of you were at Lampton House and Charlie was dancing as if biting bugs had crawled down his shirt. She displayed every sign of a lady deeply infatuated with a gentleman."

"With Colm Greenberry," Toss muttered.

"Oh, he paid her attention, to be certain. But it was not toward him that her eyes continually turned." Mater patted his hand, a gesture he remembered his own mother employing. "Her gaze was on you every bit as often yesterday at Falstone House as yours were on her, perhaps even more often. Do not abandon your hopes so readily. She sees you as a dear and beloved friend, but that does not mean she sees you *only* in that light. In fact, I am certain her feelings fall far closer to yours than you now believe."

"You will raise my hopes to dangerous heights, Mater." Contradictory emotions welled up inside. He felt himself on a precipice, not knowing how to move forward.

"Charlie's father used to say that love is always a risk, but for the right person it is a risk worth taking."

Toss breathed through the nervousness that he felt. "I don't want to lose her friendship. It has come to mean everything to me. The thought of not having her in my life anymore, even if only as a friend, is more than I can bear."

Mater squeezed his hand. "My dear boy, I would not have arranged this if I harbored the least doubt that this nudge is precisely what the two of you need."

Arranged *what*? This conversation? He suspected there was more to it.

"What is the rest of this arrangement?"

"You and I are taking Daria for a ride in Hyde Park, and, on the way, I will be decidedly distracted by a great many things while the two of you sort out a great many more."

"I'm meant to make a declaration of affection with a witness present?"

"Unfortunately, the rules of Society mean many couple's tender moments occur with other people around. You could not ride alone with Daria in a carriage, regardless, and I suspect you would be even more uncomfortable with your declaration overheard by a maid or Daria's brother or, worse yet, either of Daria's parents."

There was a tremendous amount of truth in that.

"While I know you are often able to find quiet moments when your friends are together, I also know that, as much as I adore my Charlie, should he stumble upon an affectionate interaction between you and Daria . . ." Mater shook her head. "It is abundantly clear to me that the two of you need a chance to sort all of this out. You are unlikely to accomplish that without a bit of much-needed distance from her parents, your brother, and, for completely different reasons, your friends."

Again, all very true.

The landau pulled up in front of the Mullins's London home. A nervous excitement built in Toss's chest.

"How have you arranged this bit?" he asked. "Am I meant to fetch her?"

"Her brother agreed to watch for our arrival and accompany Daria to the carriage. That way, we will avoid the difficulty of interacting with Mr. and Mrs. Mullins."

"Wise," Toss said.

"I know." She wore a satisfied smile, testament to the fact that she did, in fact, know that the arrangement was a good one while also recognizing the humor in being so obviously self-confident.

Before Toss could so much as take another breath, the door opened and Tobias emerged with Daria on his arm, walking with her toward the carriage. Seeing her was usually the very best part of any day in which he was granted the privilege of her company, but knowing the coming interlude would likely change everything about their connection, he was anxious.

"Steady on, Toss," Mater whispered. "You have courage enough for this."

I have courage enough. And he *would* rather if he had a chance of securing Daria's affection, if perhaps he actually already had, than to go on in such heart-twisting uncertainty.

Daria was soon situated, seated beside Mater as propriety insisted. Tobias offered Mater his gratitude for granting Daria an excursion. He gave Toss a nod of acknowledgement.

"Enjoy yourself, Daria," Tobias said. "And enjoy your reprieve from our parents."

She smiled back at him, "Oh, I will."

Tobias returned to the house as the carriage was set in motion.

"I have instructed the coachman to make his way to Hyde Park by an exaggeratedly circuitous route," Mater said. "You've a bit of time before we will be interrupted by others attending the fashionable hour." With that, she produced a small book from her accommodatingly sized reticule and began reading.

Daria looked at him, confused. Her pulled brow spoke of worry.

Toss could not in good conscience hesitate to begin. "Mater has kindly arranged this outing so that you and I could have some time together free of my brother and your parents."

"Oh." Daria's face brightened with relief.

Toss leaned closer so she could hear him without having to speak too loudly.

"I don't like to consider myself cowardly," he said, "but, until now, I haven't had the courage to say the things to you that I need to say in order to get the answers I wanted to the questions I have been hesitant to ask."

She looked confused again. He was already doing a poor job of this.

"You've said that you and I are the best of friends."

Her nod was minute and hesitant. He hoped that meant that she too felt the description was lacking.

"Is there any possibility, any hope that, perhaps, you might think of me, of *us* as something other than friends? Something more?"

Daria's expression was equal parts hope and nervousness, which was precisely what he was feeling. He chose to believe that was a very good sign.

He looked at Mater briefly. She gave every indication of being focused entirely on her book, but he felt certain she was fully aware of what was happening in the carriage. As she had rightly said, both the requirements of Society and the interference of their families made quiet, tender moments difficult. This was likely Toss's best opportunity to say what needed to be said.

"I've lost my future, my income, my ability to choose much of what I will do in the coming years," he said. "Laurence controls so much of my life. I still don't know if I can change that. Even with all of these difficulties, I know I would be horribly disappointed in myself if I didn't at least say . . . If I didn't explain . . ." He wasn't usually so inarticulate, but this was proving a difficult thing. Once he spoke his feelings out loud there would be no turning back. He was declaring his wish for her to be part of his future without knowing if he even had one.

"I found myself thinking of you often after the house party, and, since being in London, I doubt more than a few minutes have passed in which I wasn't thinking of you or missing you or wondering when I might see you again."

Splotches of color spread over Daria's cheeks but not in a way that spoke of true discomfort or disapproval. She seemed pleased.

"I have nothing to offer, Daria, other than my heart."

Rather than the tender look he might have expected, her brows scrunched, and her lips turned downward. "Do you truly think your heart is 'nothing'? Because that, I can tell you, is not and never has been and never will be true."

"It is a very good thing you think so, because some part of it has been yours almost from the moment I met you. And with each passing day, you claim more and more of it."

Her lovely smile, a sight he would never tire of, made a reappearance. "I have worried about letting myself imagine anything other than friendship between us. I couldn't imagine your feelings matched mine."

How well he understood that. "I had hoped I was not the only one wishing for something more, but I never could be certain. And I didn't want to lose what we did have, neither was I willing to impose upon you when I hadn't seen any proof that you wanted anything other than friendship from me."

"I was watching for proof of that from you," she said. "I didn't see any either."

Toss could have sworn he heard Mater stifle a laugh of disbelief. The knots they'd tied themselves in were a bit ridiculous, he had to admit.

Toss took Daria's hands in his. "I have begun efforts to reclaim the musical pursuits I had hoped to lay claim to. If I can manage it, I will have a future free of Laurence's interference. If I can manage it, I will have something at last to offer you."

She watched him, obvious expectation in her eyes, though he didn't know what she waited in anticipation of.

In a combination of cough and muttered words, Mater said, "Tell her you love her."

Obviously she was listening more than she was letting on.

"Be it known that I am not saying this because I have been instructed to do so."

Daria laughed lightly.

He raised her hand to his lips and pressed a lingering kiss there. "I love you, Daria. And I don't know how the coming months and years will play out, but I'm not willing to abandon hope."

"Hope is sometimes a fragile thing," she said. "But it is also resilient. Clinging to it isn't always logical, but it is very often right."

"These are the moments when I question how it is that anyone has ever dared to question your absolute brilliance."

A shimmer entered her eyes, but her smile never slipped. "How could I have possibly *not* fallen in love with you when you say things like that?"

"Does that mean you do love me?" He knew the answer, but his heart longed to hear the words.

"I do. I've loved you for weeks and weeks, I suspect."

He kissed her hand once more. "We will find a means of claiming a future, Daria. I don't know how. I don't know when. But we will. I am determined to do so."

They were approaching Hyde Park and were required to resume the expected distance.

Before they were far enough into the park for an interruption, Toss turned to Mater. "How did I do?"

She tucked her book away. "If I were to rank how well you managed to express yourself on a scale of 'a Jonquil in love' to 'Eros, Greek God of Love,' I would place you somewhere near 'Mark Antony as an Awkward Adolescent.'"

Their laughter as the landau began its circuit of Hyde Park was likely a bit more uproarious than was generally heard.

"Most people are convinced the famously funny Jonquil brothers inherited their flair for entertaining word play from their father," Toss said. "I no longer believe that is entirely true."

Mater laughed once more.

Daria leaned a bit against her shoulder, much the way a daughter would with her mother, and she smiled softly at Toss. He'd taken a risk and told her what was in his heart.

Somehow he'd find a way to reclaim enough of his future to be able to build a life with her.

CHAPTER TWENTY-THREE

Daria had spent two days on a dizzying emotional pendulum. Her ride in Hyde Park with Toss had been glorious. He'd told her he loved her and had been clearly delighted to learn that his affections were reciprocated.

And she hadn't seen him since.

With only two days remaining until the musicale, the event on which so much of her future hopes rested, having so many of her thoughts worrying over Toss's absence was wreaking havoc.

She desperately needed to regain some focus. If the evening was a failure, she would be sent so far away that two days without seeing Toss would be rendered absolutely miniscule. She would not see him or the Huntresses perhaps for years.

Mother stepped into the music room, where Daria had wandered as she'd been lost in her thoughts. For days now, Mother had worn a thundercloud expression. Being in company with her was even more distressing than usual.

"You look confused, Daria," she said. "Has taking on this musicale proven too much for you?"

"I was only reviewing in my mind the preparations remaining to be seen to." Daria didn't think that truly counted as a lie. While Toss had been foremost in her thoughts, the musicale had certainly been prominent as well.

"I hope you've written down all the needful things."

One of Father's most frequent complaints was that Daria had a mind like a sieve.

"They are all written down," Daria assured her. "And I have very recently reviewed the list."

"I shudder to think how much remains to be done. We allowed you to continue in London specifically so you could do this, you realize. It has not exactly been convenient to do so, you must know."

There was some irony in that declaration. Daria and Tobias's initial strategy for ensuring she could remain in London had depended upon their parents not wishing to be inconvenienced. That didn't seem a useful approach any longer.

"All will be seen to," Daria said. "I assure you."

"Perhaps we ought not to have brought you this Season." Mother wrung her hands. Her gaze darted about the room. "Theodosia won't be overly pleased with this delay."

"Displeased that Daria hasn't arrived yet or displeased that you have decided to send her to Anglesey at all?" Tobias asked as he stepped inside the room.

Daria ought to have been relieved to see him, but her anxiety was far too sharp, far too heightened.

"Do not make light of your great-aunt's wishes, Tobias." Mother's tone was one of warning but also of nervousness.

This was making very little sense.

"What we ought not make light of is the effort Daria has made to plan this musicale," Tobias said.

"I do not question her fervency."

"Then what, pray tell, *do* you question?" Tobias so seldom grew testy with their parents. The rarity of it worried Daria in that moment.

Mother's eyes darted from Tobias to Daria and back again as a frown grew on her face. Then, with the sudden stiffness of one making up one's mind, her expression hardened and her shoulder set. "Do not allow your brother's impertinence to make you lax in your remaining work, Daria. Focus your attention on the musicale and make certain it is a success." On that declaration, she left, chin held high.

Tobias watched her go. "Our parents do not always show you the kindness you deserve."

Daria sighed. "No, they don't."

"Have you not found their behavior strange in regard to their plans to send you to live with Great-Aunt Theodosia?" His eyes remained on the now-empty doorway. "Our great-aunt has always been a bit overbearing, and no one could argue she isn't a bit of a dragon, but I've not known them in the past to seem actually afraid of displeasing her."

"I suspect they are so convinced my musicale will be a failure that they are growing impatient to move forward with their plans." Her parents' doubts in her were well established, after all. "When it is a success, they'll likely be shocked into utter silence."

Tobias set an arm around her shoulders. "I, for one, will not be shocked."

The butler, rushed and a bit harried, stepped inside to very quickly announce the arrival of Mrs. Artemis Jonquil in the fraction of a moment before the lady herself stepped inside, bubbling over with excitement.

Artemis rushed over to them and took Daria's hands in an enthusiastic grip. "I know how much is resting upon your parents' perception of the success of your musicale, so I have raced over to offer an exciting bit of related news." Artemis led her to a sofa, and they sat together. Tobias stood nearby. "I wish to tell you of the distinguished people who are confirmed as attending your musicale. If you mention even half of this list to your parents, they will be so beside themselves with the honor of such esteemed individuals in their house that they would never express doubt in you ever again."

Daria knew her friend's tendency to grow overly expressive and dramatic when she was excited. Until she heard the list for herself, she didn't wish to get her hopes up.

To Tobias, Artemis said, "See if you can't drop a subtle hint here and there to your parents about this list. If Daria tried, they might not believe her."

"I wish that weren't true," Tobias said.

"So do I," Artemis said. Looking at Daria once more, she began reciting her list. "The Earl and Countess of Techney are attending. Lord and Lady Cavratt, the baroness being quite an accomplished musician. The Earl and Countess of Lampton, as well as the Dowager Countess. The Duke and Duchess of Kielder also."

Everyone listed was directly connected to Artemis and Charlie; their attendance was no doubt the result of those two dear people advocating on Daria's behalf. But to boast such a guest list that might also include other highly revered members of Society would be something indeed.

"Also, Lord and Lady Aldric Benick are confirmed to attend," Artemis continued. "Mr. Layton, Mr. and Mrs. Greenberry, Mr. and Mrs. Fortier, all of whom, while not titled, are revered in Society."

Daria would be declared a hostess whose invitations were highly sought after. It would be an utter triumph.

"That list will certainly impress our parents," Tobias said. "In fact, I will enjoy mentioning it to them and watching their shock turn to overawe, hopefully enough to render them quiet for a time." He dipped his head, then slipped from the music room.

Alone now, Artemis adopted a conspiratorial tone. "I have been charged with delivering a message and a note. Which would you like to receive first?"

"The message," Daria said. She was a slow reader, and if the note was long at all, Artemis would be kept waiting. Though none of the Huntresses had ever belittled her, nor expressed frustration at her struggle, Daria still found it embarrassing.

"I have received word from Cambridge that Duke and Poppy, now on term break, are coming to London." Poppy was the nickname of Charlie's friend Fennel Kendrick, the youngest of their group. That those two members of the group had not been present had been a source of disappointment for their friends. To have them here again would be delightful.

"They asked me to keep their arrival a secret," Artemis said. "They would very much like to see the looks of shock and surprise on their friends' faces when they simply appear in Town. But to render their sudden appearance as delightfully shocking to their friends as possible, I'll need your help."

"Mine?" Daria wasn't used to being the one employed in a scheme. But then, that had happened quite a lot this Season.

Artemis nodded. "They are arriving in Town tomorrow evening—they didn't think to send the letter several days before their departure; it barely beat them here—and they are hoping to make their grand appearance at your musicale and surprise their friends that evening. I do not wish to detract from the success of your event or the feeling your parents will have of it being a reflection on them. I thought we could arrange for the two missing members of our group to be here earlier in the evening when the rest of us are here so they can have their reunion before any of the guests have arrived."

Thank the heavens Artemis had already strategized. So much depended upon a successful evening that Daria feared every little disruption.

"It will be a wonderful thing to play hostess to that reunion." Daria was actually growing a bit excited at the prospect now that she knew Artemis had thought it through enough to avoid problems with Mother and Father. "Toss has expressed several times how much he's missed having them here. I think he would rather be at Cambridge with them, but his brother has made that impossible." She wasn't certain how to finish the sentence but could see Artemis understood the sentiment she was reaching for.

"Now, speaking of Toss, he has charged me with delivering a note to you. I told him to give it to you himself, but alas, he is determined to be well-behaved." Artemis sighed dramatically. "I suppose I couldn't entirely argue with that. You are both unmarried, and you are unrelated. Your parents are such difficult people. His brother is an absolutely miserable dictator who monopolizes the poor man's time." Artemis shook her head. "I decided to be cooperative this time." She held out the letter.

"Toss sent me a note?" She took it immediately.

"He did and, in so doing, further increased my good opinion of him."

"Is it ridiculous that I miss him so much when it hasn't even been an entire week since I last saw him?"

Artemis reached out and squeezed her hand. "Not at all. That is one of the ways I first realized I'd begun falling in love with my Charlie. I longed for him after even short absences."

"I don't know how I'll survive if I'm sent to Anglesey and don't see him for months and months." She pressed his letter to her heart.

"Your musicale is destined to be an indisputable success, and your great-aunt will be required to learn to live without you."

"And we will be having another house party," Daria pointed out. "I will see everyone there."

"A house party we won't have to plan," Artemis said confidently, "even though Toss will be getting a point for sending this note." Artemis rose. She gave Daria a quick hug. "Do let me know if you need anything at all as the musicale approaches."

Not ten minutes later, Daria was in her bedchamber, the door closed, sitting on the window seat with Toss's note open in her hands, illuminated by the fall of light from outside.

Daria,

I would like to begin by crowing a bit over the point I will earn for sending you this letter. It was not my motivation in doing so, but I will claim the point just the same.

She smiled, as she so often, so easily did with him.

I had a thought about your musical evening that I hope may prove helpful. It is my understanding that Lady Cavratt will be present, and I happen to know she is a remarkably skilled pianist. I also know that no matter that she is bashful and quiet, she has no objections to playing in public. Ask her if she would be willing to open the evening with a piece on the pianoforte. I'm certain she will agree, and her talent will set both a delightful and impressive tone.

Laurence has further broken his promise to allow me freedom this Season. I've chosen not to argue with him on this matter because I am hopeful that the Royal Society of Musicians will soon be sending a reply to my application for membership, and the row that will ensue is likely to reach epic proportions. I am saving my endurance for that. Unfortunately, it means I've not seen you these past days. I miss you, Daria.

I suspect you are nervous and doubting yourself. But, my darling, all will be well. I am certain of it. Your parents will see your success, and all talk of sending you away will cease.

My darling. Darling. She would never grow tired of that.

My sister's spirits have always been lifted by flowers. I wish I could send you some now, knowing the strain you are likely under. I am enclosing my admittedly inept attempt at drawing a bouquet in the hope that it will bring you a smile and help you face the difficult few days ahead.

Yours, etc.,
T

He had, indeed, drawn a very poorly executed bouquet of flowers, which, in her estimation, was the most beautiful floral offering anyone had ever received.

CHAPTER TWENTY-FOUR

USING HER SEWING SCISSORS, DARIA had very carefully cut out the hand-drawn flowers at the bottom of Toss's letter. With even greater care, she had folded it smaller and smaller until it fit in her locket. That way, she could have it with her and, even if it were found, she and Toss couldn't possibly be scolded for the note he'd sent her. The rules of such things were strict but also terribly frustrating.

She wore the locket the next evening as she sat at home alone. Mother had insisted that it would be irresponsible of Daria to spend her time on "frivolous entertainments" on the eve of the musicale. Father had dismissed all Daria's insistences that everything was well prepared and remaining at home would accomplish nothing. Her parents left for their own entertainments, none of which they labeled as frivolous.

Tobias had been gone all day and was not expected to return. His introduction to Charlie's friends had proven both a boon to Tobias's own social calendar and a relief to Daria. She wanted her brother to be happy, and having such wonderful friends would contribute to that.

Heaven willing, she would also enjoy those associations for years to come. The quiet emptiness of the house that night stood as an inescapable reminder that if her efforts the next evening did not prove successful, she would be sent to a house that was nearly always empty. And lonely.

The quiet just then was broken by light laughter, a rumbling low enough that she knew those laughing were men. Had anyone arrived other than Tobias, the butler would have preceded him and asked Daria if she were at-home.

Tobias stepped inside with Colm next to him, the two of them carrying in each arm a vase containing a glorious rainbow of blooms.

Somehow managing to bow with full arms, Colm said, "Miss Mullins, we bring you flowers from the Huntresses and are instructed to tell you they are meant to adorn the music room tomorrow evening."

"We are further told," Tobias said, "that *we* are not to decide where they are placed but are to leave that decision to you because we are . . ." He looked at Colm. "How was it we were described by them?"

"Utterly lacking in good taste?" Colm supplied.

"I do believe that was it," Tobias said.

Daria could easily imagine Artemis making a regal pronouncement like that, with laughter twinkling in her eyes.

"The Huntresses did this for me?" She hadn't asked them to, neither had she told them of her difficulties in getting Mother to agree to the expense of fresh flowers.

"They did indeed." Tobias made a show of struggling under the weight of his vases. "We have heroically carried these inside. Now, tell us where to place them."

She made a quick survey of the room. All four vases were placed in various locations until she found the perfect spots. What a difference they made—the room felt inviting. It had always been a resplendent room, but gatherings of people who weren't overly well known to each other were made more pleasantly memorable if held in a space that felt more like home.

"What is on your schedule tonight?" she asked Tobias.

"We are returning to the O'Doyles' home. Everyone is gathering there this evening since the family is leaving London in only a few days' time," he said.

Everyone. She knew he didn't mean for that to pierce her as it did. She wasn't there, yet it apparently felt as if "everyone" were. With her heart threatening to sink, she reminded herself that Gillian was also not present. There was a degree of likelihood that Newton and Ellie weren't either. Duke and Poppy were not in London. Lisette was in France. Tobias, no doubt, meant everyone *who was able*.

To her surprise, it was Colm who noticed her downcast reaction. "Everyone has said again and again how very unfair it is that you aren't with us this evening. Indeed, Eve said that were she not certain it would undermine your chances of success tomorrow evening, she would simply come here, kidnap you, and take you back home with her."

"If tomorrow goes well," Daria said as much to herself as either of them, "then I'll be able to do more things I wish to."

"You've recounted your preparations to me many times," Tobias said. "And I can say with confidence that your evening will be an unparalleled success."

"You did say I had a talent for such things."

"I meant it," Tobias said. "Our parents have far too little faith in you. There is something wonderful in the anticipation of you proving them so very wrong."

She *had* made extensive preparations. Other than being a bit pressed for time the next day, she anticipated everything running very smoothly.

"Where do you suppose our music bearer has wandered off to?" Tobias turned back to the door, apparently waiting for someone.

Colm was still facing her, so Daria asked him, "What does he mean 'our music bearer'?"

"We are not the only ones who have come bearing items for your gathering tomorrow," he said. "It seems, though, we are the speediest."

In the next instant, Toss stepped through the music room doors, a twine-tied bundle of papers tucked under one arm.

"I stopped to ask the housekeeper if the pianoforte had been recently tuned," he said as he stepped farther into the room.

Daria's heart leaped to her throat, beating out a rhythm of delight. A lump formed in her throat, and a strangled burst of emotion spilled over as tears. A single trickle, to her horror, quickly escalated to chin-quivering crying.

How was it she was crying again? She'd been rather embarrassed the last time her emotions had gotten the better of her, and Toss had been present for that outburst as well.

He set his bundle down on the pianoforte and moved directly to her. "Is this happiness or misery, Daria?" He didn't speak as one did to an overwrought child. He spoke tenderly, earnestly.

"It's unexpected, for one thing. I'm happy to see you. I really am. And relieved, but a happy relief, like I've been waiting and waiting and wasn't certain you would ever come by, and here you are. And I didn't even realize I was worrying about that, and suddenly I don't have to worry about it anymore." She shook her head, attempting to wave off yet another bit of incoherent rambling. "Father always says that if I spend less time searching for a coherent thought, I might manage to produce one more often."

"Another of his *teasing* remarks?" Toss asked quietly.

"His *teasing* is often cruel," she admitted.

Toss took hold of her hand. "It is *too often* cruel."

She wiped a tear just to find that something in his firm declaration set her crying even more.

"Tuck yourself in the doorway and look away if you must, Tobias, but I think your sister needs a hug, and if she'll let me, I mean to be the one who gives it to her."

"I'll stand guard at the door and make sure none of the servants wanders by and senses a scandal."

As they made their way to the door, Colm said to Tobias, "Perhaps we also ought to talk very loudly to one another as a distraction to the staff." Then the two of them laughed.

As soon as Tobias and Colm were ensconced just beyond the door, leaving it open with their backs to the room, Toss did as promised and set his arms gently around her. She described her feeling upon seeing him as relief. The emotion that filled her as he held her in her exhaustion, worry, and uncertainty was peace. Until that moment, she'd not guessed that a person could feel so tranquil while her heart was pummeling her chest.

"I think you've been carrying a few too many burdens for too long," Toss said quietly and gently. "Discovering you're not alone with those burdens would lead anyone to tear up."

"You carry burdens too," she said. "Your brother's despotism. Losing your parents. Worrying about your sister. Trying to discover how to pursue your music while knowing your brother will punish you for it."

She felt him kiss the top of her head. "That explains why I needed this embrace as much as you seem to."

"What if tomorrow goes poorly and I never see you again?" It was the version of her worries she'd not let herself speak out loud before.

"No matter what happens tomorrow, we *will* see each other again," he said. "It may take time, but we will."

She held tighter to him. "When do you expect to receive an answer from the Royal Society of Musicians?"

"Soon, I hope."

Soon. He would have his membership and could begin claiming his place in the world of music. If she could continue living and traveling with her family until then, she wouldn't have to be so alone and so abandoned in the meantime.

Toss leaned back a bit, his gaze sliding over her face. He brushed a hand along her cheek. "I missed you terribly these past days, my darling Daria."

My darling Daria. Oh, she liked that very much. "Artemis gave me your flowers."

He laughed again, quietly but sincerely. "I readily admit I am no artist."

"I love them. They are the most beautiful flowers I've ever seen."

Seeing his smile fully bloom once more did her heart a world of good. He'd been heavy-hearted of late, every bit as much as she had been. "I'll draw you flowers whenever you'd like."

"And you'll hold me when I cry?"

He pulled her into an embrace once more. "I'll hold you anytime you ask."

"I would like that."

"So would I," he whispered.

"Do you know why?" she asked, her heart light and her spirits soaring.

"Why?"

"Because I'm going to earn so many points for this."

Standing in a room dedicated to music, which meant so much to Toss, feeling the warmth of his embrace and the rumbling of his chest as he laughed, Daria felt at home in a way she never had before.

CHAPTER TWENTY-FIVE

THE NIGHT OF DARIA'S MUSICALE arrived. Toss was nervous for her, not because he didn't have faith in her but because so many things were out of a person's control, and so much was riding on the evening's success.

All the Huntresses and their gentlemen counterparts were meeting at the Mullinses' home one hour before the musicale was set to begin in order to offer what assistance they could and to make certain Daria had the encouragement and support she needed. Toss was grateful to offer what help he could but resigned himself to knowing there would be no opportunity to hold her again. He wanted to. He *longed* to. But he would have to wait.

Before he could leave for the evening, he was summoned by Laurence. He'd long since accepted that the "free to do as he chose" Season he'd been promised had been, in many ways, a lie from the beginning. His brother had been more difficult than usual since his less-than-flattering reception at Falstone House. Knowing Laurence would be in attendance at the musicale, Toss thought it best not to begin the evening at war with him.

"I am leaving in another moment," he told Laurence. "So I haven't time for a drawn-out discussion."

Laurence's eyes darted to the clock on the tallboy. "The musicale doesn't begin for over an hour."

"Those of us who are particular friends of the younger Mr. Mullins and Miss Mullins are arriving early to be of what assistance we can."

"You've volunteered to act as a servant in someone else's home?"

That was not at all what Toss had said, yet he knew arguing with his brother was futile. "It is my freedom-infused bachelor Season, after all," Toss said dryly.

"Within reason," Laurence reminded him for the umpteenth time. His valet was rushing about, preparing Laurence for the evening, but Laurence was so determined to give Toss a dressing down that the poor man was struggling. Was there anyone whose life Laurence didn't make more difficult?

"I know perfectly well that you are aware that friends often arrive early to such things for the express purpose of offering support," Toss said. "You can argue against that all you want, but we both know that it's perfectly ordinary and acceptable."

"And we further both know that you have a tendency to make a fool of yourself when music is involved in a gathering. I would have your assurance that you'll not commit the same misstep you did at the Brinleys' home."

"I promise to make as good a showing for myself tonight as you did at Falstone House."

Immediate anger burned in Laurence's eyes. "I don't know what you did to turn them against me, but I assure you, next Season, you will have no opportunity to do so again."

It was beyond Laurence's ability to comprehend his own role in people's dislike of him. Rosamond was lovely and kind and sweet-natured. Toss didn't think himself a complete cad. How Laurence was related to either of them defied explanation.

"I will leave you to the expert ministrations of Smith," Toss said with a slight dip of his head. "And I will see you at the Mullinses' home tonight." *Unfortunately*, he added silently. He slipped from the room and back into the corridor. Every step he took away from Laurence improved his spirits. It also further solidified his goal of living independent of his brother's financial support and the power that gave Laurence.

His steps were almost jaunty as he took the stairs to the entryway. At that precise moment, the butler stepped into the entryway with a sealed letter on a salver.

"Mr. Comstock," the man said, offering a quick bow. "This arrived for you a moment ago."

Under ordinary circumstances, Toss would have waited until after he returned for the evening, but seeing that it had arrived from the very man he had contacted at the Royal Society of Musicians, he knew he couldn't wait. He offered a quick thank-you and stepped closer to the candle sconces that lit the entryway. He broke the seal and unfolded the paper.

Mr. Thomas Comstock

We have reviewed your request for membership in the Royal Society of Musicians. Most who apply have spent time apprenticed to an established musician or have completed a recognized course of formal education. Ours is not meant to be a society for teaching people to be musicians but rather for furthering the cause of those who already are. Without the completion of your studies and without any form of apprenticeship, we are at a loss as to where you would fit in the Royal Society of Musicians.

We also do not often receive requests for working membership from those of your social standing, but we have a great many who purchase honorary memberships in support of our mission and who participate in some of our activities. We would be honored if you would consider doing that while we attempt to sort out the oddity of your application.

Yours, etc.,
M. Sanford

Toss's heart dropped to his feet. Purchase an *honorary* membership? He hadn't an extra quid to his name. He had applied for *actual* membership because he needed help achieving some financial independence and the freedom to pursue his musical hopes.

Without the completion of your studies . . .

Curse Laurence for that! Losing that final term was enough to cost him a place in the Royal Society of Musicians. He had such hopes for his future, and now everything was being snatched away again. Curse him over and over again.

Toss stuffed the letter into the interior pocket of his coat and stepped from the house. He had only until he reached Daria's home to find a means of summoning some semblance of happiness and joviality. He would not be the storm cloud that dampened Daria's evening. He would find a way despite the fact that his future—*their* future—had just crumbled around him.

He had himself sorted enough by the time he was shown into the Mullinses' music room by a footman who clearly felt he had more important things to see to. Whether that was a reflection of his earnestness to complete his duties on such an important night or the influence of Daria's parents' indifference toward their daughter, Toss didn't know. But it made him even more determined to be a source of support and encouragement for Daria tonight.

He was clearly the last of her friends to arrive, which offered him an easy way of making a lighthearted entrance. "Since Laurence always insists that we not be the last to arrive at a gathering, that being *un*fashionable lateness, I believe I have just earned a point."

That launched a laughing discussion. The Huntresses insisted he ought not get a point because while he was the last of their group to arrive, he was certainly not the last of the guests for the evening. Toss's friends countered that with the insistence that Laurence likely hadn't wanted Toss to come early at all, which Toss confirmed.

He was able to keep a smile on his face and a spring in his step, and he very nearly kept his mind off the letter mocking him from inside his pocket.

He might have had greater success in keeping his spirits truly up if Daria hadn't been so conspicuously absent. He wanted to ask after her, wanted to plead with the group to help him find her. But what would he do once he did? She would be busy the remainder of the night. He'd come to help her, not burden her. And if he were to explain to them that he just needed to know she was nearby because it kept his worries at bay, the teasing would never stop. His mind and heart were too heavy for even good-natured taunting.

So instead, he accepted an assignment to look through the printed music he had brought over the evening before for the use of anyone who wished to perform but didn't have a piece memorized.

"Sort it in a way that would make sense to a musician," Artemis further explained.

A musician. How easily this group used that word, and how desperately he needed to hear them do so. His brother thought him a failure. The Royal Society of Musicians wasn't certain he qualified to be considered a musician. His only public performance tended to support those doubts. But this group of dear and devoted people believed in him. He made a few adjustments to the order of the music, dividing it into three stacks, each containing a different style of music, as some musicians were more comfortable with one than the other.

The work quieted his mind. His ability to quickly manage the sorting assured him he had learned something during his time at Cambridge.

"I had hoped you would be here early enough to go through that." His heart swelled at the sound of Daria's voice. "I don't know the first thing about organizing printed music."

"I'm glad I could be helpful," he said, looking up at her.

"Lady Cavratt agreed to open the evening tonight," Daria said. "Thank you for that suggestion."

"I'm glad to hear she agreed."

Daria turned her head a bit, brushing her fingers over her hair, styled in a soft, intricate chignon. "Tobias at last made good on the wager he and I made before the start of the Season. I do like that he chose purple ribbon."

He smiled at her. "It looks lovely."

Daria's gaze focused more and grew a little concerned. "What's the matter?"

"Whatever do you mean?"

She set her hand lightly atop his. "You are smiling and have likely been laughing and bouncing about the room, but your eyes are sad, Toss. What's happened?"

She had seen through the mask he wore. So few did. And finding sorrow beneath it, she hadn't walked away, dismissed it, or ridiculed him.

"The Royal Society of Musicians responded to my application by saying they are not convinced I qualify for membership."

Her brow pulled sharply. "Did they give you a reason?"

He nodded. "I did not complete my education."

"But that's not your fault," she said fiercely. "That's to be laid at Laurence's feet. And besides, you completed *nearly* all of it. Surely that must be taken into consideration."

Such an ardent and immediate defense of him. How he needed it. "They haven't entirely ruled out the possibility that I might eventually be admitted as a member, but for the time being, I have, in essence, been rejected. Without their assistance, I cannot hope to have any financial independence, which means I am at Laurence's mercy."

"I'm not certain he knows the meaning of that word." Daria hadn't been distracted for a moment from her concern for him, despite the fact that the most important event of her life up to that point was about to occur and her hoped-for future hung in the balance. "I suspect you need a hug every bit as much as I needed one yesterday."

"I confess I do," he said with a sigh, seeing the same disappointment in her eyes that he felt knowing there was no possible way for such a thing with so many people about. "I promise you, I will not let this disappointment dampen my spirits tonight. By the time your guests arrive, I will have myself fully in hand. Those who spend their evening here will have no reason to be distracted from their enjoyment of it."

A look of mischievous amusement began tugging at her features. "I think I might have a means of raising those spirits even quicker."

"You have me intrigued," he said.

She took hold of his hand and pulled him away from the table on which he had placed the music. He shifted his hand enough to interweave their fingers. She called out to their friends, asking them to come join her for a moment in the middle of the music room.

Once they were assembled, she said, "Thank you for coming to help. I appreciate it so much." She looked to Artemis. "It's time you told them."

Told them? Told them what?

Everyone watched Artemis, who stepped forward, enjoying her moment of theatricality. "My dearest Huntresses and gentlemen without a name, I have kept a secret from you, a secret that would have brought you great joy but instead has brought *me* great joy in keeping it from you." She looked to Charlie. "My dear, would you mind going and giving a quick knock followed by two slow knocks on the door just over there?" She motioned toward the door leading to an adjoining room.

In the years leading up to their marriage, Charlie and Artemis had nursed a mutual dislike and distrust of each other. That Charlie immediately bounded over, excited to see what his wife had up her sleeve, was testament to how much their relationship had changed.

Toss kept hold of Daria's hand as he watched Charlie follow Artemis's instructions. Only by sheer willpower did he keep himself from wrapping his arms around Daria.

The door flung open.

A voice inside said, "I think we were in here far longer than was actually necessary."

The next instant, Duke and Fennel stepped into the room. Nothing short of the surprise arrival of two of his best friends in all the world could have torn him temporarily away from Daria. He, Newton, and Charlie rushed over to them, welcoming them warmly, shaking hands, and tossing arms around each other, all while laughing at the trick they'd played.

"How long will you be in London?" Charlie asked.

"A week," Duke said.

"When did you arrive?" Newton pressed.

"Last night. We stayed with my oldest sister," Fennel said. "And Charlie's oldest brother, of course." Those two were married, making Charlie and Fennel brothers-in-law of a sort.

"Philip kept this a secret." Charlie shook his head in amazement. "I'm shocked to hear he managed to keep *anything* a secret." They all laughed more.

Soon enough, the Huntresses joined them. Colm and Tobias were introduced to the newest arrivals, and everyone's excitement for the evening grew a thousandfold.

In the midst of it, Daria was pulled away again to see to matters pertaining to the evening. Toss watched her go, feeling his heart go with her. She brought such joy and cared so much for people. That she loved him as he loved her was remarkable and amazing.

But he'd just lost his claim to the one path that would have given them a future together. And he hadn't the first idea what came next.

CHAPTER TWENTY-SIX

DARIA STOOD AT THE BACK of the music room, keeping an eye on everything. The guests had arrived and been given ample opportunity for mingling and making certain they were seen by those they felt they ought to be seen by. The guest list was so remarkably impressive that the "be seen by the right people" needs were high.

She had watched the guests, looking for any unexpected needs or concerns, but she had also watched her parents. They had both looked unwittingly impressed, which felt like a good sign.

The mingling had given way to the point that the guests were now searching out seats. One of the footmen looked to Daria with a question in his expression, one she didn't need help interpreting. The servants wanted to know if more chairs were needed. She gave a subtle shake of her head, and the footman disappeared once more to see to his other duties.

At the front of the room, Father and Mother took their places, facing the gathering.

"How delightful for us that you are all here." Father looked over the crowd with pride. "Our music room has begged for just such a gathering as this for a long time now. We have worked tirelessly to have it ready to welcome you."

Tirelessly was the right descriptor; Daria was exhausted.

"We are honored to have Lady Cavratt open our evening." Father bowed in the direction of the lady in question.

The crowd applauded as Lady Cavratt made her way to the pianoforte. She sat and, without needing any of the music Toss had provided, began to play. The guests were enthralled, mesmerized by the music, nodding their approval to one another. Lord Cavratt beamed as he watched his wife.

One of the maids slipped past the door with a lady's wrap in hand. Daria stepped out of the room and waved her back over. Not wishing to have her words carry into the room and disrupt the performance, Daria quietly asked, "Is there a reason that is not in the cloak room?"

The maid dipped a quick curtsy. "The hook it was hanging on came off the wall, Miss."

That was not something Daria had ever heard of happening. Had needed repairs in the home been neglected?

"I'm going to dust it off before returning it to the cloakroom and hanging it back up."

"There was another hook for it?" Daria pressed.

The maid nodded.

"Very good," Daria said. "Disaster averted, it would seem." She offered a smile and received one in return.

The staff didn't often smile. She wondered if it was because Mother and Father never smiled. She'd made an effort to be more pleasant, and it had helped.

She slipped back inside the music room and was able to enjoy the remainder of Lady Cavratt's performance. The lady rose and made a quick curtsy amid the applause she received.

Toss moved to stand beside Daria. His gaze remained forward, as was proper, but he spoke to her in low tones. "I hope you know how well everything is going."

"Though I fear I might curse my good fortune, I feel entirely pleased with the evening so far."

"As you should," he said. "Lady Cavratt's opening the evening has elevated the entire occasion."

Daria smiled at him. "Are you fishing for a compliment, Mr. Comstock?"

He didn't laugh out loud, but she could see that he was tempted to do so. She liked how easily she made him laugh and how naturally he smiled when they were in company.

"I'm no expert on such things," Daria said, "but I thought her performance was very good."

He nodded. "Most musicians could only hope to achieve her level of skill. It isn't merely that she knows how to play a piece; she plays it in a way that those listening can feel what the composer intended. That is a rare ability."

"Someday, she will play something you have composed," Daria said firmly but very quietly.

His smile slipped a little, and she knew why. The unfortunate news from the Royal Society of Musicians had dealt a blow to his confidence and his hope.

She wanted him to know how remarkable he was but also knew from experience that having a family member who constantly undermined it made believing the best in himself ever more difficult.

Father was at the front of the room again, thanking Lady Cavratt and inviting others to display their talents as well. Lady Aldric rose and stepped to the front, carrying a violin. As she played, the gathered guests listened intently, seeming pleased with the performance. But through it all, Laurence continually looked back at his brother with a stern expression that could not be interpreted as anything other than a warning.

Daria whispered so as to not disrupt the performance, "Is your brother upset that you are speaking with me or warning you of something else?"

"He was quite specific that if I were to play this evening, he would not be best pleased. After the fiasco with the Brinleys' dinner party, I believe he is particularly concerned about embarrassment. My brother is losing patience with me. My wisest course is to keep the peace."

Poor Toss. To want to follow his heart and to have been so close to doing so, only to have those dreams repeatedly snatched away.

As the evening continued and more performances were offered, Daria was repeatedly pulled away to answer a question from the staff or to check on some bit of preparation or another. Toss wandered elsewhere as well, standing at times beside one of his friends or near his brother. Daria felt almost guilty being so pleased with the evening when she knew he was suffering.

Her father was now standing at the front, nearly all the performances completed, his eyes darting to Daria with a mixture of panic and impatience. No one was rising to perform next. The order of the participants had not been determined ahead of time. Did Father not remember that was how musicales were organized? How was Daria to explain that if no one wished to display, then the evening would simply progress to the food and drinks set out in the drawing room? If she said anything, that would publicly reveal that she was, in fact, the one in charge of the evening. Her parents would never forgive her for that embarrassment.

The lull was growing, and the silence was becoming uncomfortable. Father's gaze had turned to a glare. Just as Daria began to abandon hope of a solution, a voice spoke.

Toss.

"My apologies. I had forgotten I was meant to go next."

Oh, merciful heavens. What is he doing? His brother would be livid. But still Toss walked to the pianoforte.

Daria held her breath as he played. She didn't dare even look in Laurence's direction. Everyone else appeared undeniably impressed. Toss, as he always did when playing, looked entirely at peace.

Oh, please don't let him suffer for this. But she suspected he would. Her darling, caring, compassionate Toss would most certainly be made to suffer for it.

As the performance came to a close, the room erupted in enthusiastic applause. Toss quickly stood and bowed to Mother and Father in acknowledgment of their supposed roles as host and hostess, then stepped away from the pianoforte.

Father was on his feet in an instant, facing the crowd with a broad grin of triumph. "We have refreshments in the drawing room. We invite you to remain and mingle for as long as you wish. Please, enjoy yourselves, and thank you all for being here this evening."

The guests began to move about, some wandering from the music room in the direction of the drawing room, others hovering near the chairs they'd been occupying.

Daria trusted the staff to have seen to the food. Mother and Father had gone in that direction, and she knew they would tell her if anything was amiss, though she did not believe anything would be. As the music room began to truly empty, Daria caught sight of Laurence dragging his brother down the corridor and into an empty sitting room.

Daria carefully and quietly followed. She reached the door in time to hear a raised voice on the other side.

"I was very specific, Thomas. 'Within reason,' I said, and revealing yourself to be a talentless child as you did tonight is not within reason."

Daria stepped inside, head held high. "I would ask you, Mr. Comstock, to keep your voice to a civil level and conduct yourself as is expected at a Society gathering. I assure you, while the guests cannot understand the words you are speaking, they are well aware of the fact that someone is being shockingly uncouth. You are welcome to behave in this manner in your own home, but not in ours."

"This is a family matter, Miss Mullins, between my brother and me," Laurence said with palpable dignity.

Though she was quaking inside, she held herself firmly, knowing Toss deserved to have someone stand up for him. "You would contradict a lady in her own home?" she asked quietly, with enough warning to put the arrogant man on his guard.

"I certainly hadn't intended that." Laurence sputtered a little. "I was simply defending my family's reputation."

"From my position at the end of your brother's performance, I could hear the comments being made. And unless you intend to step into the drawing room and contradict the taste and discernment of Lord and Lady Lampton, Lord and Lady Aldric Benick, the Duke and Duchess of Kielder, Lord and Lady Techney, Mr. and Mrs. Fortier, and Mr. Layton, whose taste is considered absolutely impeccable, I suggest you stop telling such falsehoods under my roof." How she hoped he could not detect her shaking knees. "If you found that performance embarrassing, one must question *your* taste, not *theirs.* I will allow you thirty seconds to decide whether or not you mean to behave appropriately in the home of a gentleman and leave off misrepresenting your brother's talents or if you intend for me to return to the drawing room and let everyone know Mr. Laurence Comstock loudly calls into question the intelligence and judgment of anyone who found his brother's performance indicative of anything other than—what were the words you used?—'a talentless child'?"

Daria had not interacted with Laurence Comstock more than twice in her life, but she suspected the look of shocked uncertainty on his face was new.

Return fire. She reminded herself of the Huntresses' third battle strategy and pressed on. "Fifteen seconds remaining," she said calmly.

"I shall keep my opinions to myself." Laurence spoke through tight teeth.

"Excellent." She turned enough to motion to the open door.

Laurence offered her a very abbreviated bow as he stepped from the room.

Daria had often thought, observing Charlie, Scott, and Newton as they watched their wives, that she would love for a gentleman to look at her with the same tender pride and adoration she saw on their faces. As Toss followed his brother's path through the door, he looked at her in just that way.

If not for the fact that the house was overrun with guests and her parents were scrutinizing her every move, Daria would have thrown her arms around him and thanked him for his earlier rescue and for the risk that had been and told him how much she hoped his brother decided to treat him with greater kindness. As it was, all she could do was dip the quickest curtsy and, in response to his mouthed "thank you," silently offer a "thank *you*" in return before she slipped from the room to see to the remainder of the evening.

CHAPTER TWENTY-SEVEN

THE MUSICALE REACHED ITS CONCLUSION, and the guests had dispersed, but Toss remained, along with Colm, Fennel, and Duke. Tobias was assisting his sister in the tasks she was seeing to whilst the servants were clearing the music room and drawing room of the remnants of the gathering.

Toss likely could have left some time earlier, but he was hoping for a moment with Daria. Her fierce defense of him that evening had been remarkable, and she deserved to know that. He wanted to tell her how wonderful the evening was and how highly the other guests had spoken of it. Mostly, he just wanted to see her smile again and to spend time with her without all the others around. That seemed less and less likely to happen.

"Cambridge isn't the same without you," Duke said.

"Dull as twice-boiled cabbage, is it?" Toss asked with a grin.

"It is certainly quieter." Duke had a way of appearing entirely serious despite having an inarguable sense of humor. Those who were given the opportunity to truly come to know him saw who he was underneath the unapproachable demeanor. But few were permitted to do so.

"The flat especially," Fennell said. "The pianoforte hasn't been touched."

"Maybe dear old Mrs. Hill would consider selling it to me for far less than it's worth. I'd just have to decide where to hide it."

"Charlie said Laurence the Lout was living up to his name," Fennell said. "I still can't believe he sold the pianoforte just to spite you."

"Being spiteful was probably his favorite part."

"If he was paying the least attention tonight, he's calling himself a fool for discarding the instrument," Duke said. "You demonstrated quite clearly why the Cambridge dons saw such potential in you."

A potential the Royal Society of Musicians didn't see in him. "I can't seem to gain acceptance in my field, and I can't afford to return to Cambridge. Embarrassed or not, Laurence has managed to snatch away my future."

"I never thought I'd be grateful not to have brothers," Fennel said, "but I am in this moment."

"On behalf of the rest of us, I think I should be offended," Colm said with a laugh. "I was told this was a brotherhood. Has it been pretended all along?"

"Maybe that's what we should start calling ourselves," Duke said. His tone was serious but one that Toss recognized was also a little jesting. "The Pretended Brotherhood."

"I suspect Artemis would find that far too dull," Toss said.

They sat and chatted, quite at their leisure. It was almost like being back at Cambridge again, passing a pleasant and banter-filled evening, allowing their cares to subside for a time.

"Any idea who's winning this game you're playing with Daria?" Fennel asked.

Before Toss could answer, Duke did. "Oh, they're both winning." There was a dryness to the answer that, historically, had accompanied his philosophical observations.

"Something you'd like to share with the rest of us?" Toss did his best impression of one of their least favorite people at Cambridge, a particularly self-important man with a permanent sneer.

"We've been here only a matter of hours, and it's obvious to even the two of us"—Duke motioned to himself and Fennel alternately—"that the nature of the game has changed. You're full smitten."

"Oh, we passed the smitten stage days and days ago," Toss said in dramatically annoyed tones. "Do try to keep up."

"I am assuming, then," Fennel said, "that you have reached the point where she finds charming all those things about you that we know to be annoyances."

"What else? How could she not be utterly enthralled by a gentleman with no future, income, freedom, or the minutest idea of what in the world he is going to do with his life?"

"Who wouldn't be instantly besotted with someone boasting that list?" Fennel said.

"If you had a little less facial hair, I'd be half in love with you myself." Colm grinned, a sign, Toss hoped, that he didn't begrudge him Daria's affections.

"For me," Fennel said, "it's not the facial hair so much as the smell."

Colm nodded. "He does have a distinct odor, doesn't he?"

"We've been telling him for years."

Toss leaned back in his chair and held his arms out in a show of self-aggrandizement. "What you smell, gentlemen, is your own jealousy."

"And just a hint of whatever wood pianofortes are made of," Fennel added.

"Lud, I miss being at Cambridge with you two." Toss shook his head. "It's unfair that this pretended brotherhood of ours is fractured at the moment."

"'Pretended Brotherhood' is too depressing," Fennel said. "We need to keep thinking."

"We'd best be on our way," Duke said. "Toss's real reason for remaining behind tonight is finally free of her responsibilities." Duke rose, as did Colm and Fennel. "We'll see you at Falstone House in the morning."

Toss nodded as he, too, got to his feet. They meant to spend the next day faffing about. The Huntresses were going to meet at a dress shop to . . . shop for dresses, he assumed.

He walked with his friends to the entryway, where Tobias crossed their paths. Farewells were made as well as excitement expressed about spending the next day together. Daria stood nearer the stairs, just outside the door to a sitting room. Toss quickly abandoned the men and moved to stand with her.

"I suspect you are exhausted," he said.

She nodded. "But I think the evening went well."

"I listened as the guests mingled over their refreshments. Everyone had unending praise for the evening, and I heard not a single complaint."

Daria brushed an errant hair away from her eye. She did look tired. "We almost had a disaster at the end of the performances. Father didn't seem to realize he could simply conclude that portion of the evening. But I couldn't tell him that, as he would have blamed me for embarrassing him. But he likely would have been just as angry with me for *not* telling him and leaving him there looking befuddled in front of his very impressive guests." She sighed. "Sometimes living with my parents feels impossible."

"One of the reasons you are exhausted, no doubt." How he wanted to pull her into his arms again. That had seemed to help in the past. It had certainly helped him.

"Exhausted but not defeated." Her soft but determined smile spoke of a quiet strength too few recognized. "My parents aren't likely to change. I'm just glad to have found a way to survive that."

"You deserve to do far more than merely survive." His hand brushed her arm.

She looked up at him. "Laurence was so terrible to you tonight."

"I knew he would be," Toss said. "Turning your father's wrath away from you was well worth Laurence's lecture, I assure you."

She set her hand on his where it rested on her arm. "He ought to recognize how talented you are. But I suppose he is like my parents in that regard; he cannot see anything he hasn't already decided to believe."

"He'll forevermore believe that Miss Daria Mullins can expertly put him in his place." Toss couldn't help his grin. "I doubt the formidable Artemis Jonquil could have managed it better. It was . . . beautiful."

She laughed a little, a beautiful, heart-lifting sound. "I was terrified. I think my knocking knees were louder than my actual voice."

He leaned closer to her. "I sometimes suspect you don't realize how remarkable you are."

Even in the dim candlelight, he could see a blush steal over her cheeks. "After tonight's triumph, Anglesey doesn't loom *quite* so large and threatening on the horizon."

He took hold of her hand and pressed a light kiss to her fingers. "I would cross every county in this kingdom to spend even one fleeting moment with you, my darling Daria. And no matter how impossible it feels right now, I refuse to believe that fate will be so cruel as to tear us apart."

"I believe in you, Thomas Comstock."

How powerful those six words proved in that moment. Laurence didn't believe in him. The Royal Society of Musicians didn't. Toss himself didn't always. But Daria did.

He bent ever closer, her sparkling eyes drawing him in. The floral scent of her perfume wrapped around him, holding him there.

Tobias walked over from the now-empty front doorway. Stepping back once more was Toss's only real option in that moment. Daria seemed to regret the distance as much as he did.

"The house is all but empty now." Tobias paused for a moment at the first step at the bottom of the stairs. "Best make a quick farewell."

Unfortunately, he was right.

Toss squeezed Daria's hand. "Your musicale was a triumph, Daria. And you are, indeed, remarkable. Sleep well, and I'll see you soon."

"And if not, do you promise to send me more . . . flowers?" She set a hand on her locket.

"The very best my feeble attempts can produce." How tempted he was to embrace her before departing, but her brother was still nearby. So he contented himself with one more tender kiss pressed to her hand. "Good night, my darling Daria."

Colm was waiting outside when Toss stepped through the front door. "I thought you might appreciate not walking to your brothers' house." He motioned to the carriage nearby.

"Thank you." He'd not even thought of that complication.

They were soon seated inside and on their way.

"I hope Daria is proud of all she accomplished tonight," Colm said. "Tobias has told me of his sister's struggles to see her own value sometimes."

"Her parents' opinions are very loud in that regard."

Colm nodded slowly. "If she is victorious in your competition and we are to plan a house party, I know my parents would be happy to allow us the use of the family estate. And I think it would be good for both the Mullins siblings to spend some time in an encouraging household."

"I could use a bit of that myself," Toss said. "A lot of us, both the Huntresses and the gentlemen, could use some of that."

"I have been humbled as part of this group to realize how insufficiently I have appreciated the family I have."

"I didn't appreciate my parents as much as I should have until they were gone," Toss said. "Now my sister and I have to endure Laurence without our parents to soften that misery."

"Is your sister still very young?"

Toss nodded. "Twelve years old. We both will have to endure our brother for years. For*ever*, it sometimes seems."

"If your hopes where Daria is concerned come to be, then at least you won't be enduring him entirely alone."

His hopes had been in competition with Colm's. But his friend was being very gracious. Their group was fortunate to have Colm and Tobias among them now. The Season hadn't begun on a good footing for Toss, but it had proven beneficial in countless ways. Perhaps that was how fate found a balance in the world. The good with the bad. Ups alongside downs.

They reached Laurence's house.

"Thank you again for thinking to wait for me," Toss said. "Walking home would have been miserable, and hailing a hackney this late would have been difficult."

"You are very welcome."

As he alighted from the carriage, Toss had a spring in his step once more. The walk to the Mullinses' house earlier had been a difficult and trudging one. He felt better now, lighter.

Exhausted but not defeated.

Daria's declaration rang in his ears while the tune she had inspired played in his heart.

He fully expected to find the house quiet when he entered. Laurence had left the Mullinses' home more than an hour earlier. But that balance he had attributed to fate seemed to be leaning a bit toward the misery end of the pendulum swing.

Toss was not more than a few steps inside when Laurence appeared in the entryway, looking absolutely thunderous.

"You waited up for me," Toss said with a grin. "I'm flattered."

"Don't be." Laurence glared. "Within reason, Thomas. How many times have I reminded you of that this Season?"

Toss pretended to be confused. "Doesn't sound familiar."

"Since coming to London, you have had freedom to do as you chose, within reason. Freedom to choose your friends and associates, within reason. Freedom to hum your pathetic tunes and blubber about Cambridge, within reason."

"This sounds even less familiar."

"After your humiliating display at the Brinleys', how dare you disregard my instructions for this evening. How dare you further risk our family's good standing. How dare—"

"Could we finish the 'how dare you's' in the morning? I'm tired." Toss stepped past him, but Laurence grabbed hold of his arm, yanking him around once more. His brother had been difficult and demanding, but this was the first time he'd become physically forceful.

"Within reason." Laurence pulled out each syllable. "I have endured nothing but *un*reasonable behavior from you. Playing your inane music tonight, then setting that harridan on me afterward is the final straw."

Harridan? "You speak insultingly of a gentleman's daughter after accusing *me* of not behaving appropriately?"

"You—"

"No, Laurence, you have had your say, and now I will have mine." He yanked his arm free of his brother's grasp. "You behaved abominably tonight, and Miss Mullins rightly corrected your uncivil behavior before *you* risked our family's good standing. She saved you from your own unacceptable actions, and still you speak insultingly of her. You insist I behave 'within reason,' but I don't think you have the least idea what that means."

Laurence jabbed him with an angry finger. "I am the head of this family."

"No. You are an inferior substitute for the good people who will always be both the heart and head of our family. Our parents cared about more than themselves. They were kind and selfless. And they would be ashamed of the person you have become."

"How d—"

"I know. How dare I? Well, it is about time I dared quite a few things." *Exhausted but not defeated.* "I have done everything possible to keep the peace since you dragged me here. I have made every sacrifice, all while you have declared it not enough. I am done expecting you to change, to choose to be reasonable, to choose to be the kind of brother you ought to be. I give up."

The smallest bit of uncertainty pulled at Laurence's angry features. "If you are considering making trouble, remember that I control your income and the roof over your head. Without me, you would be destitute."

"You demand too steep a price." An unexpected calm swept over Toss. He released the tension in his lungs without so much as a hint of a sigh. "I am no longer going to pay it. I'll pack what belongings I have, and I will be gone by morning." He began climbing the stairs.

"And where will you go?" Laurence asked.

Toss paused long enough to answer. "Wherever I want . . . within reason."

CHAPTER TWENTY-EIGHT

Daria arose with a lighter heart than she'd had in weeks. The musicale had gone swimmingly. All her plans had proven a success. And Toss—dear, darling, Toss—had very nearly kissed her, she was certain of it.

Her heart had jumped about behind her ribs. If not for her brother hovering nearby, Toss might have actually kissed her. Perhaps the next time they were together, he would.

It was in this happy mood, having broken her fast and dressed for the day, that she unintentionally crossed paths with her parents. All the Huntresses were gathering at Miss Martinette's dress shop in an hour, and she'd planned to simply go directly there without interruption.

Her parents waved her into the sitting room as she passed the door. Such encounters usually rendered her rather nervous. She felt more confident now. She'd done all they'd asked of her, all they'd required of her in regard to the musicale. She had shown herself useful and had given them reason to continue living among them.

"Your father has remembered a complication we hadn't thought of," Mother said without preamble. "As you are to be away from home this morning, it would make sense for *you* to see to the matter."

They were trusting her with an errand. A surge of pride swelled in her chest. She'd proven herself to them. More to the point, she had proven herself *to herself.*

"What is needed?" she asked, holding herself with the poise she'd been attempting to show since her earliest days as a Huntress.

"You do not have a suitable coat for Anglesey," Mother said. "The weather is wetter than in Yorkshire."

Anglesey? Her lungs froze. "Why would I need a coat suitable for Anglesey?"

"If you would like to be cold whilst you are there, that is certainly your prerogative," Father muttered. "And a fitting bit of inanity."

"I was only to go to Anglesey if the musicale I planned and executed was a failure," she said. "That was our agreement."

"That was never agreed to." Mother spoke firmly.

"It was though."

"I told you I would *consider* it. Your little evening was pleasant enough but nothing I couldn't manage without you."

She shook her head. "It was declared a success by everyone present." Panic began to fill the cracks quickly piercing her confidence.

"Your removal to Anglesey is a settled matter," Father said. "Your great-aunt is expecting you, and we have delayed your departure longer than we ought."

We cannot continue to delay. Father had said that in the moments before Daria had introduced Mr. Layton to her parents. Had he been speaking, not about leaving her in Yorkshire as she'd assumed at the time but about sending her to Anglesey?

"Where is Tobias?" Worry tightened her words. "He was present when we spoke of me planning events for years to come; he will corroborate what I'm saying."

"You cannot be forever demanding Tobias's time and attention," Mother said. "He is making such inroads with the fashionable young gentlemen just now. His efforts must be focused there."

"*I* am the one who introduced him to those fashionable young gentlemen. Surely he would not begrudge me a moment of conversation."

Father's mouth pulled tight, and he shook his head in quick, jerking movements. "You are growing alarmingly high in the instep, girl. The young Mrs. Jonquil may have given you space in her circle, but that does not mean you claim her level of importance."

"I have never said that I did."

"Then, for heaven's sake," Mother said, "stop acting as if you do."

"You will be going to Anglesey, Daria," Father said. "This is not up for debate. It never has been."

"How long—How long have you been planning to send me there?"

"Aunt Theodosia wants you there," Mother said. "We cannot afford to disregard her wishes."

"What do you mean?"

Mother ruffled up at the question. "It is not your place to interrogate us, Daria."

"Theodosia is expecting you." Father's posture was rigid. His jaw was tensely set. "We will not keep her waiting any longer."

Great-Aunt Theodosia had always been dictatorial and a somewhat miserable person to spend time with, but she hadn't, as far as Daria knew, ever had this strong of a claim on Father and Mother's fealty.

"Why are you so afraid of upsetting her?"

"Enough, Daria." Father's harsh words snapped like a crack of thunder. "You are going to Anglesey even if we have to tie you to the traveling carriage."

Never, even in the midst of his often unkind words, had her father issued an actual threat until now. And his eyes were angry enough for her to believe this was not an idle one.

"What will Great-Aunt Theodosia expect me to do when I arrive in Anglesey?"

"Whatever she tells you to do." Mother spoke quickly and firmly. "Do not make her unhappy."

That did not bode well at all.

"When am I meant to depart London?" Daria desperately tried to keep her mind focused despite the whirlwind of thoughts fighting for her attention.

"The day after tomorrow." Father rose. He gave his waistcoat a quick tug, then straightened the sleeves of his jacket. "That should be ample time for you to gather whatever you mean to take with you." He walked out of the room.

Mother remained behind only a moment longer. "Do see if you can procure a coat while you are out."

"One cannot possibly be made on such short notice."

With a shrug, Mother followed Father's path from the room. "Do what you must."

Do what you must.

Her parents were sending her to live at the mercy of someone they seemed to be a little afraid of.

What you must.

Daria knew she was not the cleverest of people, but she had an idea. A desperate idea.

You must.

Careful not to cross paths with her parents, she returned quickly to her bedchamber and closed the door behind her.

In the bottom of the wardrobe was a small portmanteau. Daria snatched it out. Struggling to pull air through her petrified lungs, she filled the bag with a couple changes of smallclothes, shifts, her purple day dress, one ballgown, her dancing slippers, a hairbrush, and pins. She snatched up her reticule and placed inside the few coins she had, all the while watching her bedchamber door for any sign of her parents, listening for the sound of footsteps.

Do what you must.

Her next "must" was escaping the house without anyone realizing what she was doing. She draped a shawl over her arm and hand holding her bag. Doing so helped disguise her bundle. Her parents would surely stop her if they discovered her intentions. *"If we have to tie you to the traveling carriage . . ."* Her freedom was on the line, and she did not take that lightly. Luck was on her side. She not only managed to leave the house undetected, but she also found a hackney within a short distance.

She gave the driver directions, then sat still as stone as she felt the conveyance rattle into motion. She could hardly breathe even as she put distance between herself and her parents' house.

There was every possibility this risky escape could still go horribly wrong. Perhaps she ought not to have taken such a chance. But what did she have to lose, really? All that was likely to happen should her flight be discovered was being sent to Anglesey immediately rather than in a few days.

At least this way, there was a chance of a good outcome.

The hackney came to a stop. Daria dared a peek out the window. She had arrived precisely where she'd asked to be taken.

Do what you must.

With her bag still hidden by her shawl, she alighted and paid the driver using one of her coins, then turned to face the intimidating edifice of Falstone House.

When the butler opened the door and his staid facade broke for a moment with confused surprise, Daria realized a significant hole in her plan. Artemis would not be home, she having gone to the dress shop to meet with the other Huntresses. It was, in fact, the reason Daria had come here: Miss Martinette's was the first place her parents would look, knowing it was where she'd been expected to go. The Huntresses would be able to say she'd never arrived. Her path would be better disguised.

But with Artemis gone and Daria arriving unaccompanied by even a maid, she was in an odd position.

"Is—" *Think, Daria.* "Is—" She couldn't ask for Charlie; that would be considered shockingly inappropriate. She was too terrified of the duke to ask for him. "Is Her Grace home?"

"This is not her at-home day, Miss Mullins." Thank the heavens the butler recognized her. He would be less likely to send her away for being ill prepared to face this complication, one she should have anticipated.

"Would you ask her if—I'm not here for a formal call. I—" Good heavens, she was out of her depth already. She swallowed thickly. "Would you ask her if I could have a moment of her time, please?"

She was motioned inside. For just an instant, she thought she might be required to stand in the entryway like an interloper, but the butler indicated she should step into a small sitting room nearby.

Alone, she let herself breathe. No matter the outcome of her pleadings at Falstone House that day, she felt certain she would be permitted to remain until Artemis returned. And Artemis would know what to do. Artemis was the most ingenious person Daria knew, and the most loyal friend she could imagine.

Daria set her portmanteau on the floor beside a chair and draped her shawl over it. She attempted to stretch some of the tension out of her shoulders and back, but she suspected it was futile. Too much had happened too quickly for her to be calm.

After what felt like ages but was likely no more than a few minutes, the duchess stepped inside the room. Though her coloring was quite different from Artemis's, they looked enough alike to testify to the fact that they were sisters. "Miss Mullins. You asked for me?"

Suddenly, Daria felt terribly presumptuous. Artemis was her friend, yes. But who was she to make demands on the time of a duchess?

"I didn't mean to inconvenience you, truly I didn't. And I won't continue to do so if I can at all help it. I already have, so I suppose I can't help it to some extent. But I'll do what I can to lessen that extent. At least until Artemis arrives." She shook her head. "Not that I mean to be a nuisance *after* she arrives."

Her Grace's eyes darted to the bag at Daria's feet, not entirely hidden by her shawl. "Are you in some sort of trouble?"

Daria's breath caught in her throat as she nodded. What would the duchess think of her now? What assumptions would she make?

The duchess quickly closed the door, then crossed to Daria, taking her hand in what seemed like a very sisterly manner. She didn't know for certain, not having a sister of her own.

"Is this trouble you find yourself in the sort that would mean we would do best to keep your presence here a secret?"

Daria nodded.

"From everyone or simply from your family?"

"Certainly from my family," Daria said. "I really don't want them to know where I am."

"Then I should warn you that your brother is here. Charlie's friends are enjoying a leisurely morning together."

Tobias was at Falstone House. She hadn't anticipated that complication. Heavens, there was a reason she was not usually the one to think of schemes and execute plans. Did she want Tobias to know she was there? She couldn't imagine not telling him, and yet she needed to be certain her parents could not discover her whereabouts until she knew what to do next. Tobias wouldn't intentionally give away her location, but there was a chance he might do so accidentally.

"That you are hesitating as much as you are tells me we ought to, for the time being, not tell your brother." The duchess didn't seem to think that a terrible thing, which made Daria feel a little better. "And I suspect we also should avoid advertising your presence to the staff."

The enormity of her decision was beginning to set in. She had run away, leaving behind her family and home, and she wasn't entirely certain what came next.

"The butler knows you are here, as does my lady's maid—she was in the room when the butler told me of your arrival—but both are as reliable as the sunrise. You can pass the morning in my personal sitting room. No one will bother you there. Once Artemis has returned, I will send her directly to you."

"I didn't intend to cause you difficulty in coming here. I don't always think things through."

The duchess squeezed her hand. "If you are in difficulties enough to justify taking such drastic measures, then coming here was the right thing to do."

"Your husband will likely be angry with me." No one with even a drop of sense dared make the Dangerous Duke angry.

"I know he has a fearsome reputation, and he earned it in many ways, but he was raised by a man who was unwavering in his conviction that a true gentleman does all he can to help people in need. My husband will not only *not* be frustrated with your arrival here, but he will also insist on providing whatever assistance he can in whatever the matter is."

For the first time since Mother had mentioned the matter of a coat, Daria felt less panic-stricken. She had indeed come to the right place and, in doing so, had at least some chance of staying as far from Great-Aunt Theodosia as possible.

CHAPTER TWENTY-NINE

"AGAIN, I MUST ASK WHY you are not considering taking up the highwayman's trade?" Charlie sat slouched on a chair in the Falstone House music room, where all their group had gathered for the morning. "You'd be spectacular."

"And your brother would disapprove," Fennel added, "which would help us emerge victorious in your game with Daria."

"I think I've earned more than a few points for leaving Laurence's home for good," Toss said.

"I thought the rules didn't allow for multiple points in exchange for a single act, no matter how rebellious." Duke had an excellent sense of humor, but his character tended toward practicality over ridiculousness.

"All things considered," Colm said, "it might be time for a renegotiation."

"Perhaps, but it is *decidedly* time for a renaming." Toss wasn't overly keen to discuss his flight from home at too much depth. They all knew he'd been given refuge here at Falstone House and that his entire future was now in question. That seemed enough for the moment. "The Huntresses will hold it over our heads forever if we don't have a group name of our own."

"Can we make that decision without Newton or Scott here?" Fennel asked. "They would certainly have opinions."

"They should have thought of that before leaving the lot of us alone unsupervised." Charlie's overly stern declaration made them all laugh.

"What about 'the Hunters'?" Tobias suggested.

"Our ladies would object, I haven't a doubt," Charlie said. "Though they did find it rather entertaining when we referred to ourselves as 'the Whippers-In' at the Debenhams' ball."

Toss thought that an apt description since hunters were assisted by whippers-in and those of their group who were married to a Huntress very much filled that role during the ladies' annual arrival in Society.

"I would humbly submit the idea 'Poppy and the Poppers.'" Fennel managed a serious expression for all of two seconds. One of his nicknames was Poppy.

"'Newton and the Newts,'" Colm suggested.

"Six Englishmen and an American," Tobias tossed out. "A mouthful, yes, but very specific."

"And, unfortunately, inaccurate," Colm said. "Duke's family, after all, are Irish and have been for generations."

"Truly?" Tobias looked surprised. "How did you know that?"

Colm and Duke shrugged in near unison. "We're cousins."

That deviated the conversation for some time as the connection between the two of them was laid out. Colm's mother and Duke's father were siblings. When pressed as to why they'd not mentioned the relationship immediately, both gentlemen clammed up.

In the awkward silence that followed, Charlie very suddenly sat up, eyes a bit wide, excitement writ on his face. "I have the perfect name. Utterly and completely perfect."

"Do tell." Fennel watched him with a smile.

Toss nodded his encouragement as well.

"Playing off the Huntresses' name but without stealing their identity nor placing ourselves in the permanent role of assistants . . ." Charlie watched them all in turn, clearly enjoying the building tension. "What about 'the Pack'?"

The Pack. "As in a pack of hunting dogs?" Toss asked.

Charlie nodded. "And a pack of friends, a pack of characters—"

"A pack of cards," Colm said.

"A pack of lies," Tobias added, setting them all to laughing.

"I like it," Fennel said. "The Pack." He nodded again.

"The Huntresses and the Pack." Colm tried it from that direction.

The more Toss heard the suggestion, the more he liked it. Unless Newton or Scott posed objections, they might very well have settled the matter. *The Pack.*

"Now that you've cut ties with Laurence," Duke said to Toss, the others having launched into a discussion of their new group name and their guesses as to Newton's and Scott's thoughts, "are you considering returning to Cambridge?"

"Without Laurence's funds, I couldn't hope to pay for it." He didn't even know how he was going to pay for food to eat moving forward.

"I suspect I am about to be your best friend." Duke rested his elbows on the arms of his chair and steepled his fingers. "I did some searching after Laurence dragged you to London. There is a scholarship in honor of William

Boyce intended for a student studying composition who also plays the organ, harpsichord, or pianoforte."

"Truly?" Toss had never heard of it. But, then, he'd not been a scholarship student. Few whose families could fund their education gave much thought to scholarships and other means of assistance.

Duke nodded. "I gathered all the information I could and wrote it out for you. But I'm told the scholarship has not been claimed for next term."

Did he dare let his hopes begin to grow? "What does the scholarship offer?"

"Payment of tuition fees."

Dozens of questions flitted through his mind. "How does—How would I apply for consideration?"

"An essay of interest, a performance for the deciding committee, and a letter of recommendation from a person of adequate standing in the world of musical composition or performance."

"I could manage the essay, but a performance would require either me or the committee to travel. And blast it, I don't have any prominent musician who would endorse me."

"Don't blast things too soon." Duke was one of the most unshakable people Toss knew. "I inquired of Stuber, and he said that your professors at Cambridge could provide their own assessments of your performance abilities in lieu of you performing for the committee."

Stuber was a particularly influential professor of music at Cambridge. "And he thought they might be willing?"

Duke nodded. "And Stuber himself said he'd write the recommendation."

He could have money enough for his tuition. He could return to Cambridge and finish his studies. That would allow him to at last pursue his music in earnest.

But all the remaining complications slid over Toss in quick succession. "I wouldn't have funds for housing or for buying food or any of life's necessities."

"I can't solve that difficulty for you, but Stuber seemed to think that if your brother ever cut you off entirely, you could apply to be a fellow. That would negate the need for the scholarship but would also eliminate your living expenses."

It wasn't a guarantee, but it was a chance. It was an opportunity.

"Laurence ought not to have done what he did," Duke said. "Both what he did to you at the start of the term and the misery he's caused you since. But you have options, Toss. You have choices."

A footman stepped quietly into the room and presented Tobias with a folded missive before bowing himself back out of the room.

"Could it be Tobias has a secret admirer?" Charlie wondered out loud. "Seems to me you ought to have shared that bit with the rest of us, Colm."

"I would have if he'd shared that bit with me."

In that moment, though, Tobias didn't look entertained. His expression turned solemn before slipping into something like panic.

"What's happened?" Colm asked.

With an audible swallow, Tobias looked up at them all. "Daria's missing."

"What do you mean?" Toss was on his feet in an instant.

"Artemis came by the house to fetch her when she didn't arrive at the dress shop as planned. But she'd already left and ought to have arrived long since." Tobias looked down at the letter in his hands once more. "Father says she never called the carriage."

"She wouldn't have tried to walk, I hope," Colm said.

"I don't think so."

"What about the maid who accompanied her?" Duke pressed.

Tobias shook his head. "She never asked for a maid, and no one saw her leave, but she isn't at home."

Colm, for the first time since Toss had made his acquaintance, held himself with the fierce rigidity of a soldier. When he spoke, it was with the authority of one who had led many into battle. "Charlie and Fennel, go to Lampton House and discreetly inquire as to whether the dowager countess has heard from Daria. Tobias and I will return to his parents' home and ascertain what is being done there. Toss and Duke, you two go to Miss Martinette's and confer with the Huntresses. Determine what they know, if they know of places we ought to be looking and things we ought to be doing."

Quick as that, they had tasks and focus. But Toss's mind was growing increasingly ill at ease. Just trying to take in a breath was proving difficult. Where was Daria? How could they possibly find her in a place so large as London?

It was possible she was simply walking about the green near her home or curled up in the corner of the garden and hadn't been noticed or that she had arrived at the dress shop after all and they would soon discover all was well. He hoped they would discover her in one of those scenarios. He tried to believe they would, but he didn't entirely.

Oh, Daria. Where are you?

The others left to fulfill their assignments.

Toss held Duke back. "I think there's someone else we ought to ask for help."

"If word of her disappearance becomes widely known, it will deal tremendous damage to Daria's reputation," Duke warned.

"I know this person's discretion can be counted on. And he has resources we could only dream of."

Though he clearly didn't know who Toss was speaking of, Duke agreed without further hesitation, and the two of them made their way to His Grace's book room. Charlie's brother-in-law had allowed Toss to practice his pianoforte after Laurence had sold theirs. And he hadn't batted an eye when Toss had arrived on their doorstep that morning looking for a temporary place to stay. He would help now; Toss knew he would.

Both the duke and duchess were in the book room, and both looked up as he stepped inside.

"Please forgive the interruption," Toss said. "A friend of ours—of Artemis's—is missing, and we have come to ask if you might be willing to assist us in searching for her. Obviously, we have to be discreet, but there are so few of us, and London is so large a place . . ." He shook his head as the words trailed away. His heart demanded that he not finish the thought.

What if something had happened to Daria? What if she was in danger? Injured? Had been abducted?

The duke and duchess exchanged a quick glance. Toss truly hadn't expected hesitation. The duke's reputation was terrifying, yes, but Toss had heard stories enough from Charlie and Artemis to know that His Grace was usually the first to come to the aid of the vulnerable. And the duchess was known for her kind and compassionate nature.

"Please," Toss beseeched. "She might be in danger or injured somewhere. London is too large a place for us to search alone."

Another look passed between the couple, then Her Grace stood and excused herself, leaving the room without explanation.

"I assure you," His Grace said, "we are not ignoring your pleas on behalf of a young lady in need, just as we did not ignore your pleas on your own behalf this morning. The situation is simply more complicated than you realize."

"But you will help?" Toss pressed.

"Of course." Why was it that even when His Grace was agreeing to help a person, that person still felt oddly threatened?

But Toss would endure all the threats in the world if it meant finding Daria faster. If she were in danger, time was of the essence.

How long would they be made to wait? Without knowing the entanglement that needed to be addressed, there was no way for Toss to predict the delay.

Dropping his voice a bit lower, Duke said, "I will go consult with the Huntresses. Join us, or send word when you are able."

Toss gave a quick nod and, in a flash, was alone with His Grace. He didn't fear his admittedly fearsome host, but he also knew not to try the man's patience. Thus, he stood still and silent, waiting for the help he prayed he was soon to receive and resisting the urge to pace.

She needs me, and I'm failing her.

It felt nearly impossible to stand still, doing nothing. His mind was certainly not calm. He tried mentally tracing the path she likely would have taken to the dress shop, making note of the various places she might have stopped. They needed to discover for certain whether she had attempted to make the journey on foot, as that changed the possibilities.

The duchess returned. Staring down a lady was not precisely smiled upon in Society, but Toss watched her closely and unblinkingly, needing to know what help was at his fingertips.

"Please, come with me." Her Grace motioned him toward the corridor.

He opened his mouth to object to further delays, but the duke, who, unbeknownst to Toss, had risen from his seat and already crossed the room, set a firm hand on his shoulder. "Trust her, Mr. Comstock."

What choice did he have, really?

Quiet and frustrated, he walked with the couple out of the book room. They took the stairs up to the next floor where the family's private rooms were. Why? He needed help from the staff, who would all be found in the public rooms and belowstairs. He needed the stable staff, who would be at the mews. He needed to find Daria.

The duchess took hold of the handle of one of the doors but paused and looked back at him. "Discretion, Mr. Comstock. The more I have learned of the situation, the more convinced I am of the need for careful secrecy."

She opened the door and indicated he should step inside first. *Trust her*, the duke had said. Despite his growing frustration with the delay, Toss passed through the threshold.

Daria. She was there. In the room.

In his relief, all the fear and panic he'd kept at bay rushed over him with nearly overwhelming intensity. His heart lodged itself in his throat, preventing any words he might have spoken. His lungs emptied even as emotion threatened to pour from him. His legs felt in danger of collapsing beneath him.

Daria. *His* Daria. Safe and whole.

She rushed to him and threw herself into his embrace.

She's safe. That phrase repeated in his mind over and over again. *She's safe.*

He held her tightly, fiercely. *She's safe.* And he was determined to never let her go again.

CHAPTER THIRTY

Daria had found paradise: Toss's arms wrapped around her, the rise and fall of his chest as he breathed, the smell of his shaving soap, the warmth of his nearness. In a day that had been spent in the depths of purgatory itself, she was, for that one moment, in heaven.

"My Daria," he whispered. "I was so afraid something horrible had happened to you."

When she had been told that Toss was pleading for help in his search for her, Daria had warred with a sense of guilt intertwined with the most indisputable feeling of being cared about. "I didn't mean to cause you worry," she replied in a whisper of her own.

"I'm just relieved you're safe and you're here." He kissed her temple as he held her ever tighter. "You're whole?"

"I am now." She leaned more entirely against him, allowing the reassuring solidity of him to give her the strength she needed.

"Obviously you are *hiding* here, not merely visiting," he said. "What happened?"

"They lied to me, Toss." She swallowed back the emotion that filled her throat. "They were never going to allow me to remain, no matter how the musicale was received. It was all a ruse. They simply wished to get a bit more work out of me before sending me to Anglesey."

"You'll have to go?" He still spoke softly.

"The day after tomorrow, they said. And they spoke of Great-Aunt Theodosia in such a way that . . . They're afraid of upsetting her—truly *afraid.* I can't bear the idea of living with someone I should be frightened of. I would never feel safe again. So, I had to go where they couldn't find me."

Toss rubbed her back in slow circles. "We are birds of a feather, sweet Daria. I had a row with my brother last night. I came here as well, looking for refuge."

They were both at Falstone House, dependent on the kindness of the duke and duchess.

Daria turned her gaze to the doorway, where the duchess remained, no doubt for the sake of propriety, they having needed to close the door in order to keep Daria's presence a secret. "I have doubled the burden on your household."

Her Grace shook her head. "It is not a burden, I assure you. I have been the one in need of help many times in my life and could never countenance turning my back on others who find themselves in such circumstances. And my husband, though it will likely shock you, would probably be hurt if he thought either of you believed he would turn you away in your moments of need."

Daria felt a weight instantly lift from her heart. "Thank you." She wasn't certain to whom she was offering the expression of gratitude: the duchess, the absent duke, or Toss. Likely all three.

"What ought we to do, Daria?" Toss asked. "All our friends are searching for you. Your brother is beside himself."

"But if my parents find me, I'll lose everything."

"I do think you can trust the discretion of our friends, dearest," he said. "And I know your brother will take your part against your parents if need be."

Daria didn't straighten, nor pull away from Toss. His arms around her helped her feel braver and stronger. She looked to the duchess once more. "What do you think?"

"I agree with Mr. Comstock. Not only would you be alleviating the worries of people who deeply care about you, but you would also benefit from their help and wisdom."

It was a little unkind to leave them in such a state of worry. And heaven knew, she could use all the wisdom they could offer. "I don't think they would do so intentionally, but it is possible one of our friends might inadvertently indicate to my parents where to find me. Then what will I do?"

Her Grace smiled slowly and confidently. "Do you, for one moment, think your parents are capable of bullying my husband into doing anything he doesn't wish to do?"

Her husband was the Dangerous Duke, the Infamous Kielder, arguably the most powerful and feared man in all the kingdom, the only person whose mere presence sent the Prince Regent himself scurrying from gatherings in a posture of deference. Her parents wouldn't stand a chance.

"Set aside any fears of being dragged from this house," the duchess said. "You are entirely safe here."

With Toss holding her in his arms and the unwavering confidence of the Duchess of Kielder, Daria felt safe. And in that safety, she could begin to feel hope.

Word had been quietly sent to all who had been searching for Daria that she was safely ensconced at Falstone House. They had returned with all possible haste. Mater had arrived with Charlie and Fennel and had immediately taken on a motherly role in reassuring Daria.

Everyone was gathered in the drawing room. Toss sat on a sofa beside Daria, holding her hand in his. The few times that he'd been required to let her go, he'd been seized all over again by the worry that had all but consumed him when he'd thought she was in danger. Thinking on it again in that moment, he held tighter to her hand, needing the reassurance that she really was there and safe.

"If you do not wish to stay with us at Brier Hill after the Season," Artemis said to Daria, the continuation of a conversation that had been ongoing ever since the Huntresses' rush to Falstone House, "Gillian, I am certain, would be anxious for you to stay with her and Scott."

Daria shook her head. "Their finances are too strained as it is."

"I would be beside myself with delight if you were to stay with me," Mater said. "I live in the same neighborhood as Gillian and Scott."

"That neighborhood is the envy of many," Daria said with a hint of a smile.

It did Toss's heart good to see her expression lighten a little, but the worry in her eyes didn't abate.

He leaned closer to Tobias, who sat beside him in the drawing room, where they had all gathered. "Would your parents make a fuss if she were invited to stay with the dowager countess?" He spoke quietly, not wishing to burden Daria with thoughts of her parents.

"A fuss? Likely not. But I also don't think they would allow her to avoid Anglesey even to accept the dowager's invitation." His mouth sat in a seemingly permanent line of frustration. "Great-Aunt Theodosia's expectations are all they talked about. They weren't worried that Daria might be in danger. Our aunt was the only person for whom they showed the least concern, other than themselves." He shook his head, the quick and small sort of movement that indicated a person who wished he could dismiss the truth of an unpleasant realization. "Their dishonesty has compounded their troubles, and they have no one to blame but themselves."

"Dishonesty? For not telling Daria their plans from the beginning?" Toss asked.

"More than that," Tobias said on a sigh. "*Worse* than that."

Only when Daria asked, "What else have they done?" did Toss realize the other conversation had ended and theirs was being overheard.

"Best tell her," Colm said. "She deserves to know."

Daria was watching her brother closely, expectantly, worriedly.

"Your dowry is gone." Tobias looked more miserable by the moment. "They discovered last year that it was not specified by any legally binding agreements, and therefore, they could spend it if they chose, which they did."

"What did they spend it on?" Of all the questions Daria could have asked, that was not the one Toss would have predicted.

"Nothing of any significance." Toss's mouth twisted in disgust. "Countless different nothings. But it is gone, and they are determined to keep that fact a secret."

"But they told you?" Daria pressed.

"They didn't intend to. Mother let it slip while she and Father were fretting over what Great-Aunt Theodosia would do if you don't arrive in Anglesey when she expects you to."

And suddenly, Toss had a realization. "Something about Daria's removal to Wales is connected to her missing dowry, isn't it?"

Tobias nodded. "That's my suspicion. Our aunt is wealthy, and our parents have, it seems, mismanaged their funds. Though I cannot sort out how restoring Daria's dowry in exchange for Daria being flung far away from Society would make the least sense."

"Unless they are planning to spend my 'second' dowry."

"That would explain why they didn't want you to return to London this year." Toss met Daria's eye. "And why they are now so determined to see you as far from Society as possible as soon as possible."

"They would ruin my entire life for the sake of spending money." Her shoulders drooped.

"They are selfish people," Tobias said firmly. "And I think you should seize whatever opportunity you have to build a life free from them, whether that is at Brier Hill or the Lampton Park dower house or visiting the Huntresses in turn."

"What about you?" she asked her brother. "Don't you deserve to build a life free of them?"

"I'll manage to navigate the degree of connection I can't entirely sever, given my ties to the estate. But your escape means more to me than mine ever would."

Daria's gaze returned to Toss, watching him with worry and hope. "Will you be able to escape your brother's tyranny? For good, I mean. I know you've escaped it for now."

He was glad to be able to give her a rare bit of good news. "Duke did a little research and discovered there is a fellowship at Cambridge I could apply for and would almost certainly receive. I could return to university and complete my education, which would allow me to begin forging a career for myself."

"And you could reapply to the Royal Society of Musicians," Daria said. "They couldn't argue that you didn't have the qualifications."

He nodded. "And Laurence couldn't force me to leave Cambridge again, since my tuition fees and my living expenses would be provided by the fellowship."

Toss had hoped sharing his good news would lift her spirits, but the corners of her mouth tugged ever so slightly downward.

"I wouldn't be homeless or penniless," he added.

"And you would be able to pursue your music?" she asked softly.

He nodded. "And as the fellowship would allow me to continue beyond the original course of study, if the Royal Society of Musicians still balks at my application or if they delay their decision overly long, I could pursue a higher degree, allowing me to publish compositions and establish myself before needing to have an income to live on."

The room was quiet enough that he felt certain he actually heard her tense breath. She had been his most adamant and vocal supporter, her belief in him never wavering. Why did this heaven-sent chance to reclaim his music and the future they dreamed of not seem to please her?

After a moment, she said, "I think you should return, then, and accept the fellowship. You can't ignore the opportunity." She looked so miserable. He didn't think she was being insincere.

"I think so too," he said.

Daria's lips pressed tightly, and she swallowed visibly. She rose, slipping her hand from his. "Pardon me a moment, please." She moved quickly from the room.

"I don't think you've thought this through, Toss," Charlie said, his eyes moving from the doorway Daria had just slipped through to Toss.

"What do you mean?"

"Charlie's situation gave the Huntresses a quick and detailed lesson in the rules of study at Cambridge," Artemis answered. "Dons can't be married, but neither can fellows. Returning to Cambridge for what you have just explained may be years of study means leaving her behind. You will be surrounded by friends in a place that feels in many ways like home while actively laying claim to your future. She will be alone, without a home, waiting for you."

CHAPTER THIRTY-ONE

Daria needed a moment to collect herself. Toss was returning to Cambridge, reclaiming his musical dreams, regaining a future free of his brother's tyranny. She was happy for him, and she would not for the world undermine that in any way. But her heart hurt acutely at the knowledge that he would be so far away and that their future *together* was now years out of reach. Had she remained at his side in the drawing room, she likely would have fallen to pieces, and he needed her to encourage and cheer for him. She wouldn't return until she felt confident she could be the source of support he needed.

Her feet took her to, of all places, the music room. She couldn't imagine ever being in any music room without thinking of him, without missing him. Why could she not have absent-mindedly wandered elsewhere?

If she were truly wise, she certainly wouldn't have further tortured herself by crossing to the pianoforte. She brushed her fingers over the keys too lightly to make a sound.

Toss deserved to have his music back, to claim the dream he'd fought for. He would never be truly happy without his music, and she loved him too much to want him to be anything less than truly happy. For the time being, she would stand in this room that reminded her of him and simply breathe through her tears.

But her isolated grieving lasted only a moment.

Toss himself passed by the doorway, then rushed back, stepping inside. "I wasn't entirely certain where you'd gone." He crossed swiftly to her, a look of concern on his face.

"I needed a moment is all," she said. "I promise I don't run out of rooms in a rush of emotions nearly as often as this Season makes it seem." She had done so twice now, and the realization was more than a little embarrassing.

"And I don't usually upset ladies enough to send them fleeing from a room." He took each of her hands in his. "Daria, I didn't realize—I hadn't pieced together all the ramifications of my return to Cambridge. Yesterday evening, there didn't seem to be any possible solution to my lost education and the consequences of that. I was so pleased to hear of anything that might address it that I didn't entirely think it through. But"—he tucked their hands to his heart—"having found one possible though unsatisfactory approach gives me hope that we'll stumble on something else, something that is good for us both."

She shook her head. "This is an opportunity you cannot simply reject. Being granted a fellowship would allow you to have your independence and your music. Toss, I never see you happier or more at peace than you are when enveloped in the music you play and compose. I will not be the reason you lose that."

"My happiness could never be complete without you," he said.

"I would still see you though," she said. "Fellows can't marry, but they can travel, I would imagine."

"The only restriction on travel is the time and the funds needed."

"You would likely have very little of either." But there was hope, even though there were also a great many complications to navigate.

"Some fellowships cover more than fees and living expenses," he said. "But those that provide additional income are generally life fellowships."

She could feel the blood drain from her face. A lifetime fellowship? That meant he couldn't ever marry, that he would be tied to Cambridge and the rules of his living for the entirety of his life. "I would never see you again."

He released one of her hands and brushed his fingers gently along her cheek. "This one is not a life fellowship, Daria. If it were, I would never consider it."

She closed her eyes, letting relief settle over her for a moment. Years apart would be difficult; a lifetime of separation would be unbearable.

"And having been reminded of the restrictions of being a fellow," he said, "I can't accept even a temporary fellowship."

She looked at him once more. "This is a chance to claim your dreams, Toss. You cannot dismiss that." She brushed a finger over a button on his jacket. "Being apart while you finish your studies will be so very difficult, but it would be worth doing. I think it's *important* to do."

His hand moved slowly from her face to her neck to her back. "Would you miss me, Daria?"

"I missed you during the few minutes I spent in this room before you arrived."

He slipped his other hand free of hers and wrapped his arm around her. "And I missed you from the moment I left you in the entryway last night."

Daria pressed her palm to his chest. "I stayed there for a while after you left, wishing you were still with me, imagining what it would be like when I saw you again."

"And in your imaginings, did I get to hold you like this?" His question was somehow both soft and husky.

"If I had my way, you'd always hold me like this." She slipped her hand to his face. "Cambridge fellows are allowed embraces, aren't they?"

"I've not heard of any rules against it." Toss leaned his forehead against hers. "And what have you heard about penniless musicians? Are they allowed kisses?"

Her pulse picked up its pace. "That depends on who the musician wants to kiss."

"He very much wants to kiss *you*, Daria Mullins."

She closed her eyes once more and whispered, "I wish he would."

Perhaps it was cowardice in her that she kept her eyes closed as she waited, achingly unsure but eagerly hopeful, but Daria had, over the course of that day, called upon every bit of stored bravery she'd had.

"Daria." His lips actually brushed hers as he whispered her name. "I love you, my darling Daria."

Those words, spoken with tender conviction, sparked warmth in her heart and spread through her in an instant.

She hooked her arms around his neck. "And I love you, my dear Toss."

He kissed her, slowly, delicately. His lips were soft, tenderly touching hers, but his arms were firm around her, holding her like he never wanted to let go. The feel of him so close to her tingled over every inch of her skin. She never wanted him to let go, and even after he ended the kiss, he kept her in his arms.

"We'll find a way to make this work," he said. "I know we will."

From far in the distance, a knock echoed. Someone was likely at the front door.

"For a moment, I almost forgot we aren't alone in this house." Toss pressed a fleeting kiss to her forehead before stepping back once more.

Daria smiled at the lingering shimmer of pleasure in his expression. Her own blush of delight must have been equally apparent.

His arms dropped away from the embrace, but he took hold of her hands. "As this is neither of our homes, we don't have to be present to greet whoever has arrived. I believe we can take advantage of the distraction and avoid returning to our friends for a moment longer."

"I like that strategy."

Toss laughed. "With any luck, these visitors will be *very* distracting."

"I would suggest you work on your composition, but that might draw our friends in here, and then we'd never be rid of them."

Excitement lit his eyes. "I'm nearly finished, and I'm quite pleased with it."

If she'd had any lingering doubts that he *needed* to reclaim the musical path that had been taken from him, seeing how enthusiastic he immediately became at the very introduction of the topic would have washed them away.

"I can hardly wait to hear it," she said.

In that very instant, Artemis hurried into the room. "There you are." She spoke, not as she would if scolding them for being alone for so long but with anxiety. "My brother-in-law gave his staff very strict instructions on what they were to do should your parents arrive at Falstone House."

Daria's lungs turned to ice in her chest.

"They are in the small sitting room, waiting to be told if they will be admitted."

No words came. Her parents had come to drag her home, no doubt. To throw her into a carriage and send her off to Anglesey, never to be seen or heard from again.

"What have Their Graces decided to do?" Toss slipped an arm around Daria once more and tucked her protectively to his side.

"Whatever Daria wants them to do." Artemis looked at her. "They will allow your parents to join everyone in the drawing room, come directly here, be tossed out onto the pavement. Truly. Whatever you want."

She'd never had choices where her parents were concerned. *You always have a choice.* Rose's words returned to her thoughts once more. There was always a choice of one kind or another. In the past, her options had been between attempting to secure fair treatment or being granted any degree of peace.

In that moment, though, she had additional possibilities.

"We will all support you in whatever you choose, darling," Toss said.

Whatever I choose. She would be grateful to not see her parents, that was certainly true. But when would she have another chance to stand up to them, to defend herself, when the consequences *wouldn't* be utter misery? And when would she be more likely to insist on fair treatment and actually achieve it? She wouldn't be alone should she choose to face her parents. That wouldn't prevent Mother and Father from being hurtful, neither would it stop her from trembling with fear.

"Your sister said the duke cannot be browbeaten into doing anything he doesn't wish to do," Daria said.

"*No one* has ever or will ever force the hand of the Duke of Kielder," Artemis said with palpable conviction. "And he has declared that you are safe under his roof. That will not change no matter how much your parents might bluster."

Daria still wasn't certain what to do. "Their 'blustering' is often unkind."

"You do not have to face them," Artemis reminded her. "They can be sent away."

It was tempting. "I've often wished, though, I could have even one moment in which I wasn't powerless when faced with them, just one moment in which I could insist that I deserved better than the treatment I have endured from them without risking making it worse or being made miserable for weeks or months afterward."

"We will do whatever you want, Daria," Artemis repeated.

"Without question," Toss said. "You simply say the word."

"Your sister and brother-in-law won't let them drag me away?" Daria knew full well the question had already been asked, but she had to be certain. Absolutely certain.

"Should they make the attempt, the duke will drag *them* from the house and will, by means we would likely do best not to ask the details of, make certain they do not ever return."

This was her chance, then. A chance to say what she'd wanted to say for years. Scared and uncertain though she might be, she wanted to seize it. "I think I want to talk to them." She tightened her grip on Toss's hand as she spoke. "They've never before had to actually listen to me, and I'd like to have that happen, even just this once."

Toss pulled her arm through his. "As much as I would enjoy holding your hand, I think striking a very proper pose would make the most sense."

"As much as I would feel braver having my hand in yours," Daria replied, "I think you're right."

"Bear in mind," Artemis said, "that just because you've decided that Return Fire is your current preferred approach, it doesn't mean you cannot change strategies if you choose. And knowing when to change course—"

"Is a sign of strength and cleverness," Daria finished the well-known reassurance. It was nearly as familiar to them as Artemis's three-pronged battle strategy.

"We will follow your lead," Artemis said.

Toss set his hand on hers where it rested on her arm. "When you're ready, Daria."

She took a breath. Then another. "I think I'm ready."

With Toss at her side and Artemis a half step ahead, Daria walked from the music room, across the entryway, and to the door of the drawing room. She hesitated. Neither of her companions pushed her to keep walking, nor did they seem disappointed in her for taking an additional moment.

But that moment proved enough. Heart pounding and stomach tied in a knot, she stepped across the threshold. The Huntresses, the gentlemen, Mater, and the duchess were all inside. And just as she'd been warned, so were her parents.

"There you are." Mother didn't sound relieved or concerned. Nothing but irritation wove through the words. "You have caused an unendurable amount of bother for a shockingly large number of people."

Daria had said she wanted to say something, though she wasn't certain what, to her parents and finally be heard. But in that moment, she couldn't have spoken no matter how hard she might have tried. Too many years of finding her greatest possibility of peace in not antagonizing them was proving too unshakable a lesson.

Father watched her with something more than irritation. Far from his usual indifference, he looked angry. "You have wreaked utter havoc on our lives these past two hours. Should word of your pathetic scheme spread through the *ton*, the entire family will be humiliated."

Charlie, who seldom wore an expression that wasn't jovial, watched them with a narrowed gaze and a straight-slash of a frown. "You thought your daughter had disappeared, could possibly have been in danger, and your objection to the experience was the *embarrassment* it might cause you?"

Mother had the decency to look the tiniest bit ashamed.

Father blustered ever more. "I do not believe this matter is of any concern to you, Mr. Jonquil."

"But it is of great concern to me," Mater said.

"Which makes it of concern to me." His Grace spoke calmly from the doorway. Though he employed a conversational volume, his declaration stopped all movement in the room. Daria wasn't certain her parents were even breathing.

Mater watched Mother and Father with a look that might have been described as concern if it hadn't been obviously full of condemnation. "I fail to see how your daughter's acceptance of my invitation to be my particular guest for the remainder of the Season and then at Lampton Park when I return there could possibly be labeled a 'pathetic scheme.' Do you think *me* pathetic, Mr. Mullins?"

"Consider your response carefully," the duke warned in a deceptively quiet voice. "Even a whisper of an insult will have consequences."

The Dangerous Duke was known particularly for never making idle threats.

"We are honored at the idea that our Daria would receive so significant an invitation." Father hadn't taken even a moment to consider his words. Thus far, he hadn't landed entirely in the suds. "But she is already expected at my aunt Theodosia's house. It is all arranged. She will be going there."

"Daria did not indicate that *she* had accepted any other invitations," Mater said.

With Daria's parents' attention momentarily diverted, Toss brushed his hand over Daria's and leaned close enough to whisper, "I believe the tide is about to turn."

"And she didn't tell us about your invitation," Mother added, almost pleading. "She is a rather stupid girl. We haven't—"

"That was far more than *a whisper* of an insult," Charlie observed, locking eyes with his brother-in-law.

"I did not insult your mother, Mr. Jonquil." Daria's mother spoke quickly but with obvious confidence that the explanation of who the insult was meant for would resolve the issue. "The dowager is, I am certain, quite intelligent."

"Our daughter, on the other hand . . ." Father let the sentence dangle even as he shrugged.

"That is two insults." The duke's eyes never left her parents. "Care to make it three?"

Daria recognized the flash of ill-advised pride in Father's eyes. That expression too often preceded a harsh rebuke. Seeing it again, she wasn't certain she could even breathe.

"Three insults have already been delivered, Your Grace," Father said in haughty tones to the most powerfully dangerous man in all the kingdom. "We have been lied to, and the dowager clearly is not even ashamed of her dishonesty. One must consider the possibility that duplicity is a permanent trait of hers, which is most certainly insulting to endure."

Oh mercy.

Daria wasn't certain how the rest of the room reacted to her father's cruel words; she couldn't look away from the white-hot anger flashing bright in the duke's eyes. She'd always found him intimidating. In that moment, he was utterly terrifying.

"I will endure insults against my person." The duke strode across the room, his movements fluid yet tense. "I will stand as second for any gentleman in this room. I will swiftly respond to any mistreatment of the ladies present." He stopped directly in front of Father. Then, his tense mouth pulling at his fearsome scars, he took hold of the knot in Father's cravat, twisting it so it tightened around his neck, and pulled him so close the duke's breath must have been hot against Father's pallid face. "But no one will ever be permitted to insult the Dowager Countess of Lampton, whether in my presence or not, without answering to me."

Father choked out, "She is not even family to you."

"She has *always* been family to me," the duke growled.

Daria took a step backward. Toss was still there. He slipped his arm around her shoulders.

"I think the duke might actually kill him," she whispered to Toss.

His response was equally as quiet. "He won't, but I very much think he wants your father to know how much peril he is now in."

Mother certainly seemed to know. She was fussing her handkerchief to the point that Daria expected it to fray into a heap of threads.

"What should we do with him, Charlie?" the duke asked, still not looking away from Father.

"What do you think my father would have done if he'd heard what was just said about his wife?" Charlie was such a lighthearted and even-keeled person. To hear his voice tinged with anger was disconcerting.

Not half so disconcerting, though, as the sinister smile that spread slowly over the duke's face. "Let's go for a ride, shall we?"

"Where to?" Father's question shook a bit.

"Lampton House. Four of this lady's sons are there at the moment. Between the six of us, we ought to be able to sort out *exactly* what the late earl would have done to you." His Grace pulled Father by his cravat to where a footman stood near the door. "Have this deposited in the carriage. He's not to leave it."

"Yes, Your Grace." The footman took possession of the "prisoner" and disappeared from view.

"Gordon." The duke called the butler over. "See that the Mullinses' carriage is called up for Mrs. Mullins. She is returning home."

The butler waved a maid inside the room, offering instructions for her to accompany Mother to the entryway. He then looked to the duke once more, seeming to anticipate that there were more instructions to come.

There were.

His Grace looked back to Charlie. "Don't dawdle. Procrastination is inexcusable in matters of retribution."

Charlie gave his mother a kiss on the cheek as he passed, then stepped from the room himself.

"Your Grace." Toss took a step away from Daria and closer to the duke. "He offered insult to Miss Mullins as well."

The duke eyed Toss for the length of half a breath. "Be in the carriage when we leave."

Toss offered an abbreviated bow before turning back to Daria. "I don't truly have the right to defend you in this, but I do want to be certain he knows that unkindnesses toward you won't be ignored any longer."

Any longer. For so many years, she'd assumed his slights and insults were deserved and, therefore, were unworthy of comment. The simple acknowledgment that her pain had been wrongly ignored was a welcome and much-needed change. "Be careful."

"I will, my darling Daria." He raised her hand to his lips and, after the briefest of kisses, followed Charlie's path.

The dowager stopped His Grace with a hand on his arm. "Adam." It was very much the tone a mother used when concerned her child was about to do something ill advised. "Mr. Mullins is not worth fighting a duel with and certainly not worth causing you any trouble with the law."

The duke bent and kissed her cheek, very much as Charlie had done. Daria couldn't help but stare a little. She'd seen the duke, in moments when he hadn't realized he was being watched, show tenderness to his wife and children. But this was wholly unexpected.

"You forget, Mother Julia," His Grace said. "I *am* the law."

CHAPTER THIRTY-TWO

Toss HAD ADDED HIMSELF TO the party headed to Lampton House in order to defend Daria. Seeing the look in both Charlie's and the Duke of Kielder's eyes, he began to suspect the person most in need of looking out for was Mr. Mullins.

That gentleman, however, seemed intent on making his survival less certain. "I spoke harshly, I'll confess. But it isn't as though I said anything unflattering in front of her husband. He's been dead for years."

The duke didn't move, didn't look away, didn't speak. The only change in Charlie's expression was the slightest tensing of his jaw. Yet the air in the carriage turned icy. If Mr. Mullins, donkey-brained man that he was, wasn't very careful, he would dig himself a hole too deep to ever escape. And though Mr. Mullins deserved none of Daria's love or concern, Toss suspected she would be grieved should actual harm come to her father.

"Gads, man," Toss muttered. "Keep your mummer shut, will you?"

Mr. Mullins ruffled up. "I beg your pardon."

"It is not *my* pardon you ought to be begging. You've offered insult to Mr. Jonquil's mother and the memory of his father, and both of those people are of great importance to His Grace. The two of them might actually kill you."

"They wouldn't dare." Mr. Mullins's voice rose too steeply on the phrase to make it sound as confident as he'd likely hoped it would.

"Keep talking." The duke's invitation was clearly a warning. "You'll soon enough discover there is very little I wouldn't dare."

Somehow, they reached Lampton House without Mr. Mullins receiving a well-deserved belt in the nose. Toss and Charlie were instructed to alight first. The prisoner stepped out next, followed by the one most likely to serve in the role of executioner.

Charlie being a son of this household meant they were ushered in without hesitation. The Dangerous Duke being with them meant the ushering was undertaken in complete silence.

Three of Charlie's six brothers—Philip, Layton, and Jason—as well as Lord Cavratt, who was considered an honorary brother, were in the drawing room. So was Mr. Layton. Their laughter quieted upon the arrival of guests, but their grins didn't fade.

Philip, the eldest and by far the most flamboyant, waved them all inside. "We are celebrating the conclusion of Mr. Finley's trial. Care to join in?"

The duke grabbed Mr. Mullins by the cravat once more and yanked him to the forefront of the new arrivals, depositing him in front of the Jonquil brothers.

"Tell them," he growled at the miscreant.

"Tell them what?" Mr. Mullins's words trembled a bit.

"Tell them what you said to the dowager countess." Anyone hearing the demand would know in an instant that Mr. Mullins had not said something that would meet with approval.

The gentlemen in the room clearly ascertained as much. Five pairs of eyes were immediately trained on the man. Five mouths tightened into mere slashes.

"I—I misunderstood, and—"

"Your words, vermin. Repeat your words *for them*," the duke said, cutting off Mr. Mullins's attempt at skirting the confession.

"You had better pray they prove milder than what I suspect we are all imagining." Philip looked more pugilist than dandy in that moment. The second-oldest Jonquil, Layton, who was actually built like a pugilist, stepped up beside him. The others stood nearby, creating a united front.

A moment passed. Then another.

"The coward suddenly has no voice, Your Grace," Charlie said. "Shall I relay his message for him?"

"Better you than me," the duke said.

"Firstly"—Charlie was firm and calm, but there was no mistaking his determination—"he called his daughter stupid and pathetic while she was present and hearing everything he was saying."

"You would dare insult a lady that way?" Mr. Layton looked at him with utter disgust. "Your own daughter, even?"

Toss stepped forward. "He has shown himself utterly indifferent to his daughter's well-being and happiness. The only time he varies from that apathy is moments like the one Charlie has just described, where he reverts to insults and unkindness."

"Despicable." Jason folded his arms across his chest. "And what did he say to Mater?"

Charlie took a breath and set his shoulders once more. "He declared that she was a liar and that dishonesty was an ingrained part of her flawed character."

Philip met the duke's eye, and something silent passed between them.

"He didn't end it there," Charlie continued. "He also said that because our father is dead, Mater can be insulted with impunity."

"If we were fortunate enough to have the late Earl of Lampton still among us," Mr. Layton said, "he would address this matter personally. Instead, you have a room full of stand-ins who mean to do so on his behalf. And none of us is half as level-headed as he would have been."

"Take him." The duke flung Mr. Mullins at the brothers. "If I go with you, I'll probably kill him, and I promised your mother I wouldn't."

"Which means we likely shouldn't either." Philip took out his quizzing glass and spun it around on its ribbon. "Pity, that."

"What shall we do instead?" Layton surveyed Mr. Mullins through narrowed eyes.

"Brothers." Jason dropped a hand on one of each of his nearest brothers' shoulders and looked alternately at Charlie and Lord Cavratt. "I have a phenomenal idea." He then looked at Mr. Layton. "Care to join us?"

"It would be my honor."

Jason turned a gleefully foreboding gaze on Daria's father. "Shall we go for a walk?"

Before Mr. Mullins could answer, the duke spoke. "He worded that as a request, but do not mistake it for one."

Toss was standing near enough to Charlie to make one final remark. He did so quietly and quickly. "I have every intention of one day marrying that man's daughter. Please bear in mind her tender heart whilst doling out your punishment."

Charlie gave a single nod, then walked with his brothers and Mr. Layton out of the drawing room, the six of them flanking Mr. Mullins.

"In case you have any doubts," the duke said to Toss, he being the only one left in the room, "the late earl would not have hesitated to defend his wife. Not even for an instant. And he would have been thorough."

"No one who knows his sons could have the least doubt, Your Grace. They were raised to respect and cherish their mother."

"And he would have vehemently championed Miss Mullins and would have managed it without causing her the least distress. He was, in a word, remarkable."

For not the first time, Toss wished he'd known Charlie's father.

"And you, despite the evidence your brother offers to the contrary, were, like the Jonquil brothers, also raised to be a respectable gentleman." The duke looked directly at him. "Why, then, is there not yet an agreement between yourself and Miss Mullins?"

Not at all the topic he would have expected His Grace to raise. Toss had found over the past weeks that the duke didn't ask questions he didn't want answered. "My financial situation does not bear scrutiny, I'm afraid. Until last night, I was dependent on my brother for every penny I received. Now I simply don't have any pennies. Until we can build a life together that isn't one of poverty, we cannot truly move forward."

"Surely, the young lady has a dowry."

"Actually, she doesn't, thanks to her parents." A battle waged between embarrassment and pride. "But even if she did, no young lady wants to be—"

"Married for her dowry." The duke finished the sentence in the way one did when repeating verbatim something he had heard before. "How many times am I going to have to endure *this* conversation?"

Toss's embarrassment and pride fully gave way to confusion. "I don't believe we have had this conversation before, Your Grace."

The duke's scarred face pulled in annoyance. "I am perpetually inflicted with people who have this conversation with me. I'll tell you what I have told them. Two people who love each other and are well suited and would find happiness together and are kept apart only by the gentleman's lack of income and, thus, are able to marry only because the lady has a dowry are not at all the same as a couple who marry because a gentleman wishes to enrich his coffers with a lady's dowry and values nothing else about her. Her dowry *allowing* you to marry is not at all the same as marrying her *for* her dowry."

"Very succinctly put."

"I have had ample practice." The duke motioned Toss toward the door. "On the drive back to Falstone House, tell me more of your situation and her missing dowry."

"Are we not going to wait to see what the Jonquil brothers have in mind for Mr. Mullins?"

"I do not make a habit of loitering about in places where I have no purpose." The duke made his way back to the entryway. Toss kept pace as best he could. "I know you have an aptitude and interest in music. And I understand Mr. Fortier suggested you seek membership in the Royal Society of Musicians."

"I applied, Your Grace. They felt me insufficiently qualified."

The duke didn't look at him with pity or shock, but neither did he seem to agree with the dismissal Toss had received. They climbed into the carriage. The footman closed the door, and a moment later, the conveyance began to roll along.

"What do you mean to do now?" the duke asked. "You and Miss Mullins need an income to sustain you as the years pass, which seems unlikely to come from your late father's estate, considering the rift between you and your brother."

"If I can go back and finish my time at Cambridge, the Royal Society of Musicians would most likely allow me to join, and they do offer some financial support to musicians and composers who are in difficult straits. They also help their composers find opportunities for their works to be performed, which provides an income. But I haven't the money to return to Cambridge, and returning as a fellow would mean not being permitted to marry."

Toss found in the duke a listening ear and a very quiet companion. There was something relieving about being able to talk without being interrupted or required to justify his explanations. Worries he hadn't spoken of at length with anyone spilled from him, and none of it seemed to perplex the duke.

When there was little else to say, Toss looked at His Grace and simply shrugged. "That's the long and short of it, I suppose."

"It appears you have a few choices." The duke spoke matter-of-factly, as if being able to offer Toss multiple options for surviving a scenario in which he thought he had none wasn't shocking. "Return to Cambridge as a fellow and hope to be able to marry Miss Mullins once you have finished your time there. Or you could attempt to establish yourself as a musician without returning to Cambridge and hope to have an income soon that will allow you to marry. Or you could pursue another career, hoping to reach that level of income sooner."

"I notice you did not suggest 'Don't marry Daria' as one of my options."

"I do not waste time on pointless conversations." The duke took his hat off the seat as the carriage came to a stop. "As you have already established that Miss Mullins shares your hopes for the future, discuss the choices before the two of you. *What* you choose is not nearly as important as making the choice together."

It was exceptionally good advice. And having his options so plainly stated would simplify the conversation he needed to have with Daria. With a fair bit of luck, it would simplify the many choices remaining to be made. "I am trying to believe that we will find a means of building that life together, but I suspect doing so will require a great many risks."

"For the right person," the duke said, "those risks are worth taking."

Toss and His Grace alighted from the carriage.

"But know, Mr. Comstock, if you prove yourself a coward, I will throw you out of my house." On that final remark, the duke passed Toss on his way inside the stately home.

I'm not a coward. Toss wasn't certain if he was silently countering the duke or encouraging himself. Either way, he was determined to be stalwart.

CHAPTER THIRTY-THREE

Daria received three missives from her mother before the sun set. The first demanded that Daria tell her where Father was. Daria replied that she did not know. The second reprimanded her for the "humiliating ordeal" Father had, apparently, endured but offered no details. The third struck a different tone entirely.

Daria,

Your father insists we are to return to Yorkshire immediately and will hear no arguments. And Tobias insists he will remain in London, and he *will hear no arguments. And when Aunt Theodosia hears that you are refusing to live with her in Anglesey, as she was promised, she will make things horribly unpleasant for us.*

If the Duke of Kielder and Lord Lampton would look charitably on your father, then we could remain in Town, and that bit of nonsense would be ended. Use your influence with them. Tell them of my distress at quitting London without your brother. A family ought to be together, after all.

Do entreat them.

And do reconsider going to Wales. That would be most helpful.

Mother

A family ought to be together.

Yet Mother was insisting Daria not be with them at all.

"Another wee note from your mother, is it?" Eve sat next to Daria on the sofa in the music room.

Most everyone was still in the drawing room, she suspected. Toss was at the pianoforte, playing softly, his expression pensive. He'd attempted any number of conversations with her since returning from Lampton House, but this house was too chaotic for anything resembling a private interlude.

"Mother is asking me to use my influence with the duke and the Jonquil family to . . . I don't know precisely what I'm meant to ask them. Whatever punishment they meted out in response to my father's horridness has sent my parents scrambling to leave London, and Mother doesn't want to go. I'm meant to somehow undo that."

"'Tis rather presumptuous of them."

"I do hope the Huntresses and the gentlemen don't think ill of Tobias because of all this. He really is so very different from our parents."

Eve smiled reassuringly. "You both are."

"I want him to come to the next house party," Daria said.

Eve leaned a little closer. "Charlie and Artemis are tallying the points in your competition with Toss. If you've won, *everyone* will be at the house party."

"You and Nia would come all the way from Ireland?"

There was a moment's hesitation before Eve said, "We'll come."

Something in the answer didn't sound like one, or at least not a full answer. All Season, there'd been a secretiveness to the O'Doyle sisters. There was something they were not telling the Huntresses.

"You should go share your note with Toss." Eve nodded in his direction. "He's been watching you with concern these long minutes. 'Tisn't fair to leave him in misery, wishing to be helpful but not knowing what you might be feeling or needing."

"He has a good heart." Daria sighed a bit as she looked his way.

"As do you," Eve said. "And that is why, if you don't march yourself over there and allow your good heart and his to beat together for a spell, I'll be forced to take drastic measures."

The threat was offered with such theatricality that Daria couldn't help responding in kind. She pressed the hand holding her mother's missive against her heart and assumed a pleading expression. "I vow to rush to the pianoforte with all possible haste if you will but spare me!"

"Off with you." Eve waved her away before rising and leaving the room.

Daria walked to where Toss sat.

He stood as she approached. "From your mother again?" He motioned to the folded parchment in her hand.

Daria nodded. "She wishes me to—" Recounting the contents again weighed on her too much. She held the letter out to Toss. "You can read it for yourself."

He took it, then motioned for her to sit on the stool at the pianoforte, which she did. He brought over a small, armless chair and set it beside her, sitting as well, then quickly read the letter.

"After your mother's earlier letters berating and blaming you for the consequences of their behavior, it is shocking for her to now demand your help." Toss lowered the letter to his lap.

"My parents haven't made a habit of giving my feelings much consideration. I'm not surprised Mother is continuing that pattern."

He held up the letter. "What do you mean to do with this?"

She shrugged. "I'm not certain. It would likely be unmannerly of me to burn it."

"But, I daresay, very satisfying." He smiled at her.

"Do you know what Charlie and his brothers did to my father? Charlie has been very tight-lipped, and I'm too afraid to ask the duke."

"Though I was not present for your father's 'consequences,' as Charlie labels the proceedings, I am told it involved dragging him to his club, standing him on a table, and declaring to all present that Mr. Mullins had been declared a pariah by the Jonquil family and the infamous Duke of Kielder, that Mr. Mullins' children were above reproach, and that he had been given two days to vacate London."

"Good heavens." That must have been a humiliating ordeal for her father. Deserved, yes, but humiliating all the same.

"Your parents will have to leave Town," Toss said, "but I do believe you and Tobias will not merely be accepted in London but looked on with great approval. With the Jonquils and the Duke of Kielder and his family speaking so highly of you, your footing is as firm as it could possibly be."

There was some relief in that. Much of Daria's future was very uncertain. To know she was not to be painted with the same brush of condemnation as her parents was a small bit of reassurance.

She reached out and tapped a few keys of the pianoforte. As the sound echoed and faded, she smiled at Toss. "I do love listening to you play. Your compositions are beautiful."

"Do you like the one I've been playing this evening?"

She leaned her head on his shoulder. "You play it often. I like it very much."

He kissed the top of her head. "It's grown from the way you hummed 'English Country Garden' the night of your soiree."

"Truly?"

"I've nearly finished it, and I'm quite pleased." His arm wrapped around her and tucked her nearer to him. "I suspect I'll always think of it as your song."

While his words were touching, they didn't ease her worries or lift her heavy heart. "What are we going to do, Toss? You have no income, and I have no dowry."

"I've been wanting to talk with you on precisely that topic, but there's not been any privacy."

Daria glanced around the room. "We have some privacy now."

He took her hand and urged her to her feet. With her arm through his, he walked with her in a slow circuit around the room. "The duke offered me a succinct list of the options before us. I can return to Cambridge and complete my studies as soon as I am able. I can remain in London and attempt to establish myself without the benefit of completing my education. Or I can seek out a different means of obtaining an income, in the hope that I can do so more quickly than with my music." Toss's tone and expression were a little heavy but not to the point of looking defeated. He had such a knack for keeping his chin up, as the saying went. It helped her do the same. "Those are the options I have, and I have been thinking throughout the day what your options are in each of those scenarios."

"So have I," she said.

He set his hand on hers where it rested on his arm. "Tell me what you've sorted."

"No matter how you proceed, I will need a place to live for a time, be that years to finish your education or years to establish your music."

He nodded. "I wish it didn't have to be years, Daria."

"So do I." But she knew it was not an option for them. No matter the path Toss walked, it would be a long one. "I think you need to return to Cambridge and finish your studies there. That would give you the best chance of pursuing your music." Her breaking heart wanted her to insist he remain with her, that they both abandon any thoughts beyond the now. But music was too much a part of him for Toss to be truly happy if he abandoned it. "I intend to accept Mater's offer of living with her at the Lampton Park dower house. It would be a peaceful place, and I think she would appreciate having me."

"And Gillian will be nearby," Toss said. "That would make it less lonely for you."

"I will like that."

"I do not know how much time will be required after my education is complete for the Royal Society of Musicians to accept me," he warned.

"The waiting won't be easy," she said, "but I think we've proven these past days and weeks that we can do difficult things."

"That, my dear Daria, is because we are exceptionally amazing people."

"We." She smiled as she repeated the word. "In my family, I never truly felt part of *we*."

"We, we, we." He winked at her. "I'll say it as often as you need to hear it."

Daria turned her head enough to press a light kiss on his cheek.

"Enough of that, you two." Artemis stood in the doorway of the music room, hands on hips. "We've tallied your points, and everyone is simply dying of curiosity."

"You've not told anyone yet?" Daria asked.

Artemis shook her head. "We're waiting for you, so there's no time for *l'amour*."

Toss kept Daria's hand in his as they walked to the drawing room. She would miss him when he returned to Cambridge, and waiting until his studies were completed and his place in the world of music was established would be excruciating. But he loved her. He wanted her in his life. It was a reassurance and a promise that soothed the heartache their separation would cause.

Artemis joined Charlie where he stood in the midst of the drawing room. All the others sat or stood facing them.

"Up here with me, Toss," Charlie called out. "You and I are to represent the gentlemen's interest in this matter."

Daria took her place next to Artemis. "And we are the representatives of the Huntresses, I suppose."

Artemis dipped her head. "It has been an epic battle, I must admit."

"Tell us the results of this epic battle," Eve called out. "Torturing us seems unnecessary."

"But it's such fun," Charlie said with a grin.

"Before the tally," Fennel said, "we should tell them the name we've fashioned for ourselves—provided Scott does not write with any objections."

Daria looked at Toss, surprised to hear he and his friends had chosen a name at last. He smiled back at her, a sight she would never tire of.

"What have you decided on?" Artemis watched Charlie with wide-eyed curiosity.

"I suppose that means I am being designated the spokesman for our soon-to-have-a-name group of exceptional gentlemen?"

"Is that what you've settled on, then?" Eve asked. "'Group of Exceptional Gentlemen?'"

"That would be *far* too obvious a choice," Duke answered.

Poor Tobias stood a bit apart, looking downcast and miserable. Daria tried to catch his eye, wishing to offer a smile or some other gesture of reassurance.

It was no more his fault than hers that their parents were not the sort of people they ought to be. But he didn't look her way.

"We decided that as our paths seem unavoidably entwined with those of the Huntresses, we would do well to choose a name that compliments yours."

"An excellent idea," Artemis said.

"So we have chosen to be known henceforth and forever as the Pack."

A grin immediately appeared on Artemis's face. "As in a pack of hunting dogs?"

"Precisely." Charlie dipped his head a little in her direction.

The Pack. Daria liked it. And judging by the sparkle of amusement in Toss's eyes, so did he.

All around the room, the Huntresses expressed their approval, and the gentlemen—*the Pack*—preened a bit at having settled on such an ingenious solution to their lack of a collective name.

"Time for the point totals." Artemis set a hand briefly on Charlie's arm.

To the gathered group, he said, "Artie and I have checked our list again and again. We are certain we have remembered everything."

"And Charlie insisted on doing the mathematics an additional few times because he is an utterly bizarre person." Artemis shook her head. "Pity me, friends. I live with a mathematician."

Charlie snuck a quick kiss. "You love me, as you well know."

"Enough of that, you two." Daria used Artemis's exact words from earlier. "There's no time for *l'amour.*"

"Contrary to the besmirching my mathematical calculations have received," Charlie said to the group as a whole, "there *is* a reason I counted a few times. We have a result that is . . . unexpected."

Daria glanced over at Toss, who looked as curious as she felt.

"Daria received twenty-seven points," Charlie said.

Twenty-seven. She had done twenty-seven things of her own choosing, twenty-seven things that her parents had not dictated or required of her. Was it strange that she felt proud of that?

"And Toss," Charlie continued, "received . . . twenty-seven points."

A draw? She met Toss's eyes and saw amazement and amusement mingled there.

"What happens now?" she asked Toss.

"I haven't the first idea."

"The wagers both groups placed were dependent upon a win," Artemis said. "And if we are being quite technical, no one was victorious."

Quite without warning, Daria had an idea. Not an ordinary, fleeting one but a moment of realization that made her feel quite clever. "I received a letter from my mother in the moments before you began tabulating our totals," Daria said to Artemis and Charlie. "Which, I believe, means it arrived before the contest ended."

"It would seem so." Artemis watched her with obvious curiosity.

"Then, any action I took in regard to the letter could potentially count toward our competition."

Artemis looked to Charlie, who nodded his agreement.

"My mother has insisted I plead my father's case and pave the way for my parents to remain in London." Daria set her shoulders. "And I intend to ignore her, which, I assure you, neither she nor my father would approve of."

Toss pressed his hand to his heart and nodded, an approving and pleased look in his eyes. "That earns you a point, my dear."

"And victory," Artemis declared.

The Huntresses hoorahed and celebrated, congratulating Daria and crowing a bit over the Pack, who took their loss not merely in stride but joyfully.

Toss pulled her into an embrace. "Well done, my darling Daria."

"This means the Pack has to ensure that everyone joins in the next house party. *Everyone*." She brushed the tips of her fingers along his jaw. "They'll see to it all the Huntresses will be there and all the Pack, including Tobias. And you'll be there from Cambridge. And I'll be there from Nottinghamshire."

"We'll be together." He kissed her forehead. "My favorite place to be."

"I'm sorry we couldn't find you a musical mentor," Daria said. "Even if you had won the challenge, I'm not certain we could have managed that, though we would have exhausted all avenues."

"That you were willing to try gave me hope these past weeks." He pulled her ever closer. "And that you love me enough to wait however long is needed to make up for the loss of my income and your dowry gives me strength to face the temporary separation ahead of us."

"I do love you that much," she said, hoping to adequately communicate her sincerity. "I truly do."

"And I love you, my darling friend, my dearest love," he whispered. "My Daria."

CHAPTER THIRTY-FOUR

Falstone House was quiet the next morning. With the Huntresses dispersing for the Season and three of the members of the Pack leaving Town as well, their weeks of revelry had come to a close. Toss was choosing to feel hopeful.

He would be returning to Cambridge with Duke and Fennel, completing his studies, and setting himself on the path most likely to prove successful. A mere few days earlier, he would not have thought it possible. Doing so meant being separated from Daria. But completing the education Laurence had brought to an abrupt halt meant he could reapply for membership in the Royal Society of Musicians, this time with a very good chance of being accepted. There was no predicting how long he would need after that to secure a steady enough income for them to begin building their life together. He ached at the thought of even temporarily losing her companionship, but enduring that separation meant that in the end, they could be together for the rest of their lives. It would be well worth it.

Duke was with Toss in the Falstone House drawing room, finalizing their travel plans back to Cambridge. Duke and Fennel were also making room for Toss in their lodgings while he waited for the fellowship to be granted, though it would mean tight quarters.

"I can't thank you enough for this," Toss said. "Searching out the fellowship and a means of securing it and now giving me a place to live."

"The Huntresses are not the only group of friends who would do anything for each other," Duke said. "The Pack is simply less dramatic about it."

"We do have to admit, though," Toss said, "that the Huntresses were correct about our needing a collective name. Now that we have one, I can't understand how we went so long without it."

Duke nodded a little. "Which makes me think we are, indeed, a pack of idiots." He offered the observation with no indication of humor, though that didn't mean it wasn't a jest. No matter that Toss had known Duke for years, he still couldn't always interpret his friend's tone and expression. Sometimes he wondered if anyone really could. Toss suspected that was why people found him intimidating, even if they didn't realize the reason.

"Toss!" Hearing Daria excitedly call his name filled Toss's very heart with joy.

He turned to see her rushing toward him, smiling broadly.

"You'll never guess," she said as she reached him.

"Then you'd best tell me." He took her hands in his, resisting the urge to pull her into his arms while he was still near enough to do so.

"Charlie and Artemis have said we might have our Huntresses and Pack house party at Christmastime, and Ellie thinks she and Newton will be able to attend as well, though we'll need to hold it somewhere nearer to London, which Charlie says can likely be arranged, but we would need to find someone to host it. And Artemis says that if we have the duchess or the dowager countess in attendance, which might happen because we will likely need to borrow an estate from one of their families, then we will have all the proprieties seen to, and London Society won't be able to turn their noses up at us." She shook her head. "I've gone so long without babbling like this, but I am beginning to suspect I always will when I'm excited."

"I hope you do." He pressed their interlocked hands to his heart. "I love the way your face lights up when you're spilling all your joyous thoughts."

The smile she already wore grew ever broader. "Did you know *your* face lights up when you are playing the pianoforte? It is one of my favorite things."

Quite out of nowhere, Duke spoke. "I believe I will wander elsewhere in the room before the two of you start complimenting each other's lice or dandruff or something equally ridiculous."

Daria's brow pulled as Duke walked away. "Do you think he is actually annoyed? Or was he teasing? I can't always tell."

"Most people can't," Toss said. "The Pack can't even always manage it."

"But you like having him among you even if he confuses you?"

"He's a good gun, as Charlie is wont to say."

A look of sudden remembering pulled Daria's eyes wide. "Did you finish your composition? You said last night that you were close, and I heard you in the music room this morning playing it again."

"I did." He raised her hand to his lips, gently kissing her fingers. "Often, at this point, I begin adding other instruments and movements, but I think this one is proving to be best suited for the pianoforte exclusively."

"Sometimes the simplest approach is the best," she said.

"Precisely."

The duke stepped into the drawing room. Though it was his home, and thus, his presence was not a surprise, and though he didn't speak a single word, his arrival had the usual effect: the room grew very still and very quiet.

And His Grace didn't enter the room alone. A man Toss was certain he recognized walked at his side.

"Who is that?" Daria asked, sounding a little nervous. "You look . . . anxious or uncomfortable or something."

"Surprised, truth be told. That is Mr. Williams. He is an important member of the Royal Society of Musicians, a composer, in fact."

"Does His Grace know Mr. Williams?"

"He might, though I hadn't heard as much." Toss watched the two men as they crossed toward him. "What do you suppose he has come here for?"

"Apparently, something to do with you." Daria kept one hand in his, giving every indication she meant to stay at his side.

"Mr. Comstock, this is Mr. Williams." The duke made the introductions with his usual efficiency. "He wishes to have a conversation with you."

Toss and Mr. Williams exchanged the expected words of greeting.

"Mr. Comstock, I had hoped to speak with you yesterday, but I fear your brother was not very forthcoming about your location."

That was not surprising.

"I have received eight messages from people who were in attendance at a musicale held recently at the Mullinses's home. All wrote of your performance that evening."

"Did they?" He was too confused to say much else. Who had written? And what had they said about his moment at the pianoforte?

"What piece did you play?" Mr. Williams asked. "Even Lady Cavratt, who is well versed in music, did not identify it."

Lady Cavratt had written about him? He was only vaguely familiar with her, and what he knew of her indicated she was quite shy and reserved. What had convinced her to send the letter? And what had she said about him and his playing?

"The piece was one of his own composing." Only when Daria answered Mr. Williams's question did Toss realize he'd been too distracted to do so.

"Your application to the Royal Society of Musicians indicated your primary interest is in composing." Mr. Williams watched him quite closely, a bit *too* closely for comfort, especially when Toss didn't know precisely why the man had sought him out.

"That is correct," Toss said.

Daria squeezed his hand, bolstering his courage.

Mr. Williams turned his gaze to the Duke of Kielder. "And you stand by your words on this matter?"

"I do. And I assure you the Dowager Countess of Lampton, Mr. and Mrs. Fortier, Lord and Lady Aldric, Lady Cavratt, Lord and Lady Lampton, Mr. Digby Layton, and Lord and Lady Techney are not ones to exaggerate nor be dishonest in their correspondence."

Heavens, had all those people written about him to Mr. Williams?

"I would not imagine they would falsify their experiences," Mr. Williams said.

His Grace appeared unconvinced. "Yet Mr. Comstock's application to the Royal Society of Musicians was denied on the grounds that he was underqualified and lacked sufficient recommendation."

Mr. Williams was not cowed, but he did appear to be pondering. "Until these letters, Mr. Comstock had only the recommendation of one professor at Cambridge in a course of study he did not complete."

"Do with our words what you will." The duke dipped his head ever so slightly to them all and walked away.

"Would you be willing to play a piece for me?" Mr. Williams asked. "I would like to hear for myself what it is the impressive list of attendees heard."

Play for him. Toss sensed this was not a casually made request. It was very nearly an audition, a second chance to make his case to the Royal Society of Musicians, a possible reopening of a door that had been all but closed to him.

"Seize your moment, Toss," Daria whispered.

It was the nudge he needed to pull himself fully into the moment.

"Falstone House boasts a fine pianoforte," Toss told Mr. Williams. "If you have no immediate engagements elsewhere, I would be honored to have you join me in the music room."

"Of course." Mr. Williams motioned for Toss to lead the way.

Hoping to show dignity while not losing Daria's support, Toss pulled her hand through his arm and walked with her at his side from the drawing room to the music room. His pulse pounded a nervous rhythm in his neck. At the musicale, he'd played a sonata he'd composed during his final term at Cambridge. He'd played it well, and the selection had been enjoyable enough to earn him unsolicited recommendations from a great many influential people. It was most likely what Mr. Williams expected to hear.

And yet, it wasn't the option that his heart and mind insisted he play.

He saw Daria seated in a chair facing the instrument. Mr. Williams situated himself similarly.

"I would like to play for you my newest composition," Toss said.

"A different one from what you played two nights ago?"

Toss nodded. "I realize that is the one that brought you here, and I will play that if you would rather."

"How many compositions have you written?" Mr. Williams appeared intrigued.

"Several a year since I was at Eton."

That surprised his guest.

"I did mention that in my application," Toss said. "I was honest enough to acknowledge that my earliest efforts lacked polish, but I dedicated myself to my studies while at Cambridge, and I believe I have improved tremendously since then. I also know that I have a great deal yet to learn and anticipate improving further in the years to come."

"Are all your compositions exclusively for the pianoforte?"

"Most are for at least four instruments. I have two for a chamber orchestra."

"And you mentioned this in your application?" It wasn't doubt, necessarily, that filled Mr. Williams's question but confusion.

"I was very detailed, sir. But without completing my course of study and with no member of the society to vouch for me, there were too many questions about my abilities and understanding of the technical aspects of composition."

Mr. Williams nodded minutely. "The Royal Society of Musicians' support funds and resources are limited. We do have to take great care with how many people can draw on them."

Toss couldn't, and *wouldn't*, argue with him. He understood their hesitation even if he didn't agree with their decision in his case.

"Please play your selection," Mr. Williams said. "Whatever composition you would prefer."

With a dip of his head, Toss moved to the stool and sat. He took a quick breath. His eyes darted to Daria. She smiled reassuringly.

He set his fingers lightly on the keys, not yet pressing them. He knew what he needed to play: "Daria's Tune." How fitting that the composition she had inspired now stood at the ready as he made another attempt at securing their future together.

A feeling of utter calm settled over him as he played the opening strains. That calm warmed into comfort and peace and familiarity. He never grew entirely unaware of Mr. Williams listening and evaluating him, but foremost in his mind was Daria. She was always present in his thoughts and his heart when he played her song. Always. She'd been there as he'd written it. How was it he hadn't realized for so long that he'd fallen entirely in love with her?

The tune reached its conclusion, a soft and gentle final refrain. Applause sounded from around the room. Duke and Fennel, Charlie and Artemis, and the duke and duchess had all slipped inside as he'd played, and he hadn't noticed.

Toss stood and offered a quick bow. Raising his head once more, he looked at Daria. She watched him with her hands pressed to her heart and a smile of absolutely delighted pride on her face. He couldn't remember the last time anyone had looked at him that way.

Daria turned to Mr. Williams. Toss did as well, hope fighting with wariness. He'd been rejected by the Royal Society of Musicians once already. There was every chance he was about to be again.

"You have talent," Mr. Williams acknowledged, "and you've clearly learned technique."

Toss was very nearly holding his breath.

"How hard are you willing to work to build on that, to prove yourself to those in the society who might not be entirely convinced?"

"I have never been quelled by hard work, Mr. Williams. And working hard at my music, in particular, is more a joy than work. I have a chance to return to Cambridge and continue my studies, which I hope will help the Royal Society think better of my qualifications. And I am willing to work in the years that follow to continue to prove myself if need be."

Mr. Williams stood and crossed to Toss. "There is an apprenticeship available through the Royal Society of Musicians. The income is small but livable. The apprenticeship would serve to fill the gaps in your education *and* offer direct indications to the Royal Society of your abilities, talents, and work ethic. In a year's time, if you have indeed proven yourself, you would have the opportunity to apply for full membership."

Toss's jaw dropped, and his eyes pulled wide. "Truly?"

Mr. Williams nodded. "You could, if enough frugality were exercised, support yourself and a wife." He gave Toss a knowing look. "*Very* frugally, I must emphasize. But it would be possible."

He could complete his education away from Cambridge, meaning he wouldn't have to leave Daria behind. And he could, in a year's time, reapply to the Royal Society of Musicians. And in the meantime, he would have an income.

Toss looked once more at Daria, knowing the question that hovered in his expression. She nodded eagerly.

Hardly believing all that had occurred so quickly, he held a hand out to Mr. Williams. "Thank you for this opportunity. I promise it will not prove a waste of the society's resources."

"I have no worries on that score." Mr. Williams shook Toss's hand. "Let us see if His Grace will allow us the use of his library so I can explain the details."

As Toss was ushered out of the room, he looked back one more time at his darling Daria. A smile passed between them, a moment of silent understanding, a tying together of two hearts that finally had the hope of being together sooner rather than later.

CHAPTER THIRTY-FIVE

Falstone House was a bit chaotic that afternoon. Artemis had decided Toss's apprenticeship warranted a celebration, which sent much of the staff as well as Artemis, Daria, and the duchess into a frenzy of quick planning.

Sitting next to the duke as the preparations for the impromptu festivities swirled around them, Toss said, "I hadn't intended to cause so much upheaval in your life when I sought refuge here. For that, I am sorry."

"I assure you, my youngest sister-in-law would have found a reason to declare the necessity of a party whether you were here or not." His scarred features pulled in a pattern of vexation. "But, her exuberance appears to be providing your Miss Mullins with some enjoyment, which is important. And my wife is always happiest when her family members are happy, so I will not permit Artemis's enthusiasm to be dampened so long as she is in this house."

"My parents' philosophy on family was very much like yours, Your Grace. While they were alive, our home was a happy place."

"And now that you have the opportunity to soon create your own home and family, which philosophy do you mean to embrace: your parents' or your brother's?"

"My parents', I assure you."

The duke nodded slowly. "Good choice."

Daria, her every movement bubbling over with excitement, dropped onto the settee beside Toss. "Isn't this so very much fun?" She leaned against him, and he set his arms around her. "Duke, Fennel, Tobias, Colm, and Rose will be joining us, but otherwise it is only those of us who live here, yet we still get to plan a soiree. I hadn't thought of that before. Gatherings don't need to have a long list of guests to be delightful to plan."

He kissed the top of her head.

"And if a gathering doesn't have a long guest list," she continued, "it needn't be expensive. That makes it even more possible in lean years."

They had a great many lean years ahead of them. His income from the apprenticeship would be sufficient for them to obtain humble lodgings and eat, but little else. He'd not yet had the chance to ask her formally if she wanted to share those lowly years with him or if she would prefer to wait, as they'd originally planned, until he was more financially secure. But this moment, in which she excitedly recounted how she could plan the gatherings she loved on a budget as tight as theirs would be, gave him continued hope that they would not have to delay the beginning of their life together. Once he was able to claim a moment of privacy with his darling Daria, he would find out for certain.

Artemis called out to Daria from across the room. "Cook says he has St. Peter's fish. We should serve that at supper."

"How perfect! That is a favorite of Rose's." Daria hopped up once more, throwing a smile back at Toss before rejoining the ladies in their planning.

"At what point do you suppose I should tell them that I have invited an additional two people tonight?" the duke mused out loud.

The Duke of Kielder, famously reclusive and unsociable, had, of his own accord, invited guests to his house? It was shocking enough that, though the duke's question was likely rhetorical, Toss answered it just the same. "I suspect your reticence ought to be guided by the retribution you feel you will receive from the duchess if you delay overly long."

His Grace rose on the instant and moved with purposeful step to where his wife stood. Before he could possibly have relayed any sort of warning, two new arrivals were announced. Two *unexpected* arrivals, if Toss were to hazard a guess.

"The Dowager Countess of Lampton, and Mr. Digby Layton." The butler stepped aside to allow the two visitors to enter.

The room immediately filled with warm welcomes and declarations of delight. If the Duke of Kielder had actually thought his wife would object to the additions—and Toss firmly suspected there had been no such worry—all uncertainty would have fled.

What Toss had expected to be a simple welcome from Mater was instantly turned into a warm embrace.

"This apprenticeship is a godsend, Toss. I am so very happy for you." It was precisely what his own mother would have said, and he needed to hear it more than he'd realized.

"I am glad the duke invited you to celebrate with us." He looked at Mr. Layton. "*Both* of you. The two of you had a most welcome hand in seeing us through the difficulties of this Season."

"I am honored to have helped," Mr. Layton said.

Standing across the room, Daria was watching Toss, a look of delight on her beloved face. He couldn't begin to express how grateful he was to see her finally claim it free of her parents' interference. Throwing good manners out the proverbial window, Toss abandoned those he stood nearest and crossed directly to her.

Without hesitation, Daria set her hands in his when he reached her. "The duchess says she suspects her children will be sorely disappointed if you do not play the pianoforte for them this evening."

Toss raised one of her hands to his lips. "I would never disappoint Lord Falstone or Lady Hestia." He kissed one knuckle, then another. "But I fear I will disappoint you, my darling."

"I doubt that very much."

"I have not yet mastered the art of playing *while* dancing, so I fear I will not be able to dance with you."

She slipped one of her hands free of his and gently touched his face. "I will be happy as I can imagine being simply sitting next to you, my dearest."

And, when the time came, that was precisely what she did. Mr. Layton was dancing with the duchess. Artemis and Charlie were dancing together. Mater was undertaking the dance with a *very* earnest little Lord Falstone. His Grace was watching the scene with an inscrutable expression. Tobias, Colm, Duke, and Fennel took it in turns to spin and twirl and hoist tiny Lady Hestia in the air, looking proud as peacocks every time she giggled with delight. Rose seemed perfectly pleased to be an observer rather than a participant.

And, though Toss would have liked to dance with Daria, having her at his side while he provided the music for the evening was a delight.

Without warning, she pressed a kiss to his cheek.

"What was that for?" he asked, hoping to discover how to get her to do it again.

"Because I love you."

Toss ended the tune. It was admittedly abrupt, but he'd been prevented all day from telling Daria what was in his heart and asking her directly what her wishes were for their immediate future. She'd managed, in a quick and not entirely private moment, to speak from her heart. It was time and past he did the same.

The others in the room had stopped their dancing and had turned to look at him.

"I'm sorry," he said, his eyes darting from them to Daria and back again. "I'll resume playing, I promise, I need to— I want to—" Laws, this had gone all wrong. A not-entirely-private moment would have worked, but confessing his love and asking how and when she wanted to begin their lives together while being watched this closely by a roomful of people, including her brother, was not going to work at all. "Doesn't anyone else in this room play the pianoforte? Even very poorly?"

The duchess took pity on him and stepped away from the group. "I will take your place for however long you would like." To the others she said, "But do lower your expectations; my abilities are middling at best."

Toss offered his musical replacement a bow of gratitude. He then took Daria's hand in his and led her away from the pianoforte. She looked entirely pleased with the arrangement. The Daria he had met at the Brier Hill house party would have worried about making a misstep or word getting back to her parents that she had done something that could be construed as rude. It did Toss's heart good to see the change in her.

They'd not crossed even halfway to the door of the music room when Gordon stepped inside and, as he had done so many times during Toss's time at Falstone House, announced an unexpected visitor. This time, the butler allowed his annoyance to show ever so slightly. "Mr. Laurence Comstock."

On instinct, Toss stepped a bit in front of Daria, shielding her from his brother. Laurence wouldn't physically hurt a lady, but Toss couldn't be certain he wouldn't *say* something hurtful.

To Their Graces, Gordon said, "I did ask him to remain in the entryway while I inquired as to your availability to receive uninvited visitors."

"We are well enough acquainted with the elder Mr. Comstock to know where the blame for this breach of etiquette lies," His Grace said.

"I have come to speak with my brother," Laurence said. "Discussions with family do not require the same formality."

The duke's gaze narrowed. "Are you lecturing me on propriety in my own home?"

Unlike Mr. Mullins during his ill-fated visit to Falstone House, Laurence realized his mistake quickly. "I apologize, Your Grace. I have allowed my anxiousness to cloud my judgment."

The duke met Toss's eye, an unspoken question passing between them. The Dangerous Duke was willing to send Laurence away if Toss wished him to do so. Toss gave a slight shake of his head; he was willing to give his brother a chance.

"What is it you wanted, Laurence?" Toss asked.

"I received a letter from Mrs. Mullins, asking me to ask you to ask Miss Mullins to ask the Duke of Kielder to allow Mr. and Mrs. Mullins to return to London." Laurence shook his head. "Though I couldn't entirely make sense of it all, it sounded as though you or she might be in some sort of trouble. I was concerned."

To say Toss was shocked by Laurence's explanation would have been a tremendous understatement. It had been a very long time since Laurence had expressed any degree of concern for Toss that couldn't more accurately be described as concern for himself.

"Miss Mullins's parents have recently found themselves in a spot of difficulty." Toss didn't wish to delineate exactly what had happened, not wanting to embarrass Daria. "They have pestered everyone they can think of in the hope of extricating themselves."

Laurence's gaze shifted to Daria for a moment before returning to Toss. "They are not causing you trouble, are they?"

"No," Toss said.

"Good." Laurence offered an abbreviated bow. "I will not impose upon the household any longer." That really was all Laurence had come to Falstone House to do? He was simply concerned?

Laurence turned and left the music room, but Daria stepped out from behind Toss and followed his path, calling out "Mr. Comstock" as she did.

Toss was frozen with surprise for an embarrassingly drawn-out moment before trodding the same path.

"I would like to meet her," Daria was saying to Laurence. "And I know it would mean a lot to him. Please at least consider it."

Laurence spotted Toss approaching. "Congratulations appear to be in order."

"For what, precisely?"

"There is more than one possibility?" Laurence clearly doubted that was possible.

"I have had an eventful few days."

Looking impressed despite himself, Laurence said, "I'd be interested in hearing about your good fortune . . . good fortune*s*."

Toss gave a quick nod. "Maybe I will call on you sometime."

With an equally stiff and uncomfortable nod, Laurence said, "I hope you do."

It was the last thing that was said between them before Laurence left. Toss stared at the now-closed door. "What in heaven's name was that?"

Daria wrapped her arms around him. "With any luck, *that* was the first step toward healing your family, Toss."

"What was it you were speaking with him about before I caught up with you?"

"I asked him if he would consider bringing Rosamond to London. Her visit could, I suggested, act as a wedding gift to you."

Wedding gift? "I've been trying all day to find a private moment in which to ask you if you'd like to wait until my income is more comfortable or my membership in the Royal Society of Musicians more secure before considering things like weddings and wedding gifts and such."

"I would far rather be together in want than separated and waiting for a life built in comfort."

It was what he needed to know and what he'd hoped she'd say. He turned her enough in his arms to look into her beloved face once more. "It'll be a struggle these first months, perhaps years. But if you're willing to struggle with me, I can't imagine being happier."

"Neither can I."

Toss could not prevent the sigh of relief that escaped. "I realize this moment is meant to be romantic and poetic, that I ought to say and do something so charming that people would swoon to hear about it. But, truth be told, I'm just so grateful to know we'll be together that all I can do is stand here awkwardly hoping my fortune doesn't run out."

"You composed a song for me, Toss." She brushed a light kiss to his lips. "What could be more romantic than that?"

Toss pulled her flush with him and deepened the kiss, relishing in the warmth of her embrace and how soft and sweet her lips were. His Daria, in his arms, eager to begin their life together.

CHAPTER THIRTY-SIX

A FORTNIGHT WAS NOT A great deal of time in which to plan a wedding, but holding the ceremony so soon meant Duke and Fennel were still in Town. Having them there, Daria knew, meant a great deal to her beloved Toss. As for herself, she was happy almost beyond words. She'd resigned herself to waiting years for this moment, but fate had proven remarkably kind.

She was in the guest room she'd been granted use of at Falstone House since the day she left her parents' home. Artemis, Ellie, and Rose were there, the only three of the Huntresses still in London. Rose was helping her dress but was steadfastly refusing to attend the actual ceremony, insisting that doing so would cause more whispers than she cared to navigate. Daria wished that weren't as true as it was. While Daria would love to have their beloved honorary sister and aunt with her in the chapel and at the celebratory breakfast, she didn't wish to cause Rose any distress.

Daria's parents had not been invited, but neither had they refused the match or objected when someone—Daria didn't know who—had agreed to pay for a special license. Laurence was attending, which made everyone a little nervous. But he had agreed to bring Toss's sister, which made his presence far more welcome than it would have been otherwise. Daria would finally get to meet Rosamond, and Toss would get to see his sister again at last.

If only Gillian were here, Daria would consider the day utterly perfect.

"I don't know about you," Artemis said as she made a few minute adjustments to Daria's purple dress, "but I think the Pack still owes us a forfeit. You won the contest, yet we found Toss a musical mentor. It was, after all, your musicale that set that particular wheel in motion."

"And your esteemed guests," Ellie said to Artemis. "We should find something additional for them to do for us."

Daria met Rose's eyes in the mirror and saw the quiet amusement they had all come to enjoy so very much over the years.

"Demanding, aren't they?" Daria said with a laugh.

"Fortunately for you, their demands were made to the Pack already."

This was news to Daria. "They were?"

"And the Pack agreed." Rose tied Tobias's purple ribbon around the bouquet Daria would be carrying in the church, apparently not meaning to offer any explanation beyond what she just had.

Of all three of her companions at once, Daria asked, "What did they agree to do?"

"To make this day perfect for you." Artemis squeezed her shoulders. "They couldn't bring back all the Huntresses, but they knew there was one in particular you would most want with you."

Gillian. It had to be Gillian.

"The time frame was so tight that she has only just arrived," Artemis said. "She is quickly being freshened up and changed into a gown for the ceremony. But she'll be here with you."

"Truly?"

"Truly." Artemis motioned toward the bedchamber doorway.

Daria turned in that direction to find Gillian rushing toward her. "You're here!"

Gillian threw her arms around her. "I'm here!"

Knowing the financial straits her friend was in, Daria hadn't let herself even hope that Gillian could somehow make the journey. But having her there drove home how desperately she'd wanted her to be. For as long as she lived, she would be grateful to the Pack for making this miracle happen.

"I'm getting married," Daria said.

"To the luckiest man in all the world." Gillian gave her one more squeeze before stepping back and dropping her arms. "Give Artemis and Rose a chance to set to rights any havoc I've wreaked, then let's get you to the chapel."

When they did arrive at the chapel, Toss was there, watching Daria with unmistakable love in his eyes.

And at the end of the ceremony, when the vicar declared that they were each other's henceforth and forever, Toss's look of love somehow grew deeper.

To the hoorahs of the wedding guests, they climbed into an elegant closed carriage, lent to them by the Duke and Duchess of Kielder for the specific purpose of bringing them from the chapel to Lampton House for the wedding breakfast Mater had arranged for them there. The generosity they had received from so many was nearly overwhelming.

The carriage door closed with a click, and Daria released a slow breath, a sigh of happy exhaustion. "What a perfect morning."

Toss, sitting beside her, slid his arms around her. "I couldn't agree more."

She turned a bit, facing him more fully. "And your brother behaved, which is rather miraculous."

"My darling"—Toss nuzzled her neck—"this will be a disappointingly short carriage ride." He kissed her jaw. "I don't want to spend a single moment of it"—he trailed kisses to the corner of her mouth, her heart pounding harder with each brush of his lips—"talking about my brother."

Daria wrapped her arms around his neck. "You intend to kiss me instead?"

"Mm-hmm."

And he did. Thoroughly and enthusiastically. And as he'd predicted, the carriage ride had proven irritatingly brief.

"Do you suppose anyone would notice if we stayed in here instead of joining the celebration?" Toss kissed her neck, something she had quickly discovered she liked.

"Everyone would notice." She answered as much in response to his question as to remind herself. "And your sister would be disappointed."

He sighed. "She would be." He sat up quite straight and proper and assumed an expression of ridiculous dignity. "I shall be wonderfully well behaved." Then with a wink, he added, "For a time."

He held her hand as they entered Lampton House. No arguments about the strict requirements of propriety could have convinced her to slip her arm through his instead. They kept to the tender arrangement as the guests arrived.

Only when a young girl with Toss's dark, wavy hair and brown eyes approached with a shy smile did Daria release his hand.

He pulled his sister into a hug. "Oh, Rosamond, I have missed you."

The girl's sweet smile overflowed with adoration. There was no doubt she had missed her brother as well. "You're married, Thomas. I can hardly believe it."

"Didn't think anyone would be willing or able to endure me?"

Rosamond bumped him with her shoulder, blushing a little. "You *are* a little obnoxious."

Daria would never grow tired of the sound of Toss's laugh.

He turned his sister to face Daria, keeping an arm around the girl's shoulders. He beamed with palpable brotherly affection. "Daria, this is Rosamond."

"Our sister." Daria clasped her hands together, even more excited than she'd expected to be.

Rosamond's eyes lit. "I've always wanted a sister."

"So have I."

Toss reached out and pulled Daria to them, holding her and Rosamond in his arms. "My two favorite ladies."

"My favorite brother." Rosamond giggled. "Don't tell Laurence."

"We won't," Daria vowed on both their behalf.

The quietly charming girl remained with them only a few minutes longer before Laurence called her away. Toss watched her go with very obvious regret.

Daria set her arms around his waist and leaned against him. "We'll have her come stay with us just as soon as we are in a position to do so."

Toss kissed her quickly as they made their way to the dining room, where the breakfast would be served. "I love you. And I am unspeakably grateful that I will have the rest of our lives to keep telling you that."

"'The rest of our lives.'" She smiled at him. "I do like the sound of that."

One month later

The London Season had wound to its close, with the fine families fleeing the capital for their various country homes. The Duke of Kielder had requested that Daria and Toss remain at Falstone House to "look after the place." Daria suspected no such service was actually needed, but that the duke, being of a rather gruff nature and adamant about hiding his kind and thoughtful nature, had invented the need in order to allow the young couple to stretch their meager income a bit further.

Toss was working hard, learning all he could from his apprenticeship. They anticipated needing a year for him to earn the approval and acceptance of the Royal Society of Musicians, but once that happened, they could move forward with greater comfort. They might even be able to send for Rosamond.

Daria loved watching him blossom. Fully embracing his study of music brought him even more to life. The heaviness that had grown in his expression and posture in the weeks leading up to Mr. Williams's offer had dissipated. He was the lively and energetic Toss she'd first met at the long-ago house party, and it did her heart a world of good to see it.

He looked up from his sheets of paper covered in musical notation and spied her watching him. As was always the case, he smiled immediately. "Have I told you how much I love seeing you every day?"

"You have."

Toss set aside his quill and stood.

"Please don't let me interrupt," she said. "Your work is important."

He moved to her and slid his arms around her. "*You* are important, Daria. Essential." He kissed her quickly. "Wonderful." He kissed her again, lingering a breath's length longer. "Distracting." Longer yet. "Tempting."

"Hmmm." She made it sound like doubt.

Toss grinned. "You disapprove?"

"I was hoping for *irresistible*."

"That, my dear, should be obvious." He kissed her in such a way that, obvious or not, there was no doubt in her mind that he found her as irresistible as he said. And she kissed him in return with the same feeling of tenderness, love, and fervor.

For so long, her future had felt bleak. But with the most wonderful man she knew holding and kissing her, their future *together* felt bright indeed.

ABOUT THE AUTHOR

Sarah M. Eden is a *USA Today* best-selling author of witty and charming historical romances, including 2020's *Foreword Reviews* INDIE Awards Gold winner for romance, *Forget Me Not*, 2019's *Foreword Reviews* INDIE Awards Gold winner for romance, *The Lady and the Highwayman*, and 2020 Holt Medallion finalist, *Healing Hearts*. She is a three-time Best of State Gold Medal winner for fiction and a three-time Whitney Award winner. Combining her obsession with history and her affinity for tender love stories, Sarah loves crafting deep characters and heartfelt romances set against rich historical backdrops. She holds a bachelor's degree in research and happily spends hours perusing the reference shelves of her local library.

www.SarahMEden.com